BLOODL⎯⎯⎯⎯⎯⎯⎯⎯ HOPE

by

LISETTE ASHTON

This novel is fiction - in real life practice safe sex.

CHIMERA

BloodLust Chronicles – Hope first published in 2004 by
Chimera Publishing Ltd
22b Picton House
Hussar Court
Waterlooville
Hants
PO7 7SQ

Printed and bound in Great Britain by
Cox & Wyman Ltd, Reading.

The characters and situations in this book are entirely imaginary and bear no relation to any real person or actual happening.

BLOODLUST CHRONICLES – HOPE

Lisette Ashton

This novel is fiction – in real life practice safe sex

By the same author

THE GAMES MASTER
SERVANTS OF THE CANE
RUBY AND THE BEAST

By the same author, the first in the BloodLust series

BLOODLUST CHRONICLES – FAITH

and the third in the trilogy

BLOODLUST CHRONICLES – CHARITY

The Story so Far

Hope Harker knew there was always a price to be paid.

She sat in the manager's office, uncomfortable in her croupier's uniform of a skimpy basque over fishnet tights. Her ankles ached from the punishment of the high stilettos while the low-cut top made her feel as though her breasts were ready to spill free from their restrictive cups. The high line of the crotch, and the fact that so much of her pert bottom was on public display, left her feeling cheap, nearly naked and exceedingly vulnerable. But she knew those drawbacks were the price that had to be paid if she wanted to complete her business management degree at one of the most prestigious casinos on the *Champs Elysées*: Hope knew there was always a price to be paid.

The problem was, she also knew the price would always be higher than expected. Her business management degree was a good example; the course fees were exorbitant; the study texts were complicated; the hours were long; and the work experience on the floor of a Paris casino was demanding and mostly thankless. But she was beginning to realise that the price was much higher than the sum of those parts. The highest part of the price was the discovery that she was working for a certifiable lunatic.

Todd Chalmers put a match to his cigar and settled back in his chair. He hadn't bothered to turn on the office lights and their conversation was lit by illuminations from the *Champs Elysées* shining through the louvre blinds. The smoke from his cigar leant an atmosphere of *film noir* to the room and Hope thought they were just short of a saxophone playing sultry blues to complete that image. She studied him warily, not sure if she was supposed to laugh, agree or run screaming for help. The noises of music, money and merriment were a faraway drone at this height in the building, but Hope could hear them clearly enough in the thick silence that rested between her and the casino's owner. Diplomatically, she fixed him with an understanding expression and said, 'Let me see if I understand you correctly.'

Todd Chalmers smiled and raised his whisky glass in an encouraging salute. He looked chillingly normal and, if she hadn't just heard the lunacy he had been spouting, Hope could have believed she was having a rational discussion with a sane human being. 'You're telling me that my sister, Faith, was a virtuous vampire hunter.'

He nodded.

'You say she defeated a four-hundred-year-old vampire, but has since been turned into a vampire herself.'

Chalmers nodded again. 'That's what I'm led to believe.'

'And you think the newly established leader of this same coven is now looking for me?'

'You seem to have understood everything I said,' Chalmers grinned. 'Do you have any questions?'

Hope thought about her answer then nodded. She sat in the chair across from his desk, ankles folded as demurely as her uniform would allow, hands clutched tight together and resting in her lap. A part of her wanted to pull at the low neckline of the basque and conceal herself from Chalmers' salacious leer, but she knew that would make her look like she was intimidated and she didn't want to give him that satisfaction. 'Yes,' she said eventually, 'I've got two questions. Are you on prescribed medication, and why haven't you been taking it?'

Chalmers' smile slipped a notch. 'I don't think you appreciate the gravity of the situation...'

Hope stood up. She looked resplendent in the uniform, her narrow waist accentuated by the basque and her breasts appearing plump and desirable as they threatened to spill from their restraints. The fishnets hugged her shapely legs and defined the muscular curves of her calves and thighs. 'I think you'll find I do appreciate the gravity of the situation,' she assured Chalmers stiffly. 'You're a drunkard with a sick sense of humour and you thought it would be entertaining to scare the exchange student with spooky vampire stories.'

'Faith has been changed into a vampire. A vicious bitch called Lilah has sired her, and now Lilah is looking for you. I can train you to defeat her but you need to listen to what I'm saying. You need to do everything I...'

Hope wouldn't allow him to finish. She held up a silencing hand and shook her head. 'The guidelines of my business management degree state that I don't have to tolerate practical jokes and horseplay. Unless you have some *real* business to discuss, Mr Chalmers, I think I should get back to the floor.' She didn't give him the opportunity to reply. It seemed more sensible to turn her back on him and flounce out of the office.

But all the time she was worrying about the price she would have to pay for dismissing him so rudely. Todd Chalmers owned the casino and was regarded as a ruthless and powerful man. She knew there would be a price to pay and, as she closed the door on him, she fretted that the price would be excessively high.

Hope

Act I, Scene I

'*Faith*?'

Hope whispered her sister's name doubtfully, certain it wouldn't be heard across the casino's bustling floor. Slot machines clanged and whirred, a babble of excited chatter fought for precedence over the deafening music and she felt sure her own muted exclamation would be lost beneath all that background noise. Yet, surprisingly, the brunette turned and regarded her with a sly smile.

Hope blinked and took an involuntary step backward.

She supposed the conversation with Chalmers had to be to blame. Faith was currently in Rome – with a choir performing Tosca at *Castel Sant' Angelo* – and there was no reason for her to be in Paris. Hope told herself that the mysterious brunette just bore an uncanny resemblance to her sister, and it was only the coincidence of Chalmers' words that made her think otherwise. But, as rational as the reasoning sounded inside her mind, Hope felt sure she was looking at Faith, as the brunette raised a beckoning finger and gestured for her to approach.

Her fingernails were tipped with blood-red polish, a colour Hope knew her sister would never wear, but she guessed that argument could be applied to the rest of the brunette's outfit. She was dressed in scarlet leathers, the trousers hugging her hips and thighs while a skimpy waistcoat struggled to contain the sumptuous swell of her breasts. The vibrant red of the clothes added life to

8

her alabaster complexion and gave her appearance a vivacity that would otherwise have only rested in her sparkling eyes and full, pouting lips. Yet, although Hope knew the girl couldn't be her sister, the similarity was so striking it made her wonder.

'Faith?' she whispered again, this time with more conviction, and the brunette raised a single eyebrow.

Hope told herself that Chalmers' mention of vampires had fired her imagination and was warping her interpretation of what she was seeing. It was all too easy to think that this was an unnatural incarnation of her sister – a creature with a deathlike pallor to her complexion and supernatural hearing – and, across the distance of the crowded floor, she could imagine elongated canines glistening at the corners of the brunette's smile. Even more unsettling, and only a trick of the light Hope assured herself, were the scarlet flecks that glinted in the girl's eyes.

The brunette tossed her head, another beckoning gesture, and then walked towards the foyer door. Her flowing curls bobbed lightly and her breasts swayed provocatively as she sashayed from the room. The leather pants encased her buttocks so tightly the view bordered on being obscene. The peach-like orbs of her bottom looked firm and inviting and the skin-tight hold of the pants revealed she wore no underwear beneath.

Hope blushed at the thought that she might be ogling her own sister and finally found the strength to tear her gaze away. She could have dismissed the whole incident at that point. She was needed at the roulette table, to take over from her colleague Avril Joffre, and she was about to return to that chore when she noticed the brunette had paused and turned back to glance at her. There was something in her expression, an irresistible invitation in

9

her smile, that made Hope walk past the gaming wheel. She watched the girl disappear through the door and then hurried to follow her.

The glass-fronted foyer was eerily quiet after the hubbub of the casino. Hope glanced around, expecting to find the brunette waiting for her, but she could only see three people and none of them was the girl she'd followed. The door that led to the casino's upper floors was swinging closed, as though someone had just pushed through, but Hope didn't bother pursuing the leather-clad stranger any further. The smartly dressed trio had caught her attention and she watched them with open-mouthed amazement.

Engrossed with their own activities, none of them noticed Hope as they remained in a loose embrace. A strikingly attractive redhead, her whey-like complexion peppered with freckles, was backed against one wall, while a man and another woman eagerly kissed her. He was tall and swarthy, devilishly handsome and confidently aware of that fact. The dark-haired female reminded Hope of her sister's best friend, Claire, although it was only a passing resemblance. She quickly dismissed the similarity as another symptom of her overactive imagination and concentrated on what the three were doing.

'Nick,' the redhead breathed. There was the undercurrent of a French accent in her voice but that timbre wasn't as obvious as the tone of her lusty desire. 'Yes, Nick. Please, Nick.'

The swarthy man grinned, his smile a vicious glint of vampiric teeth.

Hope clutched a hand over her mouth to stifle a gasp of surprise. She watched the dark-haired woman press her mouth against the redhead's shoulder and saw a trickle of blood trail from between the union of her lips and the redhead's flesh. The crimson ribbon spilled against the pale skin of her chest before staining the low neckline of her dress.

The redhead turned to her, smiling with raw gratitude. 'Helen,' she sighed. Her eyelids fluttered as though she was in the throes of bliss and she arched her back against the wall. The hem of her dress had ridden up and the redhead was close to exposing herself as she rubbed urgently against Nick's leg.

Noticing every detail, Hope could see a lustre of sweat silvering the top of the woman's thighs. She'd seen exhibitionists before – her time in Paris had taught her the city was a constant parade of extroverts and show-offs – but she had never seen a display so torrid or so passionate.

Nick had one hand against the redhead's breast and he fondled her with scant regard for the lack of privacy. His thigh was between her legs and the pair writhed against each other with the urgency of desperate lovers. The prominent bulge in his trousers rubbed against the redhead's hip and they each moaned as if sharing the pleasure of the friction. Helen was clearly determined not to be left out of the intimacy, and she pressed her dark kiss against the redhead until the woman's moan turned into a guttural shriek, the cry echoing across the foyer.

Hope thought it was a curious sound, a mixture of desperate pleasure and blissful pain. As Helen continued to work her kiss against the redhead she touched the woman's breast and deftly released it from the dress. The pale flesh was covered with the same dusting of freckles that brushed the redhead's cheeks and nose, the exposed areola was a flushed, magenta circle, and her nipple stood stiff and proud.

Hope's eyes opened wide in surprise, and unaware she was doing it, she placed a protective arm across her own breasts. Inside her basque her nipples were stiffening and

11

the rush of excitement that came from the inadvertent caress shocked her. Trying not to think about her body's response, she fixed her attention more firmly on the activity at the other end of the foyer.

Helen stroked a light circle around the dark ring of the redhead's nipple. It was a teasing touch, her fingertip tracing a diminishing path until she held the hard bud of flesh between her finger and thumb.

Astounded by the blatant intimacy, Hope struggled not to cry out with astonishment. She had seen milder displays of exhibitionism before – couples enthusiastically kissing on pavement cafés and Parisian beauties dressed in outrageously revealing designer outfits – but she had never imagined three people could be so brazenly open with their passion, and she had never thought she would see such a thing in the foyer of the casino where she worked.

'Go on,' the redhead encouraged, pulling her other breast free. Nick's hand immediately fell over it, his fingers burrowing into the soft flesh as his palm rubbed against the stiffness of her nipple. She sighed gratefully, and the throaty sound turned into a chuckle of elated laughter.

Like her lovers, the redhead didn't seem to care about the public display she was making. She writhed wantonly against Nick and smiled for Helen as the woman stroked and caressed the rigid thrust of her nipple. Her lips were parted in a breathless pout and the colour in her cheeks blazed.

Reading her body language, noting the way her fingers stretched and then clenched into fists, Hope realised the woman was enjoying a blissful climax. The redhead bit her lower lip, shook her head furiously, then allowed the orgasm to rack its way through her body in a frantically slow rush. Cresting on the precipice of pleasure, she began to weep, and standing on the opposite side of the foyer,

12

Hope couldn't work out if the redhead was sobbing with frustration or gratitude. All she could decide was that the woman's predicament looked decidedly enviable. It was a shocking thought, enough to make her squirm with a rush of guilty embarrassment, but she couldn't deny that the passion was something she longed to experience firsthand.

'Let me take her,' Helen mumbled.

The words made no sense to Hope, but Nick clearly understood their meaning, shook his head and held up his hand. 'No,' he said firmly. 'Lilah's instructions were quite clear. We need to increase our numbers in this city. And we're not going to do that if you feast on every victim that comes along. We've got to do what Lilah said or there'll be hell to pay.'

'Screw Lilah,' Helen growled impatiently. 'I don't want to make this slut into another vampire. I want to feed on her. I want to take her.'

'It doesn't matter what you want,' Nick began loftily. 'Lilah said…'

He didn't get to conclude his statement, for Helen pushed him aside and pressed her mouth to the redhead's throat, and even though she had her back to her, Hope could see that this kiss was more demanding than the others. There was something about the stiffness of Helen's back and the satisfaction of the redhead's response that said this was a more powerful union than anything she had seen so far.

The redhead snatched her breath, her hands clawing at Helen's back in a way that could have been pushing her away or might have been pulling her closer. She ground her hips more urgently in Nick's direction, encouraging him to bite her with the same vital passion. He hesitated, clearly torn by other considerations, but eventually his arousal got the better of him and he deigned to press his lips against her. The couple locked their mouths on either side of the redhead's throat and twin ribbons of scarlet trailed from their kisses down to her exposed breasts. The redhead's furious need seemed momentarily boundless as she surrendered to them both, and Hope was stung by another rush of envy as she watched the woman reach climax after climax.

It was while she basked at the pique of euphoria that her colour began to fade. The excited blush that had rouged her cheekbones paled until her complexion was ashen. She groaned, an anguished wail, and then she trembled through the satisfaction of a final orgasm. Drained, she slumped back against the wall, and as soon as Helen and Nick released her from their hold she fell gracelessly to the floor.

Hope swallowed uneasily and took a step back towards the casino door. The scene had been an exciting combination of peril and arousal, but once the redhead collapsed she realised that only danger remained.

Helen wiped her mouth on the back of her hand, started turning towards Nick and then glanced sharply in Hope's direction. Nick followed the line of her gaze and his grin resurfaced triumphantly. Hope couldn't hear him speak to Helen but she was watching his lips and knew he whispered, 'Well, well, I think we've found her.' Raising his voice, smiling disarmingly as he waved across the foyer, he called, 'Hope Harker, is that you? Is that really you?'

Unnerved, Hope took another wary step back. She wanted to rush to the fallen redhead and see if she was in need of help, but a part of her knew the time for such action was already past. It would be more sensible to turn tail and flee from the danger Nick and Helen presented, but fear kept her momentarily paralysed.

'We've found her!' Helen exclaimed, wriggling her hips and clapping her hands together with obvious glee. 'We've gone and found her!'

Nick's grin broadened. 'Lilah will be pleased.'

Helen put a hand on his arm, her smile suddenly conspiratorial. 'Should we take her?' she suggested. 'Should we do that?'

'You greedy little bitch.' He nodded at the fallen redhead. 'Haven't you had enough this evening?'

Helen shrugged. 'I've had enough,' she allowed, 'but I want more than enough.'

Nick shook his head. 'Lilah would kill us both if we took her.'

Helen didn't seem troubled by the consideration. 'Maybe Lilah would kill us,' she agreed, then with an encouraging smile she added, 'but I bet it would be worth it.'

He looked as though he was pondering the suggestion, and Hope was disquieted to realise she now understood most of what they were saying. Helen was suggesting biting her – feeding from her and using her in the same way they had devoured and drained the redhead – and Nick looked ready to agree. The thought sent shivers of delicious dread tickling down her spine.

'Perhaps we should have a little taste,' Nick conceded. He sounded as though he was trying to convince himself and effortlessly winning the argument. 'It might help to keep her under control.'

Before Hope had realised the pair were moving they were virtually on top of her. Helen blocked the path to the casino door while Nick prevented Hope from rushing out into the night. The only escape route available to her was the door that led to the casino's upper floors, and after seeing the speed with which they had crossed the foyer Hope knew she couldn't reach that exit before either of the couple did. A musk of sexual excitement emanated from them and Hope drank the scent with reluctant enthusiasm.

She glanced from Nick's handsome face to Helen's pretty smile, trying to see some sign that would give away the prank the pair were playing. She had almost convinced herself they were either college students, horror film aficionados or fans of her sister's rock group BloodLust. Close up, she expected to see the telltale signs of novelty teeth and specialist contact lenses, but as hard as she studied the pair she couldn't see any indication of such accessories. And even more damning, when she glanced into the glass-fronted foyer of the casino she could only see herself in the reflection of the night-blackened windows. Nick curled back his upper lip to reveal his pronounced canines, the smile in Helen's eyes glinted crimson, and Hope realised they weren't students, aficionados or fans: she knew she was at the mercy of two genuine vampires.

'I'll scream,' she threatened.

'I'm sure you will,' Nick mused. 'But do you think it will be from pleasure or pain?' He reached out and stroked a stray lock of hair from her brow, the light caress enough to make her shiver. Hope tried to back away from him but her bare arm nudged against Helen's breast and she realised how close the woman was. Frightened and feeling frustratingly vulnerable in her basque and fishnets, she tried to cringe away from the pair.

'She's scared,' Helen observed.

Nick nodded. 'That should make her taste even better.'

Hope struggled to find the courage to stand up to the couple, but pointing to the fallen body of the redhead she asked, 'What did you do to her? Why is she still lying there?'

Helen stroked her fingers against Hope's back, the touch

light and sensitive and inspired eddies of delicious arousal to sparkle between her shoulder blades. 'We did that slut a favour,' she confided. 'We made her last moments on earth the most joyous she had ever experienced.' Pushing her face close, holding her lips so they hovered enticingly in front of Hope's, she asked, 'Would you like us to do the same favour for you? We can make the experience more than you'd ever dreamed it could be. We could make your death utterly glorious.'

Hope sighed hungrily, longing to give in to the temptation of the kiss that was being offered. Her nipples ached with frustrated arousal and she realised the excitement was being heightened by Nick's skilful caress. She hadn't noticed him slip a hand against her basque and his touch was so subtle she barely realised what he was doing. But when she glanced down and saw his palm covering the swell of one breast the torrent of pleasure began to flood through her body.

Helen pushed her face closer, extracting a long, intrusive kiss. Her tongue plundered Hope's mouth, penetrating and sliding hungrily between her lips and over her teeth. The idea of not responding was unthinkable and Hope threw herself into reciprocating. She was amazed it was so easy to enjoy the pleasure, and appalled she could give herself so easily to a pair of dangerous strangers. Yet when Helen eventually pulled her mouth away, and then allowed Nick to take over, Hope couldn't convince herself that she was doing anything wrong. She revelled in the attention of the woman's hands on her basque and wallowed in the joy of Nick's tongue sliding between her lips.

'We won't need to suffer Lilah's wrath,' Helen murmured seductively. 'We'll be telling the truth when we say this slut just threw herself at us.'

Still kissing, occasionally nibbling against her lips as his fingers continued to knead her breasts, Nick made no reply.

Helen trailed her fingertips against Hope's legs, the weave of the fishnet stockings adding a delightful frisson to the gentle caress. Hope had been enthralled by the passion that came from their kiss but this teasing promised to take her to a new realm of discovery. A fingertip traced against the crotch of her uniform and its gentle caress was infuriating. Shockwaves of pure bliss thrilled from her pussy lips and she could feel the pulse of arousal beating strongly inside her sex. Hungrily she pressed herself into Nick's demanding kiss.

'Virtue must be a family trait for these sisters,' Nick sneered.

'Lezzers and sluts,' Helen agreed scornfully. 'Every one of them.'

Hope knew they were talking about her and realised their comments were derisory and insulting, but those considerations were masked by the shadow of her arousal. Rather than worry about the couple's opinions, it was easier to give in to the joys of fulfilment their kisses promised. She revelled as another gentle caress slipped against the crotch of her outfit, and cursed the stiff fabric that stopped her from feeling the fingertips stroking her needy flesh. As Nick continued to massage her breasts she silently willed him to pull the neckline down and expose her as he had the redhead. Her eagerness was overwhelming and she wondered why the pair couldn't see she was desperate for them to take her.

Nick pressed his mouth against her throat and she shivered. The weight of his teeth, painfully sharp and perfectly placed, was the exact torment her body craved. She tried to hold herself still, bracing herself for the pleasurable pain she knew would come from his bite. Her

18

heart hammered at a deafening volume and she was aware of every subtle pressure that touched her body. The fingers that stroked her thighs, the thrust of his erection burrowing against her hip and the casual caresses that were stealing against her breasts were all urging her towards a pinnacle of release.

'What the hell do you think you're doing?' Helen demanded, and the sharp cry made Hope open her eyes. Nick moved his lips away from her throat and she almost groaned with frustration.

'I'm just tasting her,' he told Helen defensively. 'I'm not doing anything more than what we agreed.'

Helen shook her head and pulled herself up from the floor. Hope glared at her, wishing the woman would go back to stroking delicious sensations against her crotch and thighs. 'I'm having first taste of this one,' Helen told him.

Nick snorted in amazement. 'You greedy bitch. You had first taste of the last one.'

'Then it's set a precedent,' Helen said firmly. 'When we're harvesting together I have first taste and you get to finish what's left.'

He squared his shoulders. 'I don't fucking think so.'

From the corner of her eye Hope saw movement in the foyer behind Nick and Helen. She wasn't following the vampires' argument, merely wishing the pair would resolve their differences so one of them could bite her, and it was only with passing interest that she realised she was looking at Faith's best friend, Claire. The observation generated no surprise and she guessed, after seeing Faith's doppelganger this evening, then encountering a pair of genuine vampires, the sight of her sister's school friend didn't rank as being out of the ordinary.

'I'm having her,' Helen said viciously. 'And you can

take what's left.' Brusquely she pulled Hope from Nick's embrace, and Hope felt the woman's arm slip around her waist, realised a feminine hand was cupping the swell of her breast, and then surrendered to the pressure of wickedly sharp teeth scratching against her throat. The distractions and the disagreement were banished as her arousal returned with searing force. She ground her hips against the woman, languishing in the thrill of having her body squashed against another, and held herself still as she waited for the punishing pleasure of the vampire's kiss.

'Be gone!' Claire screeched, and the desperate interruption pulled Hope from her reverie. She blinked, startled by the thought of what she had been about to do, and tried to take in the situation from a fresh perspective that was purged of arousal. Claire had pulled Helen away and pushed herself between Hope and the two vampires, brandishing a small silver crucifix that looked similar to the jewellery Hope had given to her sister as a long ago birthday present.

'Be gone!' Claire cried again, waving the cross threateningly at the couple. 'Leave her alone!'

Nick raised a hand and Hope couldn't tell if he was threatening to strike Claire or defend himself from her attack. Helen's features contorted into a twisting growl as she hissed a stream of blasphemous expletives, yet despite the intimidating front they presented neither of them made any attempt to brave the cross.

Claire turned to glance at Hope, her expression a combination of concern and fury. 'Get out of here, Hope,' she urged passionately. 'Get out of here while you still have the chance.'

'What are you doing here, Claire?' Hope asked, bewildered. 'I thought you and Faith were in Rome?'

'Something terrible has happened to Faith,' Claire snapped. 'But there's still a chance we might be able to save her.' As she spoke she repeatedly glanced over her shoulder to keep a watchful eye on Nick and Helen. 'I'll tell you more about it later,' she promised, 'but for now you need to get to safety.' She turned back to face the vampires and pushed her crucifix towards them.

Realising there would be no time to ask anything further, and fairly sure she now knew the answers to her most pressing questions, Hope turned and fled through the door that led to the casino's upper floors, and didn't dare look back until she heard Claire's petrified scream. Hesitating, sure she should help but not knowing how, she prepared to go back to the foyer.

But before she could take the first steps down the stairwell, a hand fell on her shoulder.

Hope

Act I, Scene II

'You've brought vampires into my casino!' Chalmers roared, and Hope cringed from the anger in his voice.

Chalmers had caught her on the stairs and dragged her back to his smoky, dimly lit office. He seemed unnaturally well informed about what had happened in the foyer and it was only as an afterthought that Hope remembered he had private access to the casino's CCTV cameras. She shrank from the idea that he had been watching while Nick and Helen teased her to arousal, but Chalmers didn't allow her the luxury of retreating into embarrassment. His grip was powerful; his determination single-minded, and there was no choice but to go with him. She had felt a measure of relief when he secured the office door behind them but that quickly evaporated in the face of his fury. Rather than consoling herself with the knowledge that the vampires were locked outside, she was touched by the dread that she was now trapped in the room with him.

'You've brought vampires into my casino,' he growled again. 'You've put my customers, my staff and me at risk. And this is all because you wouldn't hear me out earlier.'

'I didn't bring them here,' Hope protested, but he wasn't listening. Cigar smoke plumed from his nostrils and scarlet lights from the *Champs Elysées* striped his face like bloody battle scars.

'I should have dealt with you properly an hour ago,' he said thickly. 'I should have acted on my instincts and *made* you listen. But I suppose I can address that oversight now. You've made it inevitable.'

Bewildered, Hope stared at him. She wasn't sure what he was talking about until his meaning became all too clear. Chalmers dragged her from the chair and pushed her facedown across his desk. Her breasts were squashed against the leather surface and the breath was gruffly knocked from her lungs. The revealing uniform still made her feel exposed but she knew it was now Todd Chalmers and his anger that made her feel excruciatingly vulnerable. Her bottom was raised – virtually naked save for the thin gusset of the basque and the sheer denier of the fishnets – and it only took a glance over her shoulder to see he was rolling up his shirtsleeves, his intentions sickeningly obvious.

'I told you your sister was the virtuous one,' he growled. 'I told you she'd defeated the dark one. And I told you that the coven are now looking for you.'

'How was I expected to believe all that?' Hope asked fearfully.

'You could have listened to me. If you'd shown me the courtesy of hearing me out, if you'd shown a little trust, perhaps we could have had a relationship that didn't need this discipline.'

She glared at him in disbelief but he wasn't looking at her face. His jaw was set in a determined square, his hand was raised high, and his gaze was fixed intently on her bottom. She started to protest – about to tell him not touch her and that the business management guidelines expressly forbade physical reprimands – when he landed the first blow.

The sound of his palm striking her flesh echoed hollowly

around the flat acoustics of the office. A glowing shock bristled through her buttocks and Hope was dumbstruck by the realisation that he had really slapped her. Lost for words she could only strain to see over her shoulder and gape as he raised his hand and aimed a second blow.

The pain was nowhere near as severe as she expected but the indignity was enormous and crippling. Hope bit back a cry; sure she was ready to explode with embarrassment when he struck her again. Both her buttocks were a blaze of punished flesh, her eyes filled with injured tears, and she tried to implore him with a pitiful plea.

Still not looking at her face, Chalmers slapped her backside once more. 'If you'd listened to me you might have been prepared for what happened in the foyer,' he snarled. 'If you'd listened to me we might have been able to avoid this unpleasantness.'

She trembled against the desk, shocked he had chosen to punish her in this way and amazed she was allowing him to do it. She knew her tears trailed twin lines down her cheeks, and she could see that the force of one of his slaps had laddered her fishnets, but those were only minor considerations and inconsequential in comparison to his punishment.

Shivering each time his hand landed against her rear she briefly toyed with the idea that she might be dreaming. The unexpected appearance of her sister, the confrontation with a pair of seductive vampires and now this unprecedented chastisement, all seemed so unreal it was easy to believe her imagination was running riot while she slept. But another crushing blow from Chalmers' palm made her discount that theory. The pain was enough to make her gasp with surprise and the after burn of each slap burrowed effortlessly beneath her skin. She knew

24

her dreams could be vivid but she also knew it would be impossible to sleep through such anguish.

'I take it you believe in vampires now?' he hissed, but before she could gasp her reply he drove another slap against her bottom. She clenched her teeth, determined he wouldn't have the satisfaction of hearing her cry out in pain.

So chugging breath, waiting until her respiration was under control before she dared speak, she bravely said, 'Yes, I believe in vampires now.'

'And you believe what I told you?' Chalmers demanded. 'That your sister is now one of their number and the coven is here, in Paris, looking for you?'

She flinched, knowing what to expect and not disappointed when he slammed his palm against her rear. The punishment was demeaning, hateful and unfair, and she struggled to find the strength to tell him that. It might have been easier to raise an argument if she hadn't realised that on some level she was actually enjoying the discipline, but she refused to entertain that disgusting thought and tried to shut it from her mind.

He slapped her bottom again and the force of the blow shuddered through her slender frame. Hope drew a deep breath, wishing she could distance herself from the delicious heat that burnt against her rear. Both cheeks had been warmed by Chalmers' repeated punishment and her flesh was acutely aware of every sensation. While she had been held in the thrall of Nick and Helen's caresses her body craved a sexual satisfaction she had never experienced. Now, suffering the torment of Chalmers' hand repeatedly smacking her buttocks, she realised that appetite had returned even more strongly.

Every kiss of his palm sparked a greater rush of need and the fluid fever spread quickly through her. The inner muscles of her sex clenched and brought with them an obscenely inviting desire. The sensations were galling, an affront to the way she believed her body ought to be reacting, and she cursed herself for responding so.

Her breasts remained pressed against the leather surface of the desk and the growing discomfort she felt there told her that her nipples were stiffening. A part of her was relieved her position didn't allow Todd Chalmers to see the effect he was inspiring, but there was another a part, a part she was loathe to acknowledge, that wanted him to see she wasn't immune to his discipline. Torn by confusion, she struggled to suppress a sob.

'Do you believe what I told you?' he demanded.

Nodding her head, wilfully dragging her thoughts away from the lascivious route they had been following, Hope strove to answer. After all that had happened in the foyer she was more than prepared to accept covens of vampires and Faith's unbelievable predicament, and she told him as much in a breathless gasp.

'And not before time,' he growled. 'Now, stay quiet while I take care of more important matters.'

He paused from spanking her backside, his hand resting idly against one cheek. The weight of his palm was as maddening as each punishing blow had been and she bit her lip to stop herself from moaning. The tips of his fingers brushed the creased fabric over her crotch and that light contact made her want to whimper. Glancing back over her shoulder, wondering if Chalmers knew he was firing her with desperate arousal, she was almost disappointed to see he held a mobile phone in his other hand and had it pressed against his ear. Oblivious to Hope and her responses, he stared blindly at one of the CCTV monitors as he waited for a reply to his call.

'Duval,' he barked. 'I've got a collapsed drunk in the

foyer. Kindly remove her before the paying customers start tripping over the bitch.'

He paused, his frown remaining fixed as he listened to the tinny voice at the other end of the line. Hope guessed he was speaking to Jean Duval, head of the casino's security, and although she understood the conversation the subtext was disturbing.

If Chalmers had seen what really happened in the foyer, and if he knew about the existence of vampires, she couldn't accept that he really thought the fallen redhead was merely drunk. No, his coy phrasing and ice-cool tone showed he was used to dealing with the undead, and familiar with cleaning up the aftermath of their passion, and the knowledge that she was now under the control of such a man made her ill with apprehension.

'I know you don't deal with drunks, Jean,' Chalmers growled, 'but you'll deal with this one. And once you've disposed of her you'll sweep the casino for uninvited guests.'

There was another pause, made more frustrating for Hope because Chalmers wriggled his fingers impatiently as he allowed Duval to speak. The casual caress was amplified through the crotch of her basque and sent spirals of raw delight sparkling through her pussy lips. Unable to contain her response she turned her face away, balled her hands into impotent fists and tried to hide her blushes from him.

It was bewildering to think that an hour ago she had been a promising business management student who was bold enough to confront her bully of an employer, yet now she was sprawled across his desk like some sadist's variation of an executive toy. The image was so demeaning her stomach folded with a fresh bout of shame.

Chalmers continued to glare at the CCTV monitor. 'I

told you this day might be coming, Jean,' he snapped, his tone rushed as though breaking into the other man's speech. 'You scoffed at the time but you accepted a raise in salary to protect me through the eventuality. I haven't phoned up for an argument or a discussion on the vagaries of your job description. I've called with an instruction. Just do as I've told you and keep me informed on any developments.'

Without any further words Chalmers snapped the cover on his phone closed and turned his attention back to Hope. 'Duval was being particularly dense this evening, even by the standards of the French. I trust you won't give me the same trouble.'

Not daring to look at him, fearful he would see the arousal in her expression, Hope didn't turn back. She kept her gaze fixed firmly on the surface of the leather-topped desk and watched it repeatedly blur through the swell of her mortified tears.

His fingertips stroked the burning cheeks of her rear and she struggled not to writhe beneath the wicked torment. The caress was gentle and delicate, a sublime opposite to the harsh cruelty of his spanking, and she knew it would be too easy to give in to the wayward desires he evoked. Regardless of her loathing for him, and defying her doubts about his integrity, she yearned to succumb to the temptation he presented. Her body had almost begun to relax, soothed by the idle teasing of his hand, when he brusquely tore the fishnets away.

Hope shrieked and squirmed to escape the unexpected assault and tried twisting free and scrabbling to get from the desk, but Chalmers placed a hand on her back and held her in place with insouciant arrogance. 'Stay still,' he growled. 'Your cheeks are blushing, your uniform is torn, and I won't have you leaving this office in that condition.' She fixed him with a withering glare but he missed the expression. 'And I can't have you working the casino floor with a marked arse,' he snapped. 'Stay still, stop trying to run away and let me do what needs to be done.'

Not sure what to expect, and unable to understand why it was so easy to obey him, Hope remained rigid on the desk. His fingers slipped from her buttocks, he removed the hand that had been pressing in the small of her back, and quietly stepped away. She held her breath, trying to convince herself she should take the opportunity to run, but unable to believe it would do any good. Admittedly the door was locked, and she knew Chalmers kept the key on the bunch that dangled from a chain on his belt loop, but she wanted to make some show of resistance to his brutal domination. Yet fear made her hesitate, and by the time she found the courage to act Chalmers had returned to her side and his hand fell back to the swell of her buttocks.

Hope was flinching from the shameful thrill of his touch when he placed a fat, glass jar on the desk beside her waist. Although she was unable to understand the French label, it didn't take a great feat of imagination for her to work out that he had brought some sort of soothing balm, and the thought that he might be genuinely trying to help was lost in the rush of fear that came when he popped the crotch fasteners on her basque.

'No,' she said defensively, covering herself with one hand, 'you're not doing that. I won't allow it.' But he merely pushed her fingers aside and continued as though she hadn't spoken; slipping the back of the basque up he delivered a short sharp smack to her bottom and told her to be quiet.

Hope squirmed against the desk, her unease burning

more brightly than ever. Because she knew the casino uniform was revealing, and in a futile bid to afford herself some modesty, she always took the care to wear a thong whilst working. She doubted the flimsy fabric would really conceal anything but the underwear always gave her a small sense of comfort and protection. However, she didn't think the thong would appear very modest right now and the thought that Chalmers was able to see the gusset made her shrivel with embarrassment. After all that had happened so far this evening, the excitement of encountering Nick and Helen and the hateful joy she had already experienced beneath Chalmers' hand, she feared the crotch would be dark with the moistness of her arousal. Her embarrassment burnt like acid.

'Tights, basque and a thong,' Chalmers grunted, sour amusement in his tone. 'Do you always keep this package so securely wrapped?'

Twin spots of embarrassment blazed in her cheeks as her blushes flared more furiously. She started to speak – ready to tell him the abuse had gone on long enough and that she wasn't going to suffer any further indignities – but Chalmers didn't allow her the opportunity, for his fingers went to the thong and, with a firm sweep, he pulled the underwear away.

She held herself motionless against the desk, anxious to run away and at the same time not daring to move. The knowledge that she was now completely exposed to him left her panicked and helpless. She knew he could see her sex, didn't doubt the smooth lips of her labia were glistening dark-pink beneath his gaze, and she squirmed beneath the humiliation of being laid bare for his attention. It might have been easier to tolerate if he spoke – a word of approval or some murmur of shock – but instead the air remained heavy with expectant silence.

From the corner of her eye she watched Chalmers twist the lid off the jar and scoop his fingers through the thick, white cream. The hand disappeared from view and she wasn't surprised to feel the cool balm being spread over her cheeks. Unable to stop herself, she moaned.

His previous discipline had been an exercise in suffering and made worse by her body's treacherous response, but this was unbearable. His fingertips smoothed the cream into her buttocks, soothing away the heat and leaving only a divine awareness. He traced the heated surface of each cheek, his touch firm without rekindling the discomfort. His touch was light, massaging and kneading with practiced dexterity, and Hope held herself motionless for fear of giving away her responses. It was all too easy to imagine her sex lips pouting for him, and on those occasions when his hand drew daringly close to them she tingled with unbidden need.

The soft sound of Chalmers' mirthless laughter didn't help and she considered cautioning him for mocking her. But not wanting to start the conversation, knowing he would have no hesitation in saying he was laughing at her and the blatant symptoms of her arousal, she remained silent and tried not to be won over by the growing pleasure.

He scooped his fingers through the cream again and she shivered as its fresh chill soothed her flesh. She half expected those tremors to subside as soon as he resumed his massage, but instead of diminishing they only grew more profound. His hands cupped both cheeks of her bottom, spreading the flesh around her sex and heightening her sensitivity. The casual caress of his fingertips, inadvertently sliding against her pussy lips, quickly took her to the throes of ecstasy.

Listening carefully, Hope noticed his derisory laughter had stopped. Rather than continuing to mock her she could only hear his ragged breath, underscored by a murmur of appreciation. The obvious lust in his tone was unsettling because she knew his arousal was the perfect match for her own.

He touched her again, his fingertips sliding from the cheeks of her bottom and slipping inquisitively against her pussy. Her sex was hypersensitive to every nuance and a shiver tickled through her tummy. The warm wetness she felt before returned with greater intensity and her inner muscles began to squeeze and cramp with greedy need, and when the lubricated tip of a finger slipped against her clitoris Hope was stung by a glorious rush of release.

She tried to hide the response from Chalmers, but she felt sure he was experienced enough to know what was happening. Her spine straightened, she tightened her hands into fists, and then bit her lower lip to stop herself from crying out. Her eyes were squeezed shut, but even in that world of darkness she was treated to a display of illuminations more glorious than anything she had ever seen over the Seine or along the *Champs Elysées*. Wave after wave of pounding joy soared through her body but she fought to remain motionless and maintain the charade that she was immune to Chalmers and his hateful, wonderful discipline.

He withdrew his fingers then helped her to a chair before returning to his own. They regarded one another across his desk in expectant silence. Eventually, fearing he might read something from her expression if she didn't speak first, Hope said, 'There was no need to hurt me like that. There was no need to do any of those things to me.'

Chalmers shrugged and relit his cigar. 'Report me,' he growled. 'If we live through the next three nights I'll even supply the stationery and postage for your formal complaint. Christ, I'll even give you a handwritten confession confirming everything you say. But I'll only do that if we make it through the next three nights.'

She regarded him warily. His indifferent tone reminded her that they were facing a threat greater than a mere incident of gross misconduct, and it helped to put her own response in perspective. Numbly, she realised the discipline hadn't just given her the relief of sexual pleasure; it had also taken her mind from the trauma of discovering vampires and her sister's dilemma. As the waves of unexpected joy receded, and she remembered her encounter in the foyer, Hope understood she had more important things to deal with than Chalmers' manhandling and her own perverse enjoyment. 'What do they want from me?'

'Lilah, their leader, sees you as a threat. She wants to get rid of you.'

'And what do they want with you?'

He turned away, refusing to meet her gaze. 'Lilah never cared much for me,' he said gruffly. 'I imagine she's just trying to settle old scores while the opportunity is available.' Speaking quickly, not seeming to care that Hope could tell he was deliberately avoiding the topic, he continued, 'I need to prepare you to face these vampires.'

He stepped away from the desk for a moment, poured himself a fresh scotch and filled a tumbler for Hope, before sitting back down. She didn't want the drink but she took it and hoped the alcohol would steady her nerves. 'Prepare me?' she said warily. 'What does that mean?'

'It means I need to prepare you to face these vampires,' he repeated. 'I need to help you get ready to defeat Lilah.'

'And how are you going to do that?'

His eyes glinted with mischievous charm. 'How am I going to prepare you? You've just had your first lesson, Hope. And everything else I have to teach will be equally punishing.'

She stared at him in disbelief and shook her head. 'Do you really think I'll allow you to touch me like that again?' she demanded.

'You'll beg me to do it,' he said confidently.

She glared at him, appalled by his arrogance and her own licentious response. Her insides were already trembling with anticipation and she wondered what form of illness was governing her despicable reactions. 'What makes you think I'd want your filthy hands touching me again?' she snorted.

He reached into his desk drawer and withdrew a black crystal. It sparkled like wet blood in the red lines of illumination and, although she had no idea what it might be, Hope couldn't help but be impressed by the mystical air it seemed to generate. 'What is it?' she whispered.

'The Bethesda Stone,' he replied, his tone bordering on reverence. 'It's a legendary crystal that, under the right circumstances, can reverse the condition of being a vampire.' Seeing her sceptical frown he added, 'It's possibly the one thing that can save your sister.'

Hope reached out to take the crystal from his fingers, but Chalmers pulled it away and sat back in his chair. Shaking his head he smiled sadly and added, 'You need to know a lot more about what we're dealing with before you can have this.'

'But…'

'You need to know a lot more about Lilah. You need to know about the threat posed by her coven of vampires. And you need to learn a lot more about the Bethesda Stone.'

Hope glared at him. 'It's a piece of coloured glass,' she scoffed indecisively. 'What is there to learn about a piece of coloured glass?'

He regarded her solemnly, the sardonic humour finally gone from his features. 'There's much to learn,' he said frankly. 'And I don't think you'll believe half of what I have to tell you. You've got to learn about vampires, I've got to tell you about your sister, but I think I should explain about the Bethesda Stone first and the legend that surrounds it. I think I should tell you that using it carries a price.'

Hope said nothing, unsurprised by this caveat. She already knew that everything came with a price and she considered herself worldly enough to know that artefacts like the Bethesda Stone never came cheap. But if Chalmers was correct in thinking it might save her sister, she knew it was a price she would have to pay.

Interlude

Part One

Dressed in her leathers, the waistcoat unfastened to reveal her pert breasts, Lilah looked truly formidable. She resided in one of the suite's sumptuous armchairs with one leg cocked absently over its arm and the other stretched out before her. There was a dreamy cast to her scarlet eyes, yet they still followed every detail with avid curiosity. Her enigmatic smile was at once alluring and predatory.

But, Faith thought, Lilah wasn't the most disquieting thing in the room.

Nick and Helen, recently returned from their leader's errand, joined their bodies with the lusty hunger of depraved animals. Not bothering to undress, merely unfastening the necessary buttons and pushing the nuisance of other clothes aside, they rutted on the floor with urgent abandon. They were characteristically unmindful of their audience, cursing, groaning and sighing with scant regard for the others in the room. Helen's shoulders and buttocks were buried into the plush pile of the carpet, Nick knelt between her legs, and they bucked and thrashed greedily together. Their sporadic tempo kept time with a background music of gothic rock that Faith recognised from her sister's first album with BloodLust. Helen wrapped her ankles around his back, Nick pressed his mouth against her throat, and they embraced with furious passion. The slurping of lovemaking and kisses was reminiscent of animals feeding from a trough.

But, Faith thought, the pair of excited vampires weren't

the most disquieting thing in the room either.

Marcia and the mulatto knelt on opposite sides of Lilah's chair. Since the dark one had been defeated (since Faith had ripped the cold black heart from his chest, she amended ruefully) the pair had been relegated to the roles of Lilah's attendant sex slaves. The two women were both naked and each nubile body glistened with an oily sheen of sweat. Their eyes glinted scarlet and their smiles were made menacing with razor-sharp teeth.

The mulatto's long hair clung to her scalp and shoulders in tight, mahogany ringlets. The style accentuated the shape of her skull and made her face appear delicate and desirable, but her taut muscles and an Olympian physique spoilt the illusion of fragility. Her full, pouting lips were puckered into a kiss as she repeatedly lowered her face to the toe of Lilah's boot.

Marcia – young, vibrant, and with her beauty only marred by the perpetual sneer that wrinkled her retroussé nose – knelt at Lilah's other side. She suckled against the leader's nipple, teasing the rigid bud of flesh between her elongated canines and drawing her lips greedily around its thrust. Occasionally her tongue would extend and trace against the stiff flesh until they both shivered. The exchange of pleasure was clearly a two-way street because Marcia's areolae were the flushed crimson of arousal.

But for Faith, even though their obedience was unexpected and obscene, even Lilah's pair of pliant sex slaves didn't rank as the most disquieting thing in the room.

The music playing featured her sister singing for a band that was managed by Todd Chalmers and styled to capitalise on a subculture that celebrated all things vampiric. That combination of coincidences could have unnerved Faith, but she thought those factors were nothing more than a mere curiosity compared to the most unsettling thing. She glared at the box clutched in Lilah's lap and frowned. It was old, battered – not particularly large but awkward and bulky – and fashioned to resemble a miniature pirate's treasure chest, and its presence was enough to make Faith feel nauseous.

'Why are you still holding onto that?' she asked.

Lilah lifted her gaze as though coming from a dream. The smile she flashed at Faith looked genuine and she waved a laconic greeting. 'Darling,' she cooed, 'you're back. Did you finally feed? Are you going to tell me all about it?'

Faith regarded the coven's leader with a tight-lipped smile and shook her head. She pointed again at the box and demanded, 'Why are you still holding onto that? Why don't you just throw it in the Seine, or lose it, or burn it, or something?'

Smiling, Lilah pushed Marcia away from her breast and stepped out of the chair. The tip of her boot almost kicked the mulatto in the face but the dark-skinned vampire was swift enough to avoid injury. She glared at Lilah's back, her gaze etched with fury, but the coven's leader was oblivious to the venom in the woman's expression. Lilah made her away around Nick and Helen, still clutching her prized wooden box as she strode purposefully towards Faith. 'You know I can't just get rid of it,' she purred. 'It holds a personal treasure that means so much to me.'

Faith struggled to hide her revulsion. The box was pressed between them, the contents pulsing steadfastly and with enough force to shake the small gilded latch that held it closed. 'It's disgusting.'

'I know,' Lilah agreed airily. 'But old habits are so hard to break. My brother walked in shadows for four hundred years, and he led this coven for the best part of two centuries. I don't think I'd feel right assuming the leadership if I couldn't rely on the security of keeping a small memento.'

Faith tried to step back and distance herself from Lilah and the box, but her shoulders were already pressed against the wall. She hated the dark longing Lilah aroused, and particularly dreaded that emotion when it was tainted with fear or disgust. Perversely, her revulsion and terror always spawned a deep-seated need for sexual satisfaction and she suspected that Lilah was aware of her reaction. The woman invariably capitalised on those responses whenever she encouraged Faith to submit to another indignity or depravity, and the loathsome box had now become a constant accessory whenever Lilah tried coaxing Faith to feed.

Swallowing nervously, trying to disguise her black excitement, Faith asked, 'Didn't your brother have a pocket watch or a lucky amulet that you could have taken? Do you have to keep his beating heart in that box?'

Lilah shrugged and looked set to reply when one of the vampires spoke from behind.

'She keeps his heart in the box so he can't ever come back.' The mulatto's voice was acidic. Faith couldn't work out if she was hearing scorn for her ignorance about the undeads' folklore, or contempt that Lilah had betrayed her brother. 'She keeps the box close to hand so no one can resurrect the dark one and return him to his rightful place at the head of the coven.'

Lilah glared at her. Her playful façade was gone and her features were twisted with rage. 'His *rightful* place?'

The mulatto blinked and shrugged. 'I meant his *former* place,' she corrected.

'I told you and Marcia to run an errand for me earlier,' Lilah said, squaring her shoulders and glowering furiously at the sex slave. 'I think you'd better go and do that now.'

The mulatto looked untroubled by Lilah's air of menace. She pulled herself defiantly from her place by the chair and nodded for Marcia to join her. Still naked, both tilting their chins and walking with their shoulders thrown back, the pair marched side-by-side towards the door.

Lilah grabbed the mulatto's shoulder as the woman tried to step past her. 'You don't still pine for my brother's leadership, do you?'

The mulatto's face was inscrutable. Beside her, Marcia flicked her gaze from one woman to the other and Faith understood the blonde's mounting panic. She could see that Lilah was in no mood for dissension, the mulatto was acting with her usual arrogance, and a confrontation looked inevitable.

'Do I pine for your brother's leadership?' the mulatto repeated. She laughed dryly and said, 'Of course not, Mistress Lilah.' And in a tone that dripped with sarcasm she added, 'It is now you that I live to serve.' Stiffly she tried to shake herself free and leave, but Lilah maintained her grip on the mulatto's shoulder.

'I thought you felt that way,' she said coolly. 'So, it shouldn't trouble you too greatly if I ask you to prove your loyalty.'

'Prove it?' the mulatto asked warily. 'How do you expect me to do that?'

Lilah glared at her. 'Kneel at my feet and show you respect my authority.'

Marcia gasped. Faith watched uneasily, sure the mulatto would refuse, but surprising her, the dark-skinned vampire nodded then lowered herself gracefully to her knees. She stared up at Lilah's imposing figure, her eyes wide yet still showing no sign of servility. 'Are you going to ask me to kiss your boots?' she asked. 'I'm only wondering because I've been doing that for the last hour and it's clearly not proved my obedience to your satisfaction.'

Lilah's brow narrowed, her fingers curled into claws, and Faith could see the effort the woman invested in resisting the urge to strike. But instead of hitting out, a slow smile crossed her face and she shook her head. Her eyes sparkled with Machiavellian cruelty. Pointing at Faith she barked, 'Take your pants off, girl. Don't make me tell you twice.' Not waiting to see if she was obeyed, glaring triumphantly down at the mulatto, Lilah added, 'I'm not going to tell you to kiss *my* boots.' She nodded at Faith. 'I want you to kiss hers, instead.'

Faith couldn't tell whether the air in the room was thick with tension or her own rush of excitement. She sensed the change when she tried to draw breath and realised her chest was tight with anticipation. The mulatto cast a fiery glance in Lilah's direction, and for an instant it looked like she might refuse.

Faith barely noticed the exchange as she hurried to do as she'd been told. Lilah had made her wear the scarlet leathers and insisted the clinging allure of the outfit wasn't spoilt by underwear, but Faith desperately wished she had disobeyed the coven's leader on that particular instruction. She quickly peeled the pants from her legs and, after the sweaty warmth of the leather against her crotch, her sex lips felt cool, wet and obvious. Familiar pangs of embarrassment tormented her. Even though the rest of the room's occupants were either naked or in various states of undress, and all of them had seen her in one compromising position or another, she didn't think she would ever be able to distance herself from the shame that came with public nudity. She supposed her inhibitions might fade when she began feeding, but the hunger for blood was an urge she still resisted, although knowing

41

her resolve to ignore that appetite always weakened when she was in the throes of arousal, her worries intensified when the dark-skinned vampire turned to face her. Faith's heart pounded as she stared down at the pretty woman between her bare feet.

Slowly the mulatto lowered her head and placed her lips against Faith's foot. The tight ringlets of her sleek hair brushed Faith's shins. The whisper-soft caress was maddeningly exciting and Faith urged herself to stand rigid and not be won over by the vampire's nearness. She flashed a silent plea for help in Lilah's direction, but when the coven's leader saw Faith's anxiety her smile widened.

'Kiss higher,' she demanded, wicked glee in her voice as she gave the instruction. 'Kiss her legs. And keep kissing higher until I tell you to stop.'

Faith shivered, and although she seemed reluctant the mulatto was flawlessly obedient. She placed the soft weight of her lips against Faith's bare legs and repeatedly stole delicate kisses. The pulse of Faith's arousal beat with more force and she pushed herself against the wall as though trying to escape the torment. The mulatto's scalp brushed against her legs, inched higher, and excited deep inside her. When her lips reached Faith's knees her forehead brushed tantalisingly close to the tops of her thighs. Faith could feel the ringlets mingling against her pubic curls and the movement of each follicle was amplified by arousal. She swallowed and wished she could move away, but a single glance at Lilah's stern frown told her there would be trouble if she did.

'Go on,' Lilah encouraged the mulatto. 'You know what I expect of you.'

Faith pressed her back harder against the wall as the woman obeyed. Soft lips graced her thighs, the tip of the mulatto's nose nuzzled her cleft, and then a tongue was lapping at the moist lips of her sex. The ripple of each taste bud rasped lovingly against her labia and the sudden rush of pleasure was overwhelming and unbearable.

It wasn't the first time a woman had kissed her so intimately. Before being made into a vampire Faith found herself falling into a relationship with her best friend, Claire. Their discovery of each other had been a beautiful revelation and she believed it would have developed into something wholesome and fulfilling, if not for the inconvenience of being changed into one of the undead. But because the sensitive slip of a tongue against her pussy lips would always remind her of Claire – and because memories of her friend and lover always inspired a rush of salacious thoughts – Faith wilfully pushed those recollections from her mind.

'Kiss her properly,' Lilah demanded. 'Don't just tease the little bitch.'

The mulatto placed her hands on Faith's hips and buried her face closer. The razor-sharp tips of her fingernails pressed against Faith's buttocks but the flair of discomfort didn't spoil her excitement. If anything the cruel pressure added a fresh sparkle of delight that made her yearn to surrender.

Deftly the mulatto extended her tongue. Faith could feel the tip plundering the lips of her sex, spreading the soft labia aside and burrowing deep into her wetness. The mulatto's upper lip brushed her clitoris, and when the woman pressed her fingers tighter Faith realised she was hovering on the precipice of an orgasm. Becoming a vampire had heightened her senses and she was still overawed by the way the mundane had become incredible. But now, faced with the divine bliss that was being wrought against her sex, she felt sure she was going to explode with euphoria. Gasping furiously, wanting the pleasure to continue and desperate for it to cease, Faith switched her gaze from the top of the mulatto's head to Marcia's avaricious leer, then Lilah's commanding frown.

The coven's leader smiled bitterly, looked set to make a further instruction, then cast a glance towards the suite's bedroom door. 'Enough,' she sighed, turning her frown back on the mulatto. 'Take your tongue out of her hole. For what it's worth, you've proved your obedience.'

Bewildered, Faith stared at her. She wasn't sure if she should be grateful the torment was ended or furious that it hadn't been allowed to meet her needs. Unsatisfied urges writhed in her groin like agonising cramps and with that arousal came a renewed desire to feed. She swallowed again, wishing the coppery flavour of blood was trickling down her throat rather than the flat taste of her own un-sated excitement.

Lilah ignored her, and glaring down at the mulatto she said again, 'You've proved your obedience, but your lack of gratitude remains galling.'

The mulatto snorted. 'And what the hell should I be grateful for?'

Lilah's eyebrows raised in indignation. 'When my brother ruled this coven you lived in sewers and crypts,' she pointed out acidly. 'This is only the third night of my leadership and we're already staying on the *Champs Elysées* in this damned casino's presidential suite.'

The mulatto considered this without moving from her knees. 'The location may be an improvement but the workload is still the same. I'm still bowing to the leader; I'm still kissing boots; and I have to eat pussy whenever I'm told.'

The fury on Lilah's face looked pained. She dragged the mulatto from the floor and held her so their lips were close enough to kiss. 'You're on your last chance,' she

44

snarled. 'Go with Marcia, do the errand I've instructed, and don't fuck up.'

'And then?' the mulatto asked defiantly.

'And then,' Lilah growled, 'don't give me reason to doubt you again.' She pushed the mulatto away and made her smile saccharin sweet. Waiting until the two subordinates had left the room, she linked her arm in Faith's and started to lead her away from the door.

In the three days she'd been a member of the coven, Faith had already seen enough of Lilah's mood swings to know they alternated between extremes, but she didn't think she would ever get used to them. Uneasy with the woman's nearness, and still uncomfortably aware of the fact that she was wearing only a scarlet leather waistcoat and nothing else, Faith made an attempt to retrieve her discarded leather pants. But Lilah tugged on her arm, firmly leading her away from the door.

They stepped past Nick and Helen, the pair still grunting and struggling to achieve another climax, and Lilah took Faith back to her chair. She settled herself in the sumptuous seat and encouraged Faith to kneel on the floor beside her. It didn't escape Faith's notice that she was now in the same position as the leader had kept her sex slaves, and she cringed from the thought of what Lilah might be expecting. The leader's waistcoat was still unfastened, the thrust of her nipples hovered tantalisingly close to Faith's face, and the urge to tease her tongue against one bud bordered on the irresistible. The only thing that stopped her was the wooden box, once again returned to Lilah's lap, with its repugnant contents steadfastly pulsing. Faith couldn't think of any inducement that would make her willingly go closer unless the coven's leader resolutely demanded.

Lilah reached out and stroked her fingertips against

Faith's cheek. The caress was light but she made no attempt to disguise the potential for cruelty that lay beneath her touch. In an earnest tone she leant closer and confided, 'You and I share a similar problem.' Faith snatched her fearful gaze from the wooden box and regarded the leader expectantly. 'We both have habits that are hard to break,' Lilah explained. Speaking quickly, talking over the lack of comprehension on Faith's face, she tapped the box in her lap. 'I can't conceive of ruling this coven without keeping a piece of my brother close to hand. And you can't bring yourself to do the most natural thing in the world for a vampire. You can't bring yourself to feed.'

Faith blushed and looked away, but Lilah's fingers trailed beneath her chin, tilting her face so their gazes met. 'You've been a vampire for three nights now,' she purred. 'The urge takes most of us within the first minute: the first hour at the outside. Yet you've resisted that impulse and you continue to resist.'

'I don't want to feed,' Faith mumbled, refusing to meet the other woman's eyes. 'I'm not particularly hungry. Not hungry for that.'

Lilah leaned closer, her seductive smile inching nearer. 'Are you sure you don't want to feed? You looked ever so hungry when the mulatto was tonguing your hole.'

The words reminded Faith about the wetness of her sex, and the need for satisfaction returned with brutal force. Lilah had shifted position in the chair and her bare breast was too close to resist. Not sure if she was doing it so she didn't have to reply, or acting on the instincts of a libidinous impulse, Faith pushed forward and caught the nipple between her lips.

Lilah sighed, the wordless exhalation encouraging and made Faith's arousal more demanding. The bud of flesh was solid against her tongue, and as she traced her teeth against its stiffness she was struck by a renewed need for satisfaction. She considered turning away, pulling her face from Lilah's breast, but she couldn't bring herself to move.

In the centre of the room Helen screamed. Faith shifted her gaze to the pair, managing to watch while she kept Lilah's nipple firmly between her teeth. The blonde's cry of elation was joined by Nick's sigh as he thrust deeper into her pussy. They clung to one another, trails of freshly spilt blood trickling between Helen's breasts and a smudged scarlet smile smeared across her lips. The stench of sweat, musk and ejaculate filled the room, and while she wanted to be revolted, Faith found each intake of breath only fuelled her body's craving. Her attention was drawn back to the coven's leader when Lilah caressed her cheek, the simple act of being touched enough to make Faith want to surrender, and she regarded the woman with pained hope.

'Are you sure you don't want to feed?' Lilah whispered. 'You look hungrier than any vampire I've ever seen, and now Nick and Helen have finished I could always send them out to grab a bite for you.'

With the last of her resolve, Faith managed to shake her head.

'I can call room service,' Lilah suggested. 'We could have them send up a whore or a porter, whatever takes your fancy.'

If the box hadn't been there Faith knew she would have relented. She didn't want to feed, she felt certain she would be dooming herself to great catastrophe if she did, but the temptation was almost irresistible. Yet the presence of the box – and her loathing for its vile pulse and her revulsion of its despicable contents – was enough to make her decline. Still holding the nipple between her teeth,

47

savouring the sensation and shaping her words carefully around it, she heard herself say, 'There's no need for them to find me a victim. There's no need to summon anyone from room service. I don't want to feed.'

Lilah's laughter was as soothing as the fingers she combed through Faith's hair. 'You will soon enough,' she said seriously. 'The desire will come on you and you won't be able to stop yourself until your thirst for blood is quenched.'

Faith wanted to shake her head in defiance but she was reluctant to let go of the breast at her mouth. She suspected that Lilah was right and didn't want to argue for fear the coven's leader would decide to make a point of proving her wrong. Three days with the vampires had been enough to show Faith that Lilah was ruthless and determined.

'We all succumb to that urge.' Lilah spoke with fond sadness as she continued to stroke Faith's head. The caress of nails against her scalp was light and the intimacy of the touch was maddeningly exciting. The scent of Lilah's arousal grew stronger and the rush of her own need dizzied Faith. 'Sometimes it's like a symptom of hunger, a craving that gnaws at your belly.'

Faith regarded her with sharp impatience, wondering if the woman had seen something in her body language that revealed her true desires. The ache inside her was hateful and incessant. It was a greedy pulse that beat with the same monotonous rhythm as the loathsome heart in the box. Faith believed her arousal could be satisfied by a swift and glorious climax, but she felt more certain it would be sated if she relented to Lilah's will and finally fed.

Lilah continued blithely, seemingly unmindful of Faith's growing confusion. 'Sometimes the urge comes with a hunger for blood,' she purred. 'And sometimes it comes with arousal. But for most of us it comes with a combination of those two factors. The need to feed is inevitable when a hungry vampire is faced with the right victim.' She pulled Faith's head from her breast and stood up.

Bewildered that the nipple had been taken from her, Faith could only stare at the woman. From the corner of her eye she saw Nick and Helen were watching avidly but, even though her naked bottom was exposed to them, she found it easy to dismiss the pair. Mesmerised by something in Lilah's tone, and the seductive way she extended a hand, Faith rose from her position by the chair.

'I have a gift for you in the bedroom,' Lilah confided.

Reluctant to go but compelled to follow, Faith took Lilah's hand. But she stopped at the door, terrified to go in when she saw what the vampire had prepared for her.

'I thought you might like this surprise,' Lilah purred. 'Nick and Helen brought her back for me and I thought you could make special use of her.'

Lost for words, Faith could only stare at Lilah's gift with a mixture of wonderment and horror. Naked and tied to the bed was her best friend, and former lover, Claire.

Hope

Act I, Scene III

Hope's thoughts were a chaotic jumble as she staggered along the corridor. Chalmers had spoken for too long; she was still trying to understand the spanking and her inappropriate response; she wanted to rationalise the leap in faith that had transformed vampires from an archaic myth to a contemporary danger; and there was also the issue of her sister's unbelievable predicament. It was more than she could accept in one evening, and as soon as the opportunity presented itself Hope made an excuse and left the manager's office.

She said she needed fresh air from outside the casino – perhaps the night-lit splendour of the *Place de l'Etoile*, or maybe joining one of the regular cavalcades of rollerbladers that swept through the Parisian streets – and she added that the change of scenery might help clear her mind. She didn't really believe an excursion would be of any assistance but she was anxious to escape Chalmers, the stench of cigar smoke and the scent of her own nervous excitement that now permeated his office. Borrowing his trench coat, wrapping it tight around her nearly naked body, she had excused herself and promised she would return, and those words were still ringing through her mind as she tried to decide if she should honour them, when she saw the two naked women.

For an instant she almost didn't notice their nudity. Her thoughts were distracted and the pair held themselves with such arrogant confidence it seemed only natural that they should parade unclothed through the casino's upper corridors. Their exhibitionism only registered with Hope when she absently admired the blonde's pert breasts in the same way she would have appreciated another woman's choker or brooch. The breasts were full and rounded, tipped with dusky areolae and jutting nipples, and Hope silently wished her own breasts looked as firm and buxom. When it slowly dawned on her that she was looking at the bare body of another woman, she stood rigid and gaped in disbelief.

The blonde noticed, saw Hope's incredulous expression, and paused. Her companion – a brunette with a dark-gold tan, mahogany ringlets and nipples the colour of melted chocolate – continued walking until their linked arms dragged her to a standstill. She glared at the blonde, and then glanced at Hope with avaricious intent. Their predatory interest reminded Hope of the vampires she had encountered in the foyer, and the fear that came with that memory was fully rekindled when she saw the glint of scarlet sparkling in both women's eyes.

'You look familiar,' the blonde murmured. 'Do I know you?'

Embarrassment momentarily overrode Hope's fear and she blushed. She had noticed the blonde's pubic curls were trimmed to a neat vertical line that pointed down to her sex. Unable to draw her attention away, shocked that she was so easily able to glimpse the flushed cerise of the woman's labia, she began to stammer incoherently.

The brunette gave her a cursory glance, sniffed dismissively, and pulled on her companion's arm. 'They all begin to look alike after you've fed from a few,' she snapped tiredly. 'We have an errand to run, remember? Do you really want the queen bitch getting pissed at the pair of us again?'

The brunette's body was just as attractive as the blonde's and Hope couldn't resist making a sly appraisal. Small breasts and strong thighs set off the flat stomach and athletic frame. Like the blonde, the brunette had trimmed her pubic bush to a neat, vertical line and Hope finally found the strength to snatch her gaze away before she could be caught looking at the other woman's sex. Her cheeks burnt bright crimson.

The blonde held her ground, refusing to be dragged away. 'She reminds me of someone,' she insisted. 'There's something very familiar about her face. I'm sure I've seen this one before.'

The brunette stepped by her and pulled at Hope's collar, moving with such speed and grace Hope didn't notice the vampire approaching until the shoulder of her borrowed trench coat was tugged roughly down. Hope gasped as a hand went beneath her jaw, her face was tilted from side to side and it was only as an afterthought that she realised her bare throat was being exhibited to the blonde.

'See,' the brunette said, as though proving a point. 'There are no marks on her throat, therefore you haven't seen her before. It's like I said: they all begin to look alike.'

The blonde rested her head to one side. 'Maybe I saw her and didn't feed from her,' she suggested.

'Yeah, that's likely.'

Hope realised that while they were talking she had a slim chance to escape. Both seemed suitably distracted, the empty corridor stretched invitingly in both directions, but she couldn't find the presence of mind to run. Her thoughts had been a jumble before but now they were dominated by a single, relentless fear: she was trapped in the corridor with two naked, hungry vampires. Fretfully she glanced towards the stairwell door, hoping Jean Duval might be patrolling this floor of the casino and would come to her assistance. But the empty aisle of closed doors offered no prospect for salvation.

'Maybe we should feed from her,' the blonde suggested. 'Lilah didn't say we couldn't indulge ourselves while we're out, I am kind of hungry, and…' her smile became lascivious, '…and this one looks like she's ready to be tasted.'

Hope glanced down at herself and was shocked to see how much of the trench coat had been opened. She thought the brunette was only exposing her throat, but a quick glance at her chest was enough to show that one bare breast had been exposed, looking obscenely out of place in the public corridor, and hurriedly she tried to cover herself. She wasn't sure if her hand was going to modestly conceal the breast, or pull the lapel of the coat back into place, but her fingertips didn't get the chance to reach either before the vampire caught her wrist.

The blonde's wicked smile was a combination of seduction and admonishment. 'Don't go all shy on us,' she said playfully. 'You look like you have lots of pretty things hidden under that silly coat. My friend and I could have a lot of fun before we've finished with you.' As she spoke she rubbed the pad of her thumb against Hope's nipple.

The sting of arousal was sudden and debilitating. Hope had been trying to convince herself that she was immune to the vampire's sexual charm, but as soon as the contact was made against her breast she felt ready to surrender to whatever was demanded. Every pore ached with a delicious, insatiable need, and desire beat with warm wet longing.

'If you're going to feed from her, get it done quick.'

Hope glanced at the brunette, not surprised to see a

53

frown of impatience creasing her dark brow. The irritability in her tone belied her unease as she glanced nervously up and down the corridor.

'Feed from her if you must,' the brunette snapped. 'But I'll be telling Lilah which one of us delayed the delivery of her message, Marcia.'

Marcia scowled at her companion, at the same time unfastening the trench coat's belt. Hope tried to make a token show of resistance, struggling to free her hand from the vampire's and trying to pull away, but the efforts were futile. The shoulders of the coat were pushed aside, and with a rush of cool air caressing her bare flesh she realised she was exposed to the two naked women.

The brunette turned her gaze away, staring belligerently down the corridor.

'She has a very pretty body,' Marcia said reflectively. She briefly released her hold on Hope's wrist, allowing the trench coat to fall away and puddle on the floor. Her smile broadened and she called to her companion, 'Are you sure you don't want to share her with me? She's quite an attractive little thing.'

The brunette cast a wary glance in Hope's direction, her eyes widening as she studied her. Hope blushed, her chagrin intensifying as the brunette stepped closer and stroked an icy hand against her bottom. The tips of her fingers touched the red marks Todd left when he spanked her, and even though the soothing balm had helped to lessen some of that discomfort, Hope could still feel the memory of that pleasurable pain being reborn beneath the vampire's caress.

'She's been spanked,' the brunette declared. 'And quite recently, too.'

Hope's embarrassment transcended a level of shame she had never imagined. She tried to strike the brunette's hand away but Marcia was fast and caught her other wrist before she could make contact. Both vampires leered at her with obvious hunger and appreciation.

'Spanked?' Marcia said doubtfully, then pushing Hope against the wall, forcing her to provide an unfettered view of her buttocks, she squealed happily. As her companion had done, she traced her fingers against one of the many burning handprints that blazed upon Hope's bottom. The touch was electric, inspiring a flurry of excited responses from the punished flesh. Hope tried not to be moved by the sensations the fingertips generated, but it was an involuntary response when she gasped and held herself rigid.

'My, my,' Marcia mused, and from the corner of her eye Hope could see she was addressing the brunette, 'you're right, she has been spanked.' Then she turned her attention back to Hope, giggling ecstatically. 'This is all working out too well. You've just been with Spanky Chalmers, haven't you?'

Hope tried to think how best to answer, not surprised to hear someone had given the hotel's manager such an appropriate nickname. It occurred to her that, if she'd known he was called Spanky Chalmers before, she might have been more prepared to avoid the indignity he made her suffer. But the notion was little more than a passing fancy, quickly replaced by her dread of what the pair might do now and the burden of her burgeoning arousal.

The brunette frowned. She pulled on Hope's shoulder, turning her away from the wall so they faced each other. Her eyes blazed scarlet and she made no attempt to disguise her elongated canines. Drawing a tongue slowly across the pout of her lips she asked, 'Is that right? Do you know Chalmers? Do you know where we'll find him?'

Marcia studied her with the same avaricious glint and Hope responded without hesitation. She pointed towards the end of the corridor and explained which door led to Chalmers' office. A part of her expected no gratitude, and a part of her expected one of the vampires to bite her throat and then drop her blood-drained body to the floor. She closed her eyes, shivering with dreadful anticipation, and it was only after a full minute had passed that she opened her eyes to discover the pair had left her forgotten and alone.

Feeling ridiculous for standing naked in the corridor, she retrieved the trench coat from the floor and buckled it tight around her waist. The excitement the pair had awoken continued to beat strong and unsatisfied within her and she pressed the heel of her palm against her stomach to try and smooth the desires away, and it was while she was touching herself that she realised the enormity of what she'd done: she had directed a pair of predatory vampires to Todd Chalmers' office.

Shocked from her reverie, she glanced towards his door and saw it was already closed. Hurrying along the corridor, no longer surprised that the vampires had moved so quickly, she prayed she wouldn't be too late to intervene. She reached his office then hesitated impotently as she tried to think how best to act.

The vampires had not seen her as a threat, she didn't want to simply throw herself into the middle of whatever carnage lay beyond the door, but she couldn't leave Chalmers to be maimed and tortured by the pair. Stopping herself from bursting into the room, knowing there would be no benefit in risking both their lives, she lowered herself to her knees and glanced through the keyhole.

Her view of the room left Hope cold.

Chalmers embraced Marcia while giving the brunette a perfunctory kiss on the cheek. He held one hand against the blonde's backside and squeezed her buttock with unnecessary familiarity.

Reeling from the shock, Hope kept an unblinking eye fixed on the keyhole.

'This is an unexpected pleasure,' he leered, his gaze flitting approvingly over their bodies. 'And how charming to see that neither of you have fallen victim to this season's outlandish excuses for fashion.'

Marcia pressed herself into his embrace and giggled dutifully. Her naked body moulded against the contours of his frame and she curled one leg against his thigh.

The brunette found a pair of tumblers and poured two shots from Chalmers' scotch bottle. She handed one to the blonde and swigged the other herself. 'We've come with a message,' she declared. 'Lilah wants two things from you and she wants to know how soon she can have them.'

'Don't be so rude to Mr Chalmers,' Marcia snapped, turning a winsome smile on him, yet still speaking to her companion. 'I owe Mr Chalmers a great debt of gratitude and I don't think you should speak to him like that. He's the one who introduced me to the coven and I've still got to say a proper thank you to him for that.' She broadened her smile and stroked Chalmers' chest. Her scarlet painted nails slipped between two of the buttons on his shirt and she made a theatrical show of shivering as her fingers caressed his bare flesh.

Watching avidly, Hope could see Chalmers was responding to the blonde's interest. His leer broadened and the bulge at the front of his trousers was lewdly obvious. 'I'm surprised Lilah didn't come here herself,' he confided. 'She and I share a history.'

Marcia giggled again and rested her head against his shoulder. She teased the buttons on his shirt open, starting at his throat and working her way down to the waistband of his trousers. The palm of her hand slipped easily over the swollen bulge at his groin and her merry laughter turned into a throaty chuckle.

Not missing a single detail, Hope saw the brunette was watching the pair with a stern expression as she poured herself another scotch. 'Lilah only wants two things from you,' she growled. 'Are you ready to hear what they are?'

'Lilah wants too many things,' Marcia sniffed. 'And there'll be time to talk about her and her needs after I've shown Mr Chalmers my gratitude.' The blonde slipped a hand between her own legs and drew her fingers lazily against her sex. She parted the pink pussy lips and rubbed herself obviously, and then lifting her fingers away she held them beneath Chalmers' nose. 'Can you tell how eager I am to show you my gratitude?'

The brunette rolled her eyes, and Hope watched with disbelief and wished she could move closer to get a better view. The vampires had left her aroused and unsatisfied from their encounter in the corridor. The dull ache gnawed heavily inside her abdomen and groaned with pent up excitement. Squatting on the floor, her interest escalating with each passing second, she dared to touch a hand against her sex.

Quickly she drew her fingers away, shocked by the humid warmth that lingered there, and although the caress of her own hand had promised to satisfy the needs that broiled within her, she couldn't bring herself to contemplate that act in this situation.

'You've already shown me your gratitude,' Chalmers told Marcia, taking her wrist and guiding the blonde's fingers to her mouth, and without any hesitation Marcia licked the silvering of sexual musk that coated them.

Hope wanted to be disgusted by the sight but she couldn't argue with the heightened pulse of excitement that beat between her legs. She caught her own fingers inching back to her sex, lightly caressing her inner thigh as they slipped upwards, and stopped herself before the contact became too irresistible.

'There's no need for you to thank me again,' Chalmers said firmly. His expression was difficult to read and Hope couldn't decide if he was wary of the vampires or excited by the passion they promised. Carefully observing the way he smiled indulgently for Marcia and then frowned at the brunette, she suspected he wasn't sure which response governed his actions.

'But I want to thank you,' Marcia pouted. Her fingers dropped to the waistband of his trousers and she caught the tab of his zipper between her finger and thumb. Drawing it downwards, seeming to take great pleasure from guiding her fingers over the swollen lump of his erection, she pushed her hand inside and her grin broadened.

Hope squashed her thighs together, disgusted at her libidinous response to the unexpected peepshow but helpless to control her reaction. She didn't want to touch herself – she would have equated such a response with the most despicable behaviour – yet her fingers crept back and teased idly against the down of pubic curls.

Marcia wrestled her hand inside Chalmers' trousers before pulling out the rigid length of his erection. She stroked him languidly before tugging back hard and exposing the swollen purple dome of his glans.

Hope's eyes grew wider. The tip of her index finger chased lazy circles against the nub of her clitoris and her body was quickly caught up in a swelling thrill of excitement. She could sense she was mere moments away from satisfying the need growing within her, and she rubbed more furiously as she tried to exorcise her arousal.

Marcia lowered herself to her knees. She held Chalmers' erection in one hand and maintained eye contact with him until her face was on the same level as his stiff shaft. Almost carelessly she took her drink from his desk and poured it into her mouth.

Attentive to every detail, Hope realised the vampire hadn't swallowed. There were no doubts in her mind about what Marcia intended to do for Chalmers, and mesmerised by the prospect of watching such an intimacy, she held her breath and pressed closer to the keyhole. Giving into the craving at her sex, she slipped her other hand between her legs and held the lips of her pussy apart to toy with her pulsing clitoris.

Marcia made her move swiftly, surprising Hope with her sudden display of speed. She bobbed her head forward, and without any tempting or teasing she encircled Chalmers' erection with her lips. His features were a combination of delight and discomfort, and Marcia kept one hand at the base of his length and her mouth covered his glans. Her scarlet lips looked bloody against his alabaster shaft and the colour only grew more pronounced as her cheeks dimpled when she sucked. Her lips slipped up and down his erection, and from her position outside the room Hope could hear the blonde's greedy murmurs of approval.

Needing to satisfy her desire for release, Hope pressed more insistently against the throbbing nub of her clitoris. The delicious pleasure of stroking her labia had been enjoyable, and heightened her sensitivity, but it didn't meet her body's mounting demand for satisfaction. Trying to squeeze the orgasm from her sex, determined to wallow in the pleasures of a climax, she continued to watch events in the room as she rubbed with greater urgency.

Marcia swallowed and finally moved her face away from

Chalmers' shaft, lacquered with the mingled wetness of her saliva and the scotch. Colour blazed in his cheeks and Hope guessed he was only controlling his response with effort. 'You've been learning new tricks,' he observed. Although trying to sound indifferent there was a breathlessness to his tone that revealed the depth of his true response. 'The alcohol makes that a much more spirited experience.'

Marcia smiled for him and shook her head. 'I knew that trick before I became a vampire. I learnt that while at finishing school.'

Hope could barely hear them as the first rush of her orgasm shivered between her legs. Her thighs ached from the exertion of her position and she had to clamp a hand across her mouth for fear of crying out and giving herself away. Eddies of joy swirled through her and she stiffened as the joy buffeted her body. A flood of smouldering warmth rushed from her sex, the pleasure of its egress trembling with the cramp of her muscles. The release of her orgasm wasn't quite strong enough to satisfy all the needs that lingered within her, but for the moment she conceded her appetite had been temporarily sated. She turned her attention back to the keyhole and hoped she hadn't missed anything important whilst distracted by her climax.

The brunette had ingratiated herself into Chalmers' embrace, pressing her body against his muscular form in the same way Marcia had held him before. She stroked the side of his face, guiding his mouth to kiss hers, while the blonde continued to suck on his erection.

Still concerned that Chalmers might be facing a threat from the pair, she wondered if she might be able to use their current state of distraction to her advantage. She wasn't sure what weapon she might be able to use against the vampires, or if she would be able to triumph against them in a confrontation, but she felt certain that she had to try.

Chalmers grunted, and Marcia's eyes opened wide with surprise, swallowing repeatedly as his shaft pulsed into her mouth. A trickle of semen oozed from the corner of her lips and, when she moved her face from his dwindling penis, she chased the dribble away with the tip of her tongue.

Hope pressed her thighs tight together, as the brunette extricated herself from Chalmers' embrace and the blonde deftly tucked his penis back into his trousers. Although they both remained naked and desirable, they now held themselves with a businesslike air. 'Lilah wants two things from you,' the brunette told Chalmers. 'Now that Marcia's finally said thank you, are you ready to listen to our leader's demands.'

Chalmers poured himself a drink and lit a cigar. He pulled up the zip of his trousers and grinned cheerfully at the brunette. 'Go on, tell me what Lilah wants.'

'She wants the dark one's funds transferred into accounts in her name.'

'And what else?'

'She wants the girl.'

With her eye still pressed against the keyhole, Hope frowned, arousal quickly banished as she realised she was hearing things that Chalmers would have kept from her. She strained to hear, sure she had missed some vital part of the exchange, but it seemed Chalmers was only drawing on his cigar before formulating a reply.

'Which girl?' he asked.

'The sister,' Marcia explained. She climbed gracefully from the floor, still regarding him with an expression of honest gratitude and appreciation. 'Lilah wants you to transfer the dark one's funds into accounts in her name, and she wants you to give her Faith's sister, Hope. You can do that, can't you? You do still have access to all three sisters?'

Outside the office, Hope held her breath.

'Tell Lilah I'll transfer the funds,' Chalmers decided. He moved behind his desk, dropping into his chair and propping his feet up. 'It will take a couple of days to sort out all the accounts, and I'm not going to pretend it'll be easy, but I'll honour that request for her without any problem.'

'And the girl?' the brunette pressed. 'Will you give Hope to Lilah?'

Hope struggled not to give herself away as she tried to hear how he replied. She held her breath and resisted the urge to press harder against the door.

Chalmers laughed indulgently and sipped his drink. 'Of course I'll give her Hope. As soon as I've transferred the funds, I'll make a special present of the girl.'

He might have said more if his words hadn't been interrupted by the sound of a horrified gasp from the corridor outside his office.

Hope

Act I, Scene IV

'Hope, wait!'

She thought the outcome of the chase was inevitable before it had properly begun. She fled away from Chalmers' office, hurrying out of the casino and running south west along the *Champs Elysées*. The sound of footsteps followed but she didn't bother looking back as she ran. She heard Chalmers calling, and not knowing if he was alone or accompanied by his vampire co-conspirators, she threw every effort into getting away. A sense of impending doom made her believe the outcome of the chase was a foregone conclusion but she was determined to show some resistance.

The gaudy splendour of the *Champs Elysées* quickly disappeared as she raced towards *Place de la Concorde*. Ignoring the square's brightly lit statues and monoliths, running blindly through the *Jardins de Tuileries* and on past the *Arc de Carrousel*, Hope fled along *Quai du Louvre* and across *Pont Neuf*. The bustle of traffic gave way to the lapping waters of the Seine and then preternatural silence as she hurried through the desolate streets of *Île de le Cité*.

But Hope noticed no sounds beyond the frantic pounding of her heartbeat.

'Hope!' Chalmers called. His tone was breathless and she couldn't decide if that came from exertion or fury. 'Stop bloody running!' he bellowed. 'Give me a chance to explain!'

Hurrying onto the open space of *Place du Parvis*, she found herself standing before *Notre Dame* cathedral. Its gothic splendour was intimidating in the swathes of moonlight. Stone gargoyles leered down at her and the overhanging mantles were a gallery of shifting shadows beneath the night's mackerel sky. Under other circumstances she might have smiled at the poetic coincidence – she only ever associated *Notre Dame* cathedral with tales of a grotesque creature pursuing a distressed damsel – but her nerves were too fraught to let her appreciate the irony. Not hesitating to admire the imposing architecture, only hoping there might be some way to get into its sanctuary, she ran to the first of the three magnificent doors.

The Portal of St Anne was securely locked and the Portal of the Virgin remained steadfastly closed. Before she could reach the Portal of the Last Judgement, Chalmers' hand fell on her shoulder.

His cheeks were flushed with exertion and a film of sweat glistened on his forehead. He drew two rasping breaths before grunting, 'Finally.'

She whirled from his embrace and tried to hurl a slap at his face, but he caught her wrist before she could strike him then held her with quiet authority. 'Get away from me,' Hope cried. 'I don't want anything to do with you, you Judas!'

He cast a glance around the deserted square, and although there was no one around he seemed uncomfortable with the lack of privacy. His eyes lit on something in the shadows, a grim smile crossed his rugged jaw, and he dragged her from the cathedral steps. She tried to resist but her efforts only succeeded in unfastening the belt of the trench coat, her naked body revealed in snatches and relief, and as she struggled to wrap it back around herself Chalmers managed to wrestle her out of the public square. There was the jangle of keys and the protesting creak of an aged hinge, then he was leading her through a doorway into darkness, down a flight of stone steps and into a spacious cellar.

'Let go of me!' she insisted. 'I heard what you were saying and I won't have you make me into anyone's special present.'

Keeping her body pressed tight against his own, seeming to realise she would run if he gave her the slightest opportunity, Chalmers patrolled the unlit room with contemptible familiarity. Carefully he applied the flame from his cigar lighter to sconces on the walls. The flutter of orange light slowly illuminated their grim hideaway and Hope stopped struggling when she realised where they were, the tombs that lined the walls and the stench of musty decay enough to make her fall respectfully silent.

'This is one of the cathedral's private crypts,' Chalmers explained. He patted the jumble of keys on his hip and smiled grimly. 'I'm one of the few who has private access to this place.'

She snorted, surprised to find she still had the courage to show contempt and indignation. 'That's only to be expected,' she sneered. 'A man in league with vampires would be bound to have access to all the cemeteries and crypts in the city.' Valiantly she tried to pull herself away but his grip was unrelenting and she sensed her remarks had finally spurred his anger.

A stone sarcophagus dominated the centre of the room and he dragged her to its closed lid. Hope didn't want to be taken near the macabre tomb and fought every inch, but Chalmers was equally determined and he had the advantage of greater strength. Despite her best

66

endeavours, he quickly stripped the trench coat from her and bent her over the stone.

She was shocked by the easy way he manhandled her and equally disturbed by the fiery glare in his expression. The flames from the sconces burnt bright in the gloom and their orange flicker reflected in his eyes. A feeling of vulnerability made her shiver, and although she was adamant he wouldn't make her suffer any further indignities, her intent was swiftly thwarted when he slapped her bottom, a furious warmth erupting against her chilly flesh, and she was appalled to find her shame awoke a hateful need within the pit of her stomach.

Chalmers slapped her bottom again. 'We're not going to stand a chance against these vampires if you don't show me a little trust,' he growled. 'I thought I'd made that clear the last time I reddened your arse.'

His palm struck her buttocks again and she clenched her thighs together. Both cheeks were already burning from the punishment and the heat had quickly spread to her sex. She was acutely aware of her labia, tingling with a need to be touched and already moist with excitement. The despicable tug of arousal simmered within her loins and she cursed herself for responding to him in such a way. Desperate to disguise her reaction she glanced back over her shoulder and fixed him with a scowl. 'Trust you?' she scoffed. 'You promised me as a gift to your vampire girlfriend. How am I expected to trust someone who does that?'

He spanked her again and the force trembled through her body. Unwilling to watch him raise his hand again, not wanting to be stung by the delicious thrill of anticipation the sight aroused, she glared into the dusty shadows that lurked in the corners of the crypt. The sarcophagus was frigid beneath her breasts, the cold stone freezing her front.

But every smack he landed against her rear invested her with a vile and despicable warmth.

'I take it you were eavesdropping on my private conversation.'

'I heard you sell me out, if that's what you mean.'

Angrily he caught her by one shoulder and turned her over. The ancient stone pressed into her back, and spread out beneath him, exposed and available, she was swept along by the need to experience more of his cruel domination. She made no attempt to conceal her inviting breasts and didn't even consider placing a modest hand over the flush of her swollen, pink labia. A part of her wanted him to see that she was no longer scared and she lay on the tomb's lid in a posture of challenging defiance.

The appreciation in Chalmers' gaze was momentarily unsettling. His smile inched wider and his lips parted to reveal genuine approval. Then he scooped up her ankles with one hand, lifting both her legs high, and raised his other hand ready to strike again.

She choked back a cry of protest and tried to twist free from the threat of another slap. At the back of her mind she knew she wasn't making a real attempt to pull away and she was sickened by her body's need to feel him spanking her bottom – and when he finally struck she grimaced with pained delight.

'Did you really think I was selling you out?' he gasped.

She blinked back furious tears and glared at him. 'I *still* think that. I *know* you were selling me out. I saw you with those vampire sluts. I heard everything you said to them. You promised to make a special present of me to that bitch Lilah.'

His open hand struck her again, the echo resounding from the walls and the shock rippling through her body. Her legs were beginning to ache from the awkward position, the flesh of her buttocks felt savagely red, but her arousal was undeniable. She stared at him through a swell of fresh tears and the crypt's shifting shadows. It was all too easy to remember the way he had kissed and caressed the dark-skinned vampire while the blonde sucked his erection. Mentally picturing those clandestine moments, the pulse between Hope's legs beat with renewed force. It briefly crossed her mind that she had masturbated while she watched Chalmers with the two vampires and she recalled wishing she'd been more involved in what was happening. The stream of dark thoughts left her giddy with desire.

Another slap to her buttocks brought her mind back to the crypt but it didn't detract from her growing excitement. Chalmers glared down at her. 'What did you expect me to say to them?' he demanded. 'Don't you realise I had to tell them something to buy more time? If I hadn't said I was delivering you as a special present they'd have insisted on taking you tonight.'

She glared at him, hating the fact that his reasoning seemed plausible and almost convincing. He swept his hand down again and she flinched, expecting to feel another crushing blow against her punished bottom, but when his hand simply rested there, the fingertips lazing dangerously close to her sex, she held herself tense and rigid.

'I used to work for Lilah's brother, the dark one,' Chalmers explained, his expression unreadable in the light from the sconces, but Hope could see he wasn't boasting – only stating facts. 'Some older vampires find it difficult to deal with the mortal world. The aversion to daylight makes many things impractical, so they employ non-vampires to organise various aspects of their lives.'

She willed herself to concentrate on what he was saying, painfully aware that his fingertips were slipping closer to her sex. The inner muscles of her pussy throbbed and she prayed he wouldn't glance at her cleft, scared he would see she was almost melting with need for him. She could picture her labia glistening with a glaze of musky arousal and the thought that he would notice left her ready to squirm with shame.

'The dark one trusted me with many responsibilities when he ruled the coven,' Chalmers continued. 'I organised travel and accommodation. I researched those projects he grew interested in. And I handled all his finances.' His expression turned grim. 'But, now Lilah is head of the coven, my services are no longer required. Lilah is comfortable handling her own affairs in our modern society and she wants to take personal control of the purse strings.' Speaking sternly, not allowing Hope to miss his emphasis, he added, 'She wants her brother's money, and she wants you.'

He released his hold on her ankles and snatched his other hand away. Her feet dropped to the floor and she was left sprawled across the sarcophagus feeling violated and discarded. For an instant she was stunned by the way he could excite her and then turn his back, and she wondered if she had done something wrong to make him reject her so easily. He had chased her, caught her and spanked her until her need for him was intense, and then seemingly oblivious to her desire, he simply walked to one of the sconces and lit a cigar from its guttering flame.

Shivering with frustration she sat up on the tomb and crossed her legs, then glanced around the gloom of the crypt. Chalmers snatched the discarded trench coat from the floor and tossed it to her. Hope caught it as it flew through the air and truculently wrapped it around her shoulders. 'Why does this Lilah woman want me?' she asked, glaring at him, resenting him for having awoken her arousal and then leaving the need unsatisfied.

'She believes you're a threat. Some gypsy told her that

you're the only obstacle that endangers her leadership of the coven.' With meaning, he added, 'You're an obstacle that Lilah intends to remove.'

Hope considered this before speaking. She realised he had carefully shaped his words but there was no missing the disdain in his tone. 'Am I a threat to her leadership?'

Chalmers shrugged and regarded her from behind a veil of drifting cigar smoke. 'Faith proved herself virtuous, and as it turned out the dark one had every reason to be worried about her. Several of the shaman I spoke to suggested Charity is the virtuous girl that the original gypsy prophesied, but most of them were stoned to the eyeballs on home-grown incense, so I don't put a lot of stock in their predictions.' He paused, suddenly seeming to see that his words might be hurtful. Forcing a smile he said, 'Not that any of that's important. You're related to both Faith and Charity. I'm sure you must have some virtues.'

Hope glowered. 'You're not just saying that to make me feel better?'

Smoking his cigar, Chalmers said nothing.

She sat quietly for a moment, growing more uneasy at the thought of trusting him and his advice. Even if Chalmers was no longer in league with the vampires it was clear he had once been heavily associated with them. His talk of shaman disturbed her, not because the idea of destiny, divination or mystics was unsettling, but because it sounded as though he had already spent a great deal of time investigating her and her sisters.

She knew Chalmers had been part of the production team involved with Faith's choir trip to Rome, and it was because of his management of Charity's band that she had been able to complete the work experience element of her course at his casino. But the discovery that he had been slyly researching the three Harker sisters made her suspicious.

Putting her reservations aside, knowing there were other issues to deal with ahead of her lack of trust, she tried to think of a way forward. 'Perhaps Lilah has good reason to be scared of me,' Hope suggested. 'Perhaps I can do something that Faith wasn't able to do? Perhaps I'm the most frightening of the three of us?'

He shook his head and held up his cigar to make a point. 'Lilah's not scared of you. She just sees you as a threat. If she were scared of you I don't think she'd have come to Paris to track you down.'

Undeterred Hope continued, standing up, trying to appear brave in the face of a daunting situation. 'Maybe I should seize the initiative. Maybe I should go and challenge her now.'

He shook his head. 'You're not ready. She'd feed you to a neophyte.'

Hope studied him scornfully. 'Pep talks and confidence building really aren't your strong suits, are they?'

Chalmers acted without warning – Hope watched him cast his cigar to one corner of the room and then he pounced on her. The trench coat was spread out over the lid of the tomb as he roughly laid her down. Her initial reaction was to struggle and try to beat him away, but he avoided the first of her ineffectual blows then held her hands above her head. As he ingratiated himself between her legs the coarse weave of his trousers irritated her inner thighs. The weight of his thigh brushed against her pussy lips and she nearly screamed when a fresh surge of longing soared through her body.

He held his face mere inches over hers and glared down. 'Lilah's a twisted bitch of a vampire who feeds on the flavour of sexual excitement.'

Hope moaned, barely hearing him and only aware of his

nearness and the promise of satisfaction. Chalmers' face loomed closer; he stole a kiss from her, and then pressed his lips against her throat. Every inch of her flesh was receptive to him and she wallowed in the friction of his clothes rubbing against her bare body. His jacket brushed the swollen tips of her nipples, his trousers rubbed back and forth between her thighs, and the presence of his concealed erection nuzzled fervently against her sex. Her craving for him had never been stronger and it took every ounce of willpower to resist the urges he aroused.

'Challenge Lilah now and she'll devour you and spit out the bones,' he warned. She writhed against him but he seemed unmindful of the need he'd awoken. His kisses moved further down from her throat, towards the fullness of her breasts. His lips shocked her with their heat, and when his mouth encircled her stiff nipple she wanted to beg him to fuck her.

Chalmers moved his mouth to her other breast, suckling noisily against the nipple. He still held her by the wrists, keeping both arms pinned above her head, and she wished he would release his unnecessary hold. The urge to fight free was no longer an issue, and if he'd allowed her the chance to move she would have embraced him and welcomed him as a lover.

'She'll excite you and arouse you,' Chalmers warned. 'She lured your sister into her trap and she'd easily be able to ensnare you too.'

Hope was trying not to listen. She wanted him to release her hands so she could unfasten his trousers and reveal his erection. The need between her legs was now an ungovernable demand and nothing else mattered beyond the moment when he'd penetrate her, the thought making her weak with hunger.

'She'll make you beg for her.' He spoke while holding

her nipple between his lips and the tremor of every word thrilled her. Unable to stop herself, caught in the throes of a frenzied arousal, Hope ground her hips against him, the shape of his concealed erection rubbing against her, and she bit back a sigh of desperation.

Chalmers maintained his hold on her wrists – slowly moving his face from her breast – while his other hand slipped downwards. Spirals of mounting joy erupted beneath the touch of his fingertips as he stroked her ribs. Almost tentatively he traced the flat plane of her stomach, caressed one hip, then brushed his knuckles through her neat triangle of pubic curls.

Unable to stop herself, Hope groaned, and when he finally reached the moist haven of her pussy she held herself motionless. She needed him to touch her febrile warmth and yearned for him to plunder her. The pad of his thumb brushed her clitoris, two fingers toyed lazily with the dewy lips of her labia, and she held her breath in anticipation.

'You're not ready to resist the sort of treatment Lilah can hand out,' Chalmers muttered, and then briskly he stood up and lit a fresh cigar, his teasing ceasing so abruptly that she was momentarily stunned. His sudden lack of interest in her hurt more than any of the smacks he'd delivered to her tingling bottom. She glared at him, but he'd moved to a corner and in the shadows she couldn't be sure if he was looking at her. Hurt and aching with frustration, she lifted herself from the sarcophagus and wrapped the coat around her shoulders again. The bitter taste in her mouth and the knot of tension in her stomach made her feel weak and nauseous.

The point he had been trying to make dully registered above her subsiding arousal, and resentfully Hope realised Chalmers was correct. If she couldn't resist the torrid stimulation he had just inspired, she knew she would have

74

little chance against a predatory vampire. She fought against the feeling of despondency but it was a difficult struggle. 'If I can't go and challenge Lilah now, what am I expected to do?' she asked, cocking her head towards him, waiting until she sensed he was looking at her.

'You'll face her soon enough,' he vowed, walking from the shadows and sitting beside her on the lid of the tomb. His nearness had filled her with an insatiable need for satisfaction before, but she resisted the temptation to be swayed again. The frustrated ache within her was too crushing a penalty for her to risk suffering such torment again.

Chalmers placed an avuncular hand on her leg and patted reassuringly. 'You'll face Lilah all too soon,' he said quietly, 'but for now, you're expected to wait and prepare.' He produced the Bethesda Stone from his jacket pocket and held it out for her. 'You're expected to learn how to use this, and you're expected to endure my discipline until you reach a point where Lilah's influence can't effect you.'

She considered his words carefully as he offered the crystal. She didn't fully understand what he meant when he said she would have to endure his discipline, but she suspected he'd make his meaning clear. Knowing she had no other option, resigned to doing whatever was necessary to save her sister, Hope grudgingly took the stone.

She regarded its curious shape – like two ovals fused together to make the silhouette of a figure eight – and wondered how it was supposed to help her sister. She reasoned that because she had already allowed herself to believe in vampires and the cult of the undead, she should have no problems accepting that the irregular piece of crystal might be able to cure Faith. But the doubts still weighed heavily on her mind.

'You'll wait to challenge Lilah?' he asked, and she nodded. He drew on his cigar and the tip glowed brightly in the crypt's gloom. 'You'll wait until I say you're ready?' he pressed, and reluctantly, Hope nodded again. He smiled. 'I'm pleased we've reached an understanding. The next thing you know, you'll be telling me you trust me.'

She glared at him in the gloom. Although prudence dictated that she should do as he said, and although she was willing to submit to any indignity to save her sister, she still didn't believe she could trust Chalmers.

Interlude

Part Two

Claire was spread-eagled over the divan. The bindings at her wrists and ankles secured her naked body to the four corner bedposts. Her large breasts were vulnerably tempting, her thighs were taut with the effort of trying to pull herself free, and Faith knew the dark triangle of her pubic curls concealed a haven of delight. Unable to stop herself, Faith licked her lips.

Claire stared up, eyes wide with horror, a rubber ball-gag filled her mouth and the harsh black straps contrasted sharply with her pale face. She shook her head and made a renewed effort to pull free from her bindings, but the knots at her hands and feet remained secure and she eventually gave up with an expression of spent resignation.

A barrage of questions flashed through Faith's head. She had half-expected Claire to arrive in Paris – since they parted she'd sent countless text messages explaining all that had happened after she defeated the dark one – but she hadn't thought she would encounter her in this situation. Her initial reaction was to run to Claire's side. She wanted to remove the ball-gag, ask what she was doing in the casino, find out which of the coven had captured her, and ascertain that she was unharmed and well. But rather than doing anything so altruistic, Faith found herself driven by a different motivation.

'Claire,' she purred, a sinister smile blossoming on her lips as she glided closer. One of the many pleasures she had discovered since becoming a vampire was a heightened perception that benefited every sense. She inhaled lightly and was stung by a rush of sensory overload. The fragrance of Claire's perfume was only subtle but it was synthetic and annoyingly intrusive. More enjoyable were the scents of her nervous perspiration – emanating in waves from her throat and wrists – and the feral musk of her arousal. They were rich bouquets, more revealing than any scent she had ever caught before becoming a vampire, and Faith wallowed in their heady essence. Drinking in those aromas was enough to make her dizzy and she paused by the bedside.

Claire continued to regard her with obvious apprehension but Faith was no longer looking at her face. Her fingers were extended, ready to caress Claire's leg, but she stayed herself. Her hearing was attuned to every sound, from the faraway hubbub of the night's dwindling traffic to the distant clatter and clang of slot machines on the casino's ground floor. From within the room she could hear Claire's frightened respiration and the frantic pulse of her heartbeat. The rhythmic pounding reminded her of the backing tracks to some of her sister's most acclaimed songs: the ones Lilah darkly referred to as 'stroke music'. It also told Faith that the young woman trussed out on the bed was growing more intimidated and aroused with each passing second.

Faith flexed her lips, exposing a razor-sharp smile, and waited until Claire's horrified gaze met hers before whispering, 'Hello, lover.' She could hear the accelerated pulse of Claire's terror and smell the fresh sweat from her fear. There was no doubt in her mind that Claire was frightened even before she made a fresh attempt to tear herself free from her restraints. The bed's joints groaned as though making the sounds Claire couldn't manage from

78

her gagged mouth. For a brief instant, when Claire found the strength to arch her back from the mattress, it looked like she might be triumphant in her struggle. But then she collapsed back on the sheets with a tormented moan of frustration.

Gently, Faith lowered her hand to Claire's ankle. The flesh was warm and smooth, and she could tell that Claire had shaved her legs within the past twenty-four hours. The pad of her index finger stroked a small, healed cut and Faith shivered when she thought of how that might have happened. The image was more intoxicating then the whisper-soft contact because Faith could picture her friend, alone in a hotel bathroom, with a white towel wrapped around her wet hair and a matching towel modestly fastened around her breasts. Faith knew Claire would have sat on the side of the bath, lazily soaping an extended leg before drawing a razor against the smooth skin. It was all too easy to imagine her accidentally nicking herself, a pen-line of blood dribbling down her calf. The thought made Faith ache with renewed hunger.

If she closed her eyes she knew she would be able to see the scene with perfect clarity and inhale the rich, coppery fragrance of her friend's spilt blood. Even with her eyes open she could easily imagine the dark scarlet ribbon and could almost taste its intoxicating flavour. But she stifled her imagination, not sure she could resist the urges it inspired. Instead of dwelling on what had happened to her friend, she drew her fingers higher.

Claire stiffened on the bed. She glared at Faith, trying to impart some message that she couldn't get past the ball-gag, and shook her head.

It wasn't the response Faith expected and she frowned, momentarily puzzled. Before she was a vampire, less than three days earlier, she and Claire were developing their relationship. Their intimacy hadn't gone as far as she wanted – and had left her with an appetite for much, much more – but those encounters they enjoyed still blazed brightly in her memory. The two nights when they grew close had been magical occasions filled with mystery, broken taboos and marvellous discoveries. Even the days, when they were struggling to conceal their affection, had been blissfully infuriating. It never took more than accidental contact to make Faith giddy with longing. The inadvertent caress of an arm against her breast made her sex grow moist. A platonic hand on her shoulder or leg turned Faith weak with desire. It seldom took more than Claire's nearness to make Faith tremble with arousal, and in the few moments they had managed to steal alone together, Claire told Faith she felt exactly the same way.

But now Claire's reaction seemed to fly in the face of those responses, and perturbed, Faith wondered if her friend was genuinely reluctant to suffer her touch. There was the possibility that she might have lost interest in her since they were last together, or maybe met someone else on her journey between Rome and Paris. Faith even thought there was a chance that Claire no longer found her attractive now she was a vampire. But none of those explanations felt quite right and, Faith thought, the conflicting signs of Claire's body language made understanding even more difficult.

Although Claire was shaking her head and battling with her restraints, her nipples were still rigid and the wetness on her labia remained slick and dewy. Even though her eyes were wide with trepidation Faith could see the shine of arousal sparkling in her gaze. The heady fragrance of sexual excitement was now almost palpable. Claire's heartbeat had slowed from a frantic pulse to a dull, desperate demand. Her breasts rose and fell with each drawn out gasp, and despite her denials Faith felt sure that Claire wanted her.

Inadvertently confirming those thoughts, Claire groaned. The sound broke Faith's reverie and she glanced down to see her hand had been daringly close to her friend's sex. The pads of her fingers stroked a silky thigh, the tips of her nails dimpled the smooth flesh, and her knuckles brushed lightly against the triangle of curls covering Claire's sex mound. Shocked, she snatched her hand away. She was appalled to realise what she was doing and commonsense told her she should be rushing to the door and fleeing the room. The idea appealed to her, and she knew it would help her avoid the temptation Claire presented, but she couldn't bring herself to move away from the bed.

Almost as though acting of its own volition, her hand returned to Claire's thigh. The slight contact inspired a crackle, like a minor electric shock, and then Faith made her grip more forceful. She pushed the heel of her thumb against the swell of Claire's pelvis, and relishing every moment of the exploration, she stroked upward.

Claire sighed, the sound muffled by the ball-gag but Faith could hear the undercurrent of arousal that carried the cry. Encouraged by the response, wanting to provoke another sign of Claire's enjoyment, she stroked her friend's stomach, then stole a caress against the underside of her breasts. The skin felt silky, pliant and ready to yield.

Warming to the exchange, and growing hungry for more, Faith climbed onto the bed and knelt between Claire's legs. Their thighs rubbed together with a sultry friction that made them both gasp sharply. Faith stared hungrily at Claire's breast, her fingertips drawing circles around one areola. She stroked the swollen orb, aching to touch the nipple and doggedly resisting the temptation. The pulsing bud was already standing hard and she longed to touch it with her fingers. Daringly, she lowered her mouth and rubbed her bottom lip against the stiff flesh. Claire writhed helplessly beneath her, and as Faith took the nipple into her mouth, sucking gently then teasing the tip with her tongue, Claire threw fresh efforts into trying to break free. The bed shook beneath them, the springs and joints groaned loudly in protest, but Faith kept her lips pressed to Claire's breast. Stretching a wicked smile around the rigid teat, she nibbled lightly.

Claire's body grew painfully tense. Faith was aware of every muscle straining against hers and could even see the pulse in her friend's throat. The temptation to bite was suddenly too strong, and knowing she couldn't give in to her impulses she pulled away and rushed to the bedroom door.

Her fingers twisted the handle and she was infuriated to realise that Lilah had locked her in. She understood the leader's motives – Lilah was anxious for Faith to have her first feed – but understanding didn't help Faith escape the room. Not wanting to lower herself to that level, but knowing she couldn't continue to resist the temptation Claire's body represented, Faith pressed her back against the door and tried to look at anything except her friend.

The glittering night-lights of Paris twinkled through the window but she was already tired of seeing only nightscapes. Turning from the window she caught a glimpse of the vanity mirror and walked over to study its reflection. Since becoming a vampire she had been wary of mirrors, uncomfortable with reflections in which she was no longer included. But, she thought, staring into an empty mirror had to be better than tormenting herself with the lure Claire's bound body offered.

Folding her arms over her breasts, unmindful of her semi-nudity in Claire's presence, she stood in front of the glass and cocked her head to one side as though studying an art exhibit in the *Louvre*. This mirror, like every other she had seen over the past three days, only showed the room behind her. It didn't return her image.

That thought was going through her mind, saddening her as she considered that she would never see herself again, when she realised that wasn't quite true. There was a shadow on the surface of the glass, little more than a smoky blur, and at first she thought it might be a smear room service had overlooked. Yet when she concentrated on the dark smudge, narrowing her eyes and trying to make shapes from the indistinct blur, Faith could just make out the haze of her reflection.

It wasn't a proper mirror image – it was as easy to overlook as the watermark on bonded parchment – but Faith felt sure she could see something. Touched by unexpected hope, anxious to see what was hidden in the reflection, she leant closer. Briefly she thought she could see the shape of her own face, and even the garish red leather waistcoat Lilah had instructed her to wear. There was a moment of misty clarity, a glimmer of her deathly pale skin made ghostly by translucence, and she also caught the predatory leer of her vampire's smile.

But as soon as her fingers touched the glass the shadow of a reflection melted like smoke. All that remained was the image of Claire, naked and bound, spread across the bed. Not wanting to dwell on what she might have glimpsed in the mirror, sure that she didn't really want to understand what it implied, Faith turned her thoughts back to her friend, and Claire's expression of helpless vulnerability made her hungrier than ever.

The distraction of her reflection and all her efforts of

denial were easily brushed aside as she returned to the bed with renewed determination. This time she didn't delay the moment with coy exploration or gentle teasing. No, this time she climbed swiftly between Claire's spread thighs and lowered her mouth to her sex.

Claire's muffled cries were indignant and strident, but not listening to them, or at least not heeding them, Faith extended her tongue to her friend's inviting pussy lips. Marvelling at the beauty of her sex, she only paused to savour the aroma. Faith could detect the scent of true excitement simmering within the glistening pink depths and knew she would be able to taste that intimate flavour as soon as she lapped the dewy lips. Beyond hesitation, determined to satisfy every appetite regardless of how craven or carnal it might be, she nuzzled Claire's cleft and inhaled deeply.

The moan of approval could have come from the girl beneath her, from the depths of her own throat, or might even have been a duet of their united cries. It was an animal sound, eager for more and encouraging Faith to bury her tongue deeper.

Hungrily, she allowed instinct to take over. Her hands remained in constant contact with Claire's body, smoothing against the bare flesh and exploring her full, womanly curves, but her nose and tongue stayed buried against her pussy. The wetness grew more profound, forcing Faith to drink more deeply and allowing her to act without thought. It was easy to forget those temptations she was trying to resist and much more simple to just give in to the moment. Her mouth and chin were coated with the wet remnants of Claire's arousal and the sweet-scented musk only made her eager for more. She squirmed her tongue against the throbbing nub of Claire's clitoris and trembled as she savoured its vital, urgent pulse. The labia leaked against her tongue and lips and the folds of flesh yielded to each penetration.

Claire sobbed around the ball-gag but Faith was beyond caring if the sounds were protests or invitations. She drank with a passion she had never known before, revelling in each delicious discovery of pleasure and determined not to stop until her need had been sated. She paused occasionally, pressing kisses against her friend's thighs while her fingers continued to explore. Her palms cupped buttocks, stroked breasts and smoothed thighs, but the focus of her attention remained firmly on devouring Claire's sex.

Claire suddenly squealed around the ball-gag, and Faith glanced up in time to watch the orgasm shuddering through her friend's body. Claire held herself rigid on the bed, pulling tight against the restraints as she rocked from side to side in a desperate explosion of release. Her cheeks were flushed with ruddy colour and the tendons in her neck were taut and obvious. She jerked her pelvis in gratuitous convulsions and sobbed as freely as the gag would allow. Twin tracks of tears trailed from the corners of her eyes and she finally sagged against the mattress with a sigh of spent gratitude.

Panting hungrily, still savouring the taste of the juices she'd been drinking, Faith delicately wiped her mouth with her fingertips. Her face felt sticky with Claire's dewy residue and the scent of her musk lingered in her nostrils. Sighing contentedly to herself, she smiled dreamily down at her friend.

Claire looked to be in a state of bliss. Even with the ball-gag filling her mouth – even with the glimmer of trepidation still lurking in her eyes – it was impossible not to see that she was languishing in a haze of satisfaction. Her pussy lips were flushed and wet, her nipples remained rigid, and the pulse in her throat throbbed with a strong, irresistible invitation.

Unable to stop herself, Faith pressed her body over Claire's. The leather of her waistcoat stopped her from fully enjoying the delicious caress of naked flesh against naked flesh, but that was only a minor irritation and easily overlooked. She pressed her thigh against the slick folds of Claire's pussy and relished the slippery contact. Claire's hips ground towards her and they writhed together with fevered urgency. If Claire had looked spent a moment ago, Faith now thought her friend looked more than ready to enjoy further pleasure. She momentarily cursed the bindings, wishing Claire could embrace and touch her in the same way that she was being caressed. But rather than worrying about what was wrong with the situation, Faith urged herself to enjoy all that was right.

She raised one hand and stroked the taut muscles on Claire's throat. The skin was deliciously smooth, the pulse of her jugular beat just beneath the surface of the flesh, and the shiver of arousal that sparked through Faith's fingertips exhilarated her. Simply caressing the pale blue line of the vein was enough to carry her to the brink of a climax and if she'd thought how it would feel to bite against that pulse, she knew she would be wallowing in her own joyous release.

But the excitement was cut short when she touched Claire's crucifix. A stab of burning pain seared her fingertips and she snatched her hand away indignantly. The discomfort was almost enough to make her forget her arousal and she glared at Claire with an injured pout. 'That bloody hurt,' she complained, rubbing her fingers. Small blisters were already forming and she winced as the pain throbbed through her hand. 'That really bloody hurt.'

Claire gazed blankly back. For an instant Faith

considered ripping the crucifix away. She told herself she could ignore the agony that would come from touching the hateful jewellery and would then be able to easily place her mouth over Claire's throat. The prospect was so tempting she almost surrendered to the impulse, and her hand was reaching out to the chain when she saw the expression in Claire's eyes and hesitated.

The ball-gag gave her features a startled expression, but looking beyond that peculiarity and seeing more than the fear dilating her pupils, Faith wondered if her friend might be willing to help. Making a swift decision she leant across Claire's naked body and began to unfasten the bindings. She released the knots quickly, already adept at the task after working alongside Nick and Helen over the previous three nights, and pulled the rope free from Claire's wrists. An expression of relief crossed her friend's face, but Faith didn't notice because she was unfastening the awkward buckles of the gag secured behind Claire's head.

When Claire was finally able to tear the rubber ball from her mouth Faith could no longer contain herself. She saw Claire's lips, moist and pouting, and dared to kiss her. It crossed her mind that she might meet with refusal; that Claire might continue to fight and make her resistance more hurtful now she could use her hands and her tongue. But because she needed to enjoy her friend's kiss she risked the rejection.

The exploration was everything she had hoped. Their tongues met and caressed in a forbidden intimacy. The greediness of both their appetites were as powerful as Faith had expected and her arousal returned with renewed vigour. Claire wrapped an arm around her and Faith responded by placing a hand over her breast. The nipple's gentle pulse rekindled the urgent throb of her excitement and they both sighed as if sharing the pleasure.

'You came looking for me,' Faith whispered between kisses.

'I came to help you,' Claire sighed.

Faith nodded, not knowing what difference her friend's reply suggested, and beyond caring. Taking advantage of her superior position, not bothering to release the bindings at Claire's ankles, she pushed her friend to the bed and hovered over her. 'Take off the crucifix,' she hissed. 'I need to get to your throat and the cross is getting in my way.'

Claire's eyes widened with shock and she clutched a protective hand around her throat. She shook her head and silently stuttered before finding her voice. 'You want to get to my throat? What for?'

Faith smiled uncertainly, wondering if Claire was really so dense that she didn't know. 'Follow the plot, Claire,' she said. 'I'm a vampire: you're naked and tied to a bed. Why do you think I need to get to your throat?'

Claire regarded her with fresh horror, but Faith wouldn't allow herself to acknowledge the expression. 'I want to make you,' she explained patiently. 'I want to give you the dark gift that has been bestowed on me. I want to drink from you and change you into a vampire, so we can be lovers forever.'

Claire pulled herself out of Faith's embrace and shrank back against the sheet. 'You mustn't feed from me,' she said stiffly. 'You simply mustn't.'

Faith studied her with wary caution, then smiling slyly she again stroked Claire's breast and they both shivered from the electricity of the contact. 'It doesn't hurt too much,' she promised. 'And you do want that, don't you? I thought it would be something we would both want.'

Claire groaned and pushed Faith's fingers aside. 'You

couldn't know how much I want that,' she whispered. 'But you mustn't do it. And not just for my sake. You mustn't do it for your own sake. The damage would be irrevocable.'

Faith stared at her uneasily. 'I don't understand what you're saying. I want to make you, I know you'll love being made, why are you fighting me?'

Claire shook her head. 'I'm not fighting you. I'm here to help you.' She drew a deep breath, letting Faith hear a range of emotions that included frustration and exasperation. 'There might be a way to cure you. There might be a way to reverse the process of you being a vampire. But it will only work under certain conditions.'

With a tremendous effort Faith pulled herself away from Claire. She remembered the smoky image in the mirror, a half-glimpsed reflection that seemed to be telling her something she wasn't ready to hear. Deciding she had to know what Claire was talking about, she nodded solemnly. 'Go on. How can you cure me from being a vampire?'

Rather than unfastening her bound ankles, Claire flexed one wrist back and forth while stroking Faith's arm with her other hand. Then she took a deep breath and smiled doubtfully. 'I've organised a ritual to be performed.'

Faith nodded. The concept of rituals and magic had been little more than myths and fairytales a week earlier, but she reasoned once a person was able to accept the existence of vampires archaic lore didn't stretch the imagination too greatly.

'You'll need to be on hallowed ground,' Claire continued.

'Okay.'

'The timing will be crucial.'

Faith considered this, and then nodded.

'But most important of all…' Claire's hand tightened around her wrist, as though she was trying to impress the enormity of this point. 'Most important of all: it's vital that you remain pure.'

Faith frowned, shook her head, and then laughed. 'I don't understand that final part. How could I even be considered pure? Forget all those nasty things I did before I defeated the dark one. Just look at the situation as it is now. I'm a vampire. I've willingly submitted to every despicable pleasure that's crossed Lilah's mind. I no longer have the self-control to resist any demands she makes of me. It would probably be impossible to find anyone less pure than me.'

'Pure in the vampiric sense,' Claire explained patiently, her smile rich with compassion. 'In order for the Bethesda Stone to work it's vital that you don't feed. It's imperative that you don't take a victim.'

Faith regarded her solemnly. 'What are you telling me, Claire?'

'I'm telling you, if you want to retain any hope of becoming mortal again, you mustn't take one victim. Spill one drop of blood and you'll be damned as a vampire for all eternity.'

Hope

Act II, Scene I

'*A rien ne va plus,*' Hope cried. 'No more bets.'

Avril Joffre stepped to her side and whispered, 'Monsieur Chalmers has just called with a message for you.'

Hope stood over the spinning wheel, watching the numbers blur into an indistinguishable stream of red and black. The casino was always quiet this early in the evening, twilight had barely ended outside, and there were less than a handful of customers playing the roulette table. She glanced up at Avril and smiled without enthusiasm. Reluctant to show any interest she grudgingly asked, 'What did Spanky say he wanted?'

Avril's brows knitted together. 'No. No one called Spanky. The message was from Monsieur Chalmers.'

Hope nodded, not bothering to explain. The language barrier could be difficult at the best of times and she had no enthusiasm to work through her reasons for using Chalmers' nickname. Such a conversation would either become unbelievably embarrassing or simply unbelievable, and she was in no mood to face either option. 'All right,' she conceded tiredly, 'Monsieur Chalmers. What did Monsieur Chalmers want?'

'He wants you in his office. He said you are to go there now.'

Grimfaced, Hope shook her head. 'Tell Monsieur Chalmers I'm busy.' The roulette wheel slowed and finished its revolution with a clatter as the ball settled and came to rest. She called the number and the colour for the benefit of the few customers who were still playing then motioned for Avril to clear the losers' chips from the table.

Obligingly Avril did as she was asked, then returned to Hope's side. 'Did you not listen me?' she said, speaking in an urgent hush, her command of English far better than Hope's negligible grasp of French, and it was only when she became flustered that she made any mistake in her otherwise flawless pronunciation. 'Monsieur Chalmers wants to see you in his office. He said you must go there now.'

'I know exactly what Monsieur Chalmers wants,' Hope said coolly. 'And he won't be getting it from me tonight.' With quiet defiance she added, 'I'm not going.'

Avril looked horrified, and after working with her for the past few months Hope wasn't surprised the minor act of rebellion unsettled her colleague so greatly. Avril was meticulous about her work and a firm believer in the ethos of obeying all the management's instructions. Hope's refusal to go rushing up to Chalmers' office clearly flew in the face of everything Avril considered proper for the workplace, and under other circumstances she might have found the reaction quaint or funny. But this evening her thoughts weren't prone to amusement. She didn't want to be in the casino, she didn't want to be near Chalmers, and she certainly wasn't going to deliver herself to his office.

'Monsieur Chalmers will not be happy,' Avril said ominously.

Belligerent, Hope didn't reply. It was only when Avril had turned her back that she felt a pang of remorse for taking out her anger on her colleague. She didn't want to argue with Avril – the woman was dependable, and one of the few friends she'd made in the lonely city – and Hope knew she was simply being diligent and repeating the manager's instruction. But the events of the previous evening were still a jumble in her mind, and although she'd spent the day trying to work out what had happened, she still believed she needed some time to think and put the situation in its proper perspective. And while she wasn't clear on all the details of what she now needed to do, she felt sure it would be easier to gain some clarity if she spent as little time in Chalmers' company as was practicable.

Yet that rationalisation didn't make her feel any better about upsetting Avril. Spiked by guilt, she thought of offering some excuse that would make an allowance for her rudeness. She was reaching out to touch Avril's arm, trying to recall enough French to make a sincere apology, when movement from the casino's main door caught her eye and immediately she forgot about the croupier's injured feelings.

Her first thought was that Faith had returned. The sheen of chandelier lights glistening against leather was enough to make her remember the garish clothes her sister had worn the night before. It wasn't Faith – a single glance at the commanding figure who strode into the casino was enough to tell her that much – but Hope was nevertheless mesmerised by the sight of the woman bearing down on her.

Strikingly attractive, athletic and slender, she held herself with more confidence than seemed decent. Her jet-black hair was stark against her alabaster complexion, but because it framed her pretty face and gleamed with the same silky shine that reflected from her leathers, the tresses seemed to complete her ensemble. Her figure was unremarkable; a narrow waist, small breasts encased tightly inside her waistcoat and muscular thighs in figure-hugging leather jeans; but she walked with such haughty pride it was obvious she held herself in the highest regard.

And for some reason she couldn't understand, Hope found herself agreeing with that unspoken verdict. She watched the woman cross the casino floor, unable to tear her gaze away. She wondered how it was possible for a stranger to have such an effect on her and so easily attract her undivided attention. It was only as the brunette stepped closer that she noticed the scarlet flecks dancing in the woman's eyes, and that single detail told her exactly why her attention had been drawn and she instantly understood the secret of the woman's appeal.

Hope took a wary step back as, smiling assuredly, the brunette marched boldly to the roulette wheel. Before taking a seat she placed a small wooden box on the table. Hope glanced at it, wondering why the miniature chest seemed to throb sporadically, but rather than dwelling on the anomaly, briefly chilled by something unpleasant about the box, she lifted her gaze and met the woman's expectant smile.

'Hope?' Her tone was crisp and businesslike but not unfriendly. 'Hope Harker?'

'Do I know you?'

The brunette extended a hand. Her fingernails were exquisitely manicured, dripping blood-red polish that made her skin look unbearably pale. Her palms looked smooth and free from lines, and for some reason that observation made Hope wonder how it would feel to have such hands caress her naked body. She blinked quickly, trying to shut the image from her mind, but it remained insidious and every thought afterwards was tainted by its hue. She could easily see herself and this woman, alone in the dark, their bodies swathed with sweat as they toiled together towards a pinnacle of pleasure. She knew the brunette's vampiric eyes would gleam brightly in the dark and it was easy to picture their gleeful appraisal during a passionate kiss. The image came with such clarity Hope thought it was almost as though she had just lived through the experience. 'I don't know you, do I?' she asked, shaking her head, swallowing thickly and trying to compose her thoughts. 'Who are you? How do you know me?'

The brunette's hand remained in the air, waiting for Hope to take it. 'I'm a friend of your sister,' she smiled, and with heavy emphasis she added, 'I'm a very close friend.'

It had been automatic to reach out and shake the offered hand, but as soon as she realised what she was doing, Hope snatched her fingers back as though they had been burnt. Understanding came to her with frightening speed and she glared at the woman. 'You're Lilah,' she hissed vehemently. 'You're the one who changed Faith. You're the hideous bitch who made my sister into a vampire.'

Lilah nodded. Her smile blossomed more fully and revealed a pair of piercing canines at the corners of her lips. 'It's good that you know who I am; we don't need to waste time with introductions.' Resting one hand across the miniature treasure chest she strummed her fingers against its top and glanced around the casino.

Hope wasn't sure but she thought she saw the box throb again.

'Where can we talk?' the brunette asked.

'Nowhere.' Hope shook her head. 'We can't talk. I have nothing to say to you.'

'You want to see your sister again, don't you?'

Hope glared at her. It was automatic to suspect duplicity but she was unable to see any glimmer of deceit in Lilah's placid smile. She had to repeatedly snatch her head away whenever she glanced at the woman because her gaze was too enchanting. Something in her eyes promised all manner of passion, excitement and forbidden pleasures, and Hope knew if she toyed with that temptation for too long she was likely to surrender.

'You want to try and help your little sister, don't you?' Lilah coaxed.

'Where is she? What have you done with her?'

'Come with me,' Lilah offered. 'We need to talk.'

She reached across the roulette table and placed her hand on Hope's. Her touch was cold enough to inspire a shiver and Hope could see gooseflesh erupting on her forearm. Yet even though Lilah's caress was chilly, the smooth fingertips were the exciting balm she had expected. A delicious tremor ran through her flesh filling her with a sudden, urgent craving. The momentary thrill reminded her of the intoxicating images that struck her when she first saw Lilah.

'We can talk more easily if we're away from here,' Lilah murmured. She drew an invisible pictogram on the back of Hope's hand while her smile lilted playfully. 'Perhaps we could go for a drink at the bar? Or would you prefer that we went somewhere more private?'

Hesitant, but knowing she had no other option, Hope came to a quick decision. She told Avril to take over at the roulette table and the croupier acknowledged the instruction curtly. Hope distantly noted that she would have to work hard to win back the woman's friendship, but she knew there were more important matters to deal with first. She stepped away from the table and waited for Lilah to retrieve her wooden box.

Surprising Hope, the woman offered her arm, and Hope told herself that she shouldn't be touching the vampire and that she was courting a very real danger by remaining

96

in Lilah's company, but she was unable to resist the invitation. So knowing it wouldn't help if she appeared churlish or intimidated she warily linked arms, and trying not to be swayed by the aura of excitement that emanated from the woman, Hope walked with her away from the casino floor.

With every step the vampire's hip brushed against hers and Hope felt ill with a rush of dark arousal. She could feel herself being drawn to some seductive aspect of Lilah's personality, and she knew it would be a struggle to continue resisting. 'What did you want to talk about?' she asked, desperate to end the torment before she did something to regret. But Lilah shook her head and carried on leading her into the foyer, so Hope stopped walking, forcing Lilah to pause in mid-stride. 'I asked...'

Lilah placed a finger against Hope's lips, and its cool touch inspired a shiver that made her feel weak, secretly relishing the intimacy and longing for it to progress further. The contact made her aware of her lips, pouting with a need to be kissed and tingling with anticipation. As Lilah gently smoothed her fingertip from side to side Hope grew giddy with need for the woman.

'We'll talk soon enough,' Lilah assured her. She drew her finger away slowly and edged her lips close to Hope's. The promise of further intimacy lingered between them, and as she stared longingly at Lilah's succulent smile, Hope struggled against her yearning to submit. They were standing so close their breasts were touching, and through the stiff confines of her uniform basque Hope could feel her body being charged by an icy electricity that radiated from the vampire. The sensation was strongest around her nipples and she eventually had to step back to stop herself from being crippled by a delicious spasm of bliss.

She lowered her gaze, shocked by the fresh flood of

torrid images tumbling through her mind. She was sure that Lilah was responsible for the obscene visions, and when she glanced up again the woman was gracing her with a knowing smile. Hope blushed, fearing the vampire might be reading her thoughts, there was something in Lilah's smile that said she knew exactly what she was thinking, and at the same time there was no hint of disapproval.

The door to the casino bar was open and its subdued lighting was a pleasant contrast from the harsh brightness of the casino floor. Confidently taking the lead, Lilah commandeered seats at a discreet booth and ordered two glasses of wine. She placed her wooden box on the table between them, waited until the drinks were served – a glass of the house white for Hope and a blood-red Bordeaux for herself – before breaking the silence. 'I believe you have the Bethesda Stone,' she said, her voice as rich and lustrous as her wine.

Hope was shocked from her silent admiration of the woman and almost reached into the small pocket of her basque to retrieve the mentioned item, but deliberately stopping herself she tilted her jaw defiantly, and trying to match Lilah's cool composure she feigned indifference as she challenged, 'What if I have?'

'Do you know anything about the power of the Bethesda Stone?'

Hope had spent a day searching the Internet and struggling through reference books at the *Bibliothèque Nationale* only to find there was no mention made of the stone. 'Do any of us really know about the power of the Bethesda Stone?' she said, not wanting to expose her ignorance to Lilah, but suspecting the woman would detect an outright lie.

A flicker of hesitancy flashed in Lilah's eyes before she

98

laughed, then reaching beneath the table she placed a hand on Hope's thigh and patted condescendingly.

Hope was torn by conflicting desires: needing to snatch her leg away and wanting Lilah to make her touch more demanding, but she fought to keep the emotions from her face, determined Lilah wouldn't see the reactions she was inspiring.

'You should give this up now,' Lilah said earnestly. 'You have no chance of winning.' She stroked her fingers over the intrusive weave of the uniform fishnets, and Hope determinedly resisted the delicious sensations tickling her thigh, though it wasn't easy to suppress every response. The hairs on the nape of her neck tingled and she knew it would take little more than a single command and she would be down on her knees and trembling at Lilah's feet. And when the hand crept higher, insinuating over the toned muscles of her inner thigh and stroking daringly close to the crotch of her basque, she made an even more determined effort to maintain her composure.

Seeming to take her response as a challenge, Lilah stroked her fingers back and forth and drew a line against the gusset of the basque, carefully tracing the gentle swell of Hope's tightly concealed sex mound.

Pulses of furious anticipation lurched through Hope's tummy and she grabbed her wine glass to try and stop her hand from shaking. Inhaling deeply, and hearing the undercurrent of arousal carrying each breath, she struggled to resist Lilah's mesmerising charm.

'You should give this up while you still have the chance,' Lilah whispered, her tone as much a silky caress as the feather-light touch of her fingertips. 'The Bethesda Stone always demands a price, and I don't think you'll be willing to pay.'

Hope invested every effort into appearing unmoved.

'Aside from the words that made perfect sense,' she snapped scathingly, and with a heroic effort she pulled herself from the chair and started towards the bar exit. Her legs felt weak and it was difficult trying to walk without a faltering step, but she felt she accomplished the departure with more dignity than anticipated.

She was quietly congratulating herself on resisting her true urges when she realised Lilah was standing in the bar doorway, blocking her exit. It was only natural to glance back at the table, her mind frantically wondering if there might be two Lilahs, when she recalled Chalmers telling her that vampires were favoured with unnatural speed and stealth.

'Make it easy on yourself,' Lilah purred. 'Give me the Bethesda Stone and I'll give you something in return.'

'You'll give me my sister?' Hope asked.

Lilah shook her head. 'I'll give you something better than your sister.'

Her smile resurfaced and Hope knew, whatever exchange Lilah was proposing it would involve being bitten by that smile, but rather than frightening her the idea was perversely appealing.

Lilah held the miniature treasure chest under one arm, and with the other she reached out to touch Hope's wrist. 'I can make you, Hope Harker,' she said earnestly. 'I can make you and educate you, and then we can spend the rest of our days together in a paradise of ecstasy. Your sister is already enjoying the bliss of a life that I've given her. You could know that pleasure too. All you have to do is give me the Bethesda Stone.'

For an instant Hope was tempted. She didn't know why Lilah wanted the stone, and she couldn't recall why she was fighting so desperately to keep hold of it, but it suddenly seemed unimportant and well worth the bargain

Lilah was presenting. She was about to reach into her basque, ready to prise the stone from its pocket, when the vampire moved closer.

Lilah's fingers slipped to the shape of Hope's breast. She pressed the yielding flesh and encouraged the stiff bud of Hope's nipple to stand proud beneath the fabric. A couple pushed past them, and someone whispered disparagingly about their lack of decency, but Hope barely heard any of what was said. She was revelling in the bliss of Lilah's touch and on the brink of handing over her sister's last chance of being cured of her vampirism.

And it was that thought that made her hesitate. With a gargantuan effort she found the strength to tear her gaze away and she lurched past Lilah and stumbled into the foyer. It was all too easy to remember the scene she'd witnessed between Nick, Helen and the redhead, and Hope was suddenly scared that she might suffer the same fate as the woman that pair had drained. And that fear grew more profound when Lilah appeared in front of her again. Her bloody smile was still as enticing as it had been before, but Hope could now see the patience behind it was growing strained.

'Don't fight this,' the vampire whispered. 'Your sister didn't fight me, and she's currently revelling in her role as one of my subordinates. You don't even have to subject yourself to the same indignities I made her suffer.' Lilah pushed herself closer, easing a leg between Hope's thighs and moulding their shapely bodies together. Then placing her lips to Hope's ear she brushed a gentle kiss against the lobe before whispering, 'I'm only asking for the stone. And in return I'm offering you a whole new world.' Slowly, drawing her kiss from Hope's ear and down, Lilah pressed her teeth against the upward sweep of the girl's slender throat. 'It's a very exciting world,' she murmured seductively. 'There are all manner of pleasures to be had, and I'm sure you'll enjoy every one of them.'

With all the strength she could muster Hope wrenched herself from Lilah's dangerous embrace and fled into one of the casino's lower corridors. She didn't have any idea where she was going, focusing only on the knowledge that she had to escape Lilah before the temptation proved too irresistible. Her body ached with desire for the woman and she couldn't understand how or why she was resisting the seductive invitations. The impulse to give in bordered on the unbearable and she felt sure her resolve wouldn't be able to withstand another confrontation with Lilah.

When the vampire appeared in front of her for a third time Hope didn't know if she should sob with frustration or gratitude. Lilah was still smiling and her eyes sparkled with wicked mischief. 'Why don't you follow your sister's shining example?' she suggested, again pressing her body close to Hope's, writhing gently and sparking an electric frisson between their scantily clad figures. Where their bare flesh caressed Hope thought she had never felt any sensation more invigorating. Where their clothed bodies touched Hope was stung by the need to remove all the obstacles that stood between her and the vampire.

Slowly lowering her face, Lilah placed her teeth against Hope's throat again and the girl shuddered submissively.

'Why don't you yield to me now?' Lilah asked, and this time Hope couldn't find the strength to resist. The vampire inspired a host of responses, from fear and revulsion right through to desire and an urgent, inarguable need. She knew what the woman wanted from her – and she knew it was more than just the crystal stashed in her pocket – and in that moment she was more than willing to make any sacrifice. Almost fainting with the effort she took a step back from the vampire, and started to reach for the

Bethesda Stone.

'I don't think so.'

Hope shook herself from a dreamy haze and realised Todd Chalmers had appeared. He stood between her and Lilah, extending a crucifix with one hand and brandishing it menacingly in Lilah's direction.

'Toad,' Lilah purred, her tone saccharin with effected warmth. 'I'm surprised to see you here. I thought you were busy organising the transfer of my late brother's estate into my name.'

Chalmers seemed not to be intimidated by the vampire. 'I am working on the transfer,' he said stiffly. 'Last night I told your naked errand girls it would take me a couple of days to finalise all the details. They did get the message back to you, didn't they?'

Lilah shrugged as though she didn't care. 'If I have to wait until tomorrow night for my money, I can be patient for another twenty-four hours.' Stroking the back of her hand against Hope's cheek she smiled hungrily. 'I was just trying to deal with some other unfinished business while I had the spare time.'

Chalmers took hold of Hope's arm and pulled her to his side. Lilah glared at him with animal ferocity but he seemed indifferent to her display of temper. Still holding the crucifix he pushed it closer to the coven's leader until she grudgingly took a step back. 'If you got the message about the money, then you'll have received the message about this girl: you don't get her tonight. You can have her when I say you can have her.'

Lilah's eyes narrowed to cruel slits. 'Are you dictating to me, Toad?' she growled. 'Are you trying to issue me with commands?'

He shrugged. 'The deal is simple. Feed from Hope before tomorrow night and I won't finish transferring the funds.'

She glared at him as though he'd slapped her face. Hope could see the vampire was aching to step forward and deal with both of them and it was only the presence of the cross that made her hesitate.

'Feed from Hope before tomorrow night and I'll transfer all your brother's funds to a charity,' Chalmers promised. 'Which good cause do you think he would have preferred to benefit from his passing? A church – one with plenty of crucifixes hanging around the chapel? Or maybe one of those sanctimonious organisations that helps fallen women? That would be more appropriate, since your brother couldn't help himself with fallen women.'

Lilah raised a finger and jabbed it towards his chest, but Chalmers swatted at her hand with his crucifix.

'You'll account for every penny of that money before we cease trading together,' she snarled. 'You'll account for every penny or I'll drain the compensation from your throat.'

He pulled Hope more tightly into his embrace. 'It will be easier to do the necessary accounting if you allow Hope to assist me,' he stated calmly.

'Is that what she's doing?' Lilah asked guardedly, a glint in her eye that Hope understood. She could see the woman was looking for a way to retreat from the confrontation without losing face, and it seemed clear that Chalmers' impromptu lie offered her that escape route. 'She's helping you transfer my brother's accounts?'

Chalmers nodded. He glanced at Hope with a look of censure. 'That's what she was supposed to be doing, but it appears she was a little reluctant to leave the casino floor this evening.'

Lilah looked to have accepted the lie. 'You should punish her for that,' she remarked. 'I know I would if she was one of my subordinates.'

Todd tightened his grip on Hope's arm and began to drag her down the corridor. He remained facing Lilah, keeping his crucifix extended to prevent her the opportunity of attacking as soon as his back was turned. 'Don't worry about punishing her,' he called cheerfully. 'I intend to take care of that before we get on with anything else.'

And although she wanted to believe he had made the remark for Lilah's benefit, Hope couldn't help but worry that his threat was sincere.

Hope

Act II, Scene II

The discipline was the hateful ordeal Hope had expected. Chalmers hauled her into his office, bolted the door and then dragged her to his desk. The stale smell of cigar smoke and whiskey were perpetual ghosts lingering in the room and she found it all too easy to associate those pungent scents with the shame of being beneath his hand. Once again he didn't bother turning on the lights and the office was lit by slats of reds and golds filtered through blinds at the window.

Hope protested and tried to struggle free but Chalmers was powerful, determined and in absolute control. He tightened his grip on her arm and pulled her roughly behind his desk. As soon as he had dropped into his chair he silently urged her to bend over his knee. Hope didn't want to demean herself in the way he was indicating, but when he tugged hard on her wrist she was forced to fall across his lap. The position was undignified and humiliating and left her cold with dark foreboding. Her shame was already intense and Chalmers had yet to deliver the first blow of her punishment. She didn't dare brood on how bad she would feel by the time he'd finished, but wondering if there might be a chance to plead with him she glanced meekly over her shoulder.

His features were masked by shadows. 'You've brought this on yourself,' he said tersely, slapping her bottom, the sound of palm striking buttock filling the dull atmosphere.

A shockwave of discomfort trembled through her rear, and she clenched her teeth trying to suppress a squeal of dismay. She turned away from him and studied the floor, not wanting him to see the upset he was causing.

'You've brought this all on yourself,' he repeated, bringing his hand down again, and she didn't argue with him because she suspected he might be right. 'I knew Lilah was going to be on the prowl this evening,' he stated, landing another smack as if to punctuate the declaration, and through the flimsy protection of her basque, panties and fishnets the blow stung and she grimaced unhappily. She chugged breath in an effort to deal with the discomfort, but the dull ache continued to linger.

'I knew she'd be heading to the casino tonight.'

Another slap reddened her blazing buttocks.

'And I knew she'd be trying to get her teeth into you.'

He concluded the sentence with a further smack.

She had hoped her clothes would cushion the impact somewhat, but instead they only made the torment worse. The friction of her panties made her fearful to squirm and the coarse weave of the fishnets was an accelerant to the heat of each blow. Unable to stop herself she writhed against him, kicking her legs and determined to show that she was unhappy with the discipline, but he held her firmly over his knee and continued to assail her with firm, methodical blows.

'And yet, in spite of the agreement we reached last night…' he went on in a tone of calm fury, this time with more weight behind the slap, '…even though you assured me of your trust…' she stifled a moan as he smacked her fully on her left cheek, '…you still ignored my instruction when I told you to come to my office.'

With punishing force he struck the tops of her thighs. Her buttocks had almost become acclimatised to the weight of each dull slap, and the shock of his hand smacking such a sensitive area was infuriating. Startled into protest, Hope shrieked with indignation.

'Stop whining,' Chalmers snapped, landing another smart shot, and she instantly fell silent. Her flesh was ablaze from the searing punishment, and hating the dominance he wielded over her she shifted position to find enough leverage to try and tear away. But rather than creating the chance to break free she only seemed to place herself more firmly over his lap. The thickening bulge of his arousal grew stiff from his groin and Hope blushed when she realised she was feeling its presence against her stomach. It was all too easy to remember that, the previous evening, she had seen his cock exposed in this same office. The vampire sucking on him remained bright in her memory and the pull of that image was ominously exciting. Valiantly she tried to shut the thoughts from her mind, and willed herself to concentrate on his words rather than the growing swell of his obvious enjoyment.

'You could have avoided this unpleasantness,' he said, driving his hand hard down upon her rear, and although she couldn't see she felt sure his broad palm print would be emblazoned across both cheeks. 'All you had to do was show some trust and obedience,' he said as he caught her backside with another slap.

She stiffened against him, wanting to protest but unable to find her voice. His hidden penis pulsed beneath her tummy each time he landed a blow, and she shrank from the idea of what that response indicated. It was disconcerting to discover he was gleaning so much pleasure from spanking her but it was more worrying to realise that his reaction matched the swell of her own mounting need.

'There would have been no need for this if you'd just

come to my office when I called for you.'

As his hand cracked across her bottom again, Hope remembered the message Avril had passed on. It was painfully easy to recall her own stubborn refusal and she quietly cursed the rebellious urge that made her ignore him. She choked back a sob of despair when she realised that simple act of defiance had resulted in her having to suffer this despicable indignity.

'I've asked you before, and I'll ask you again: What do I have to do to make you understand the gravity of this situation?'

He growled the question as he swept another brutal slap against the tops of her legs. She could hear him grunt with the effort and noticed his erection twitched more forcefully against her stomach. Determinedly she tried not to think about his excitement or how it perfectly reflected her own awakening desire.

'How severe do I have to make this punishment before you understand the danger we're facing?'

She could barely hear him. Her buttocks were glowing with punished warmth and the spreading heat radiated to her sex. Delicious shivers tingled through her pussy lips, heightening her sensitivity and increasing her need for him. The pounding pulse in her temples made it impossible to listen and she groaned with muted fury as she succumbed to the thrill of unwanted arousal.

'Perhaps a mere spanking isn't enough to teach you the lessons you need to learn,' he suggested, and she glanced back over her shoulder, uncomfortable with the ominous threat in his tone. His face was in shadows, making his eyes unreadable, but she could see the solemn cast of his frown. 'Perhaps you need a proper exercise in discipline.'

She was going to ask him to explain what he meant when he suddenly pushed her from his knee. Falling to the floor, sprawling inelegantly on the carpet, she glared miserably up at him.

Ignoring her, Chalmers rose from his chair. With his figure in silhouette Hope could see the thrust of his erection pushing at the front of his trousers and she quickly turned away in case he noticed her peeping. She heard him walk to one of the cupboards that lined the darkened walls, and from the sound of the soft squeak she guessed he was opening a door. It was only when he returned to the desk and she dared to glance up at him that she saw what he'd retrieved.

'No,' she said defiantly, 'you're not using that on me.'

In the faltering lights his face was stern and sombre as he used the cane to point. 'Bend over the desk, Hope. Don't make me tell you twice.'

It was instinctive to try and refuse, but she knew that wouldn't do any good. As much as she wanted to argue she was willing to concede that, on some level, she probably deserved to be punished. And even more galling, and a fact she was loath to accept, she silently yearned to experience the sting of the cane he was wielding. But she shook her head, determined to deny that thought and face him with all the resistance she could summon.

'Bend over now,' he said flatly, 'or I'll strip you and then cane you.'

Hating herself for obeying, but determined that he wouldn't tear the clothes from her body, Hope grudgingly climbed from the floor. She didn't know if he could see her face, or the venom of her glowering expression, but he didn't show any reaction to her obvious distress. Bending over the desk, pressing her breasts against the leather surface and raising her bottom, she took three deep breaths as she prepared to suffer the despicable torment.

'Spread your legs,' he ordered, and inwardly she groaned, her body reluctant to obey, and although she put every effort into trying to shuffle her feet apart, she couldn't make the muscles work.

Chalmers growled impatiently and pushed his free hand between her thighs. She stopped herself shrieking with surprise but it was a close call. Rigid with apprehension she dutifully surrendered as he pushed and forced them further apart. His touch was hatefully close to her sex and Hope fretted that he might notice her heat. When the back of his hand brushed her crotch a sparkle of raw delight blossomed through her pussy lips, and this time it was a lot more difficult to keep her cry of frustration contained.

'That's more like it.' Chalmers' voice was edged with approval and Hope was disgusted to note that his praise made her feel bizarrely flattered. Cursing her body for responding to his discipline she tried to tell herself that she was unmoved, but the argument lacked conviction. She was acutely aware of her backside, and the gratuitous view she was presenting him with. 'That's much more like it.'

The atmosphere in the office was thick and electric. From the corner of her eye she watched him disappear behind her and she tried to brace herself for the inevitable sting of the cane. A part of her was worried the thin length of wood would prove to be an unbearable agony, but another part was slyly anticipating the experience.

'You can't carry on defying me,' he whispered, and she mumbled insincere accord, not knowing to what she was agreeing and not particularly caring. Her focus was centred on her expectation of how the cane would feel when he sliced it against her, and he could have been talking in a foreign language for all she understood. She flexed her fingers, tightening and then relaxing them as she waited. Her buttock muscles were clenched in readiness for the first strike.

'Tell me that was the last time you'll defy me,' he ordered, and she opened her mouth, not sure what she was about to say, only hoping she could find words to appease his foul mood. But before she could manage the first syllable he slashed the cane against her poor bottom.

The pain was enormous. A piercing wire of white heat blazed across her cheeks and left her writhing against the desk. She had thought the spanking a punishing ordeal but it was a lover's caress in comparison with the vicious sting of the cane. Eyes wide with disbelief, mouth open in silent protest, she thumped her balled fists hard against the surface of the desk.

'Tell me that was the last time you'll defy me,' he said again, and she began to dread each of his sentences, knowing it preceded a blow of one sort or another. This time was no different and he sliced the cane across her cheeks for a second time. His aim was true – surprisingly true considering the low lights – and he landed the second stripe directly over the line of the first, and she hadn't been aware that the pain was subsiding until it was reborn with the fresh fury of exquisite agony. Silently shrieking, desperate to make some audible protest but unable to force the air from her lungs, she suffered a third strike across the top of her thighs as he repeated the question.

'That was the last time I'll defy you,' she managed to gasp. 'I promise. I promise. That was the last time I'll ever defy you.'

'You can't continue defying me,' he said calmly, driving another stinging blow against her rear. The cane bit the lower sweep of her buttocks and fresh starbursts of anguish sparkled from her punished flesh. She struggled to keep her knees locked, not wanting them to buckle and leave her hanging from the edge of the desk. Each slash of the cane fuelled an insidious warmth she was loath to suffer. His spanking had excited an appetite she didn't want to acknowledge, but the torture of the cane took that to a new and unimagined realm.

'I won't,' she gasped, hurrying the words for fear he might hear the arousal in her tone. 'I won't defy you ever again. I promise I won't.'

He hurled the cane down again, scoring her cheeks with vicious ferocity. 'Promise me I'll see your trust in future,' he demanded. 'Promise me.'

She drew stilted breaths and repeatedly slammed her fists against the top of the desk. Her sex throbbed with a need for satisfaction and she wished he would simply accept her reassurance and then sate the vile need he had awoken. She briefly considered telling him that much: turning around, spreading herself across the desk and demanding he fuck her. But although she felt sure Chalmers would need no encouragement, she didn't think he would consider that an end to the punishment. More likely, she thought, he would screw her for his own pleasure and then take malicious glee from the torment of her frustration.

'Promise me I'll see your trust in future,' he repeated.

'I promise,' she wailed. 'I promise.'

'Promise me I'll have your trust,' he growled, but she wasn't listening. The need for satisfaction weighed more powerfully than ever and every breath seemed to inch her closer to the release of an orgasm. The pulsing ache in her bottom only added to her excitement and she wondered if she dared touch herself. She didn't doubt Chalmers would disapprove but such a consideration didn't make her discount the idea. She glanced back over her shoulder and watched him slice down another blow. The impact made her spine stiffen and she relished the cruel barb that burrowed beneath the flesh of her buttocks.

'Promise me I'll have your trust,' he repeated.

Because the room was in shadows she was tempted to give in to the salacious impulse. She conceded that Chalmers would most probably notice but there was a chance he might not. Rather than worrying about his opinions and approval she was more swayed by the certainty that her body needed the release of a climax. She didn't doubt it would only take a single touch, the caress of her fingertip trailing lightly against the crotch of her basque, and she knew she would be writhing in the divine bliss of an orgasm.

Her breasts began to ache as she brooded on the idea and she felt painfully aware of her pussy clenching in hungry anticipation. She half-turned, easing one arm down by her side and stroked the taut muscle of her upper thigh. A shiver of delicious bliss rippled through the flesh and she held herself still, suddenly fearful of what she was planning. Her sex ached to be touched. The lips were swollen inside her panties, crippling her with desperate need, but she didn't dare.

Chalmers hurled the cane so hard it whistled through the air. The impact was scorching, and although Hope had been trying to contain her cries it was impossible not to shriek as this slice slammed into her body. All thoughts of touching herself were forgotten as she realised the blow had pushed her beyond the need for self-pleasure. The flood of release soared through her and she groaned as waves of satisfaction ebbed and flowed through her quivering frame.

'Promise me I'll see your trust,' Chalmers said again.

'I promise,' she sobbed, unable to tell if she was

addressing him with impatience, obedience or gratitude. 'How many more times do I have to say it? I promise.'

He threw the cane to the corner of the room and she heard it land with a noisy clatter. 'Fair enough,' he said. 'I'll trust that you're speaking the truth and we'll end the punishment now.'

She glanced round at him, unable to believe the torment was finally ended. Bewildered that he hadn't made her suffer more, and amazed that he hadn't tried to take advantage of the need he'd inspired, she whispered, 'Have you finished punishing me?'

'Unless you want me to cane you some more?' he suggested, but hastily she put a protective hand over her rear.

'No,' she told him, trying to make her tone convincing. 'I think I've had enough of that for one evening.' She felt sure her words revealed the real truth and she lowered her gaze, scared he might see the sparkle in her eyes.

Chalmers nodded. 'Good. It's about time we reached an understanding. Now, take your clothes off.'

She glared at him, her jaw dropping with disbelief. 'But you've spanked me and caned me,' she protested. 'How much more punishment do you think I deserve?'

He sniffed and shook his head. 'This isn't punishment. You have the Bethesda Stone, and if you want half a chance of saving your sister we have to perform the ritual as soon as possible.'

Hope glared at him. She hated the way everyone seemed to use the hook of her sister's salvation to try and bend her to their will, but she was powerless to refuse the obligation. 'Are you telling me I have to be naked to use the Bethesda Stone?' she asked.

Lighting a cigar he nodded, the ferocity inside him when he spanked her now gone, and she could only see weariness about him. 'Activating the Bethesda Stone involves a specific ritual in which you will be the conduit,' he said quietly. 'The timing is crucial, the location is important and the details have to be exact. I've consulted experts who say the conduit must be naked for this ritual, so I don't see the point in taking chances.'

She placed a protective arm across her breasts. She considered asking him what might happen if she refused, then remembered he had extracted a promise that she would obey his instructions. So bitterly realising there was no other choice, knowing she had to do it for the sake of her sister, she began to unfasten the clasps of her basque.

Chalmers turned his back as she started to undress. 'It's not so bad, is it?' he said. 'Who knows, excite me enough while we're performing the ritual and I might even give you the fuck you're so desperate to enjoy.'

Her cheeks burnt more brightly than before and she didn't trust herself to respond. She eased out of the basque and then began to slip the fishnets and panties down her legs. The office suddenly felt cold and it was only the heat of her blushes that stopped her from shivering. The dim lighting, or Chalmers' gesture of turning away, didn't lessen the embarrassment of being naked. She still felt exposed, embarrassed and exceedingly vulnerable, and when he turned to face her she folded one arm across her breasts again and covered her sex with the other hand.

Even though his back was to the dim light and she couldn't really see his face clearly, Hope felt certain Chalmers was grinning. However, there was no indication of mirth in his voice when he finally spoke.

'Thank you,' he said tonelessly. 'It's about time you started doing as you're told.'

Not wanting to fuel another confrontation, still painfully

116

aware of how punishing his discipline could be, Hope said nothing. She watched Chalmers drop his cigar into the ashtray on the desk, and followed him with her gaze as he walked past her to the door. 'W-where are you going?' she asked, panicking slightly.

'Wait here,' he told her. 'There's equipment needed to make this ritual work.'

'Equipment?' She couldn't understand why but his casual use of the word conjured up images of leather harnesses and all manner of torture devices. She didn't know if it was a product of her torrid imagination or the result of having spent time in the company of Lilah. 'What sort of equipment?' she asked nervously.

Rather than answering her question he paused in the open doorway. 'I'll be ten minutes – fifteen at the most. Why don't you show a little of that trust you promised and let me get what's needed?'

She thought of arguing, and then decided there was no point in delaying him or causing another confrontation. Nodding grudgingly she indicated that he should go. 'I guess I can wait like this for ten minutes,' she murmured, and he slipped through the door and closed it softly behind him.

She wanted to sigh, expecting to feel relief that Chalmers had finally left her alone, but it was impossible to think like that. Rather than being grateful he was gone, she felt uneasy that he was no longer there to offer protection, and when the door opened only moments later she felt immense relief. 'That didn't take ten minutes,' she said. 'Or have you forgotten something…?'

'Forgotten something?' Lilah asked sweetly, her scarlet gaze brightening as she appraised Hope's naked body. 'I haven't forgotten anything. No, it seems more likely that I've just found exactly what I was looking for.'

Interlude

Part Three

'What do you think to this one?' Helen asked. 'Would you like to try him?'

Hunger and temptation were weakening Faith's resolve and she considered the question seriously. After Claire had warned her about the dangers of feeding – and that, once she took her first victim, she would never be able to go back – Faith had vowed to resist the impulse until a cure could be effected. But that conversation happened the previous night and now, twenty-four hours later, she was no longer sure she could abide by the promise. The temptation to give in was constant and her need was gradually growing worse.

'Stop taunting her,' Claire said defensively. 'If she doesn't want to feed you can't make her. Why do you have to be such a bitch all the time, Helen?'

Helen had delayed their journey to seduce a young man. Since they'd left *Boulevard de Rochechouart*, and ventured onto *Boulevard de Clichy*, the vampire seemed to recognise something about the *Pigalle* district that appealed to her predatory instincts. Her smile had become more vulpine and she looked to be regarding each passer-by as a potential conquest. Faith didn't know what it was about the area that appealed to Helen – she thought the *Pigalle* had a tawdry feel; redolent of poverty, drugs and prostitution – but she wasn't greatly surprised that the vampire felt comfortable in such a locale.

118

'Bonjour,' Helen whispered, as she passed a youth in jeans and a denim jacket.

He cocked his head in her direction and was instantly captivated by some promise in the glint of her eyes. Helen welcomed him into her open embrace and they were soon writhing against a closed shop front as they joined in a torrid and passionate kiss. Faith thought that, if Helen had shown this initiative a few streets earlier, she and her newfound friend would have looked like a live attraction outside the *Musée de l'Érotisme*.

'Try him,' Helen insisted. 'You might like him.'

'Stop being such a bitch,' Claire complained.

Helen paused from her pleasure for long enough to flip a finger in Claire's direction, and then divided her attention between the young man and Faith's reluctant interest. 'He's a good kisser,' she said with honest approval. Her lips glistened with saliva and glowed the colour of polished rubies. The flush in her cheeks burnt bright and it seemed obvious to all of them, except the young man in her arms, that she was ready to feed. Stroking her hand against the bulge in his trousers she added, 'He's also got a fair sized cock on him. Should we see how good he is at using it?'

Faith turned away and Claire snorted as she followed her friend. In a loud voice, loud enough to be overheard, she said, 'I can't believe I'm related to such a slut.'

'And I can't believe I'm related to a fat, pious lezzer,' Helen called after her.

Claire didn't bother rising to the insult. She kept her back to Helen and linked a defensive arm with Faith, and in the lowest voice she could manage, trying to keep her conversation unheard by the others, she asked, 'How are you bearing up?'

Faith made every effort to keep the stress from her expression. 'I'm bearing up,' she lied. 'But it's not as easy as I thought it would be.'

'And you're still cool with the plan for tonight?'

It was hard to maintain the expression she knew Claire wanted to see, but Faith struggled to smile complacently. 'I'm cool,' she said, sure her reply sounded like a blatant lie. 'I just hope it works.' She would have said more but the eye contact threatened to be too much.

As well as trying to disguise her slipping resolve, Faith was also trying to contain other emotions. The desire she had always felt for Claire continued to glow within her yet she didn't dare acknowledge its presence. Although she considered the emotion to be pure she couldn't trust the greed of her vampiric appetite not to take things too far. The yearning need to kiss Claire, to hold her and make love to her, could easily turn into a feeding frenzy she wouldn't be able to control. It wasn't that she wanted to drink from her best friend, although the idea was painfully tempting, but she didn't think she could keep a constant rein on all the voracious hungers that tortured her soul. Adamant that her willpower wouldn't be put to that test, Faith tore her gaze away before her longing proved too strong.

Claire's gentle sigh told her that she was trying to understand her dilemma. 'It's a shame these rituals don't come with a guarantee,' Claire said glumly. She looked set to add something else but Helen chose that moment to shriek happily and they both turned to glance back at her.

'Faith!' Helen cried. 'Seriously, you ought to try this one! He's a joy to use. He really is quite gifted.' Laughing with malicious delight, she added, 'He might even be able to cure the fat lezzer!'

Faith glanced at the vampire and saw Helen had taken the intimacy further. The young man's trousers were unzipped and his erection speared through the gap. Helen hoisted her skirt and spread her legs so she could accept him into her sex. He penetrated her awkwardly but his thick girth and obvious enthusiasm clearly compensated for any detriment the position might otherwise have caused. Each time he pushed forward Helen squealed and squirmed greedily onto him. She made no attempt to contain her obvious joy even though they were on a public street and in full view of occasional pedestrians and passing cars.

Faith didn't want to see what Helen was doing but she felt compelled to watch. Her gaze was drawn to the sight of the youth's length penetrating the vampire. He slipped easily between the melting lips and his shaft glistened with the liquid silver of her arousal. The squelch of their coupling was infuriatingly loud, and because of her supernatural sensitivity Faith could detect the musk of Helen's wetness and the tang of the young man's sweat.

'Come and try him,' Helen spat the words between eager grunts. 'Or try him and come,' she giggled. 'I'll bet he could satisfy the pair of us before we drained him.'

The young man's eyes widened with lecherous confirmation but Faith wasn't watching. She turned her back again and allowed Claire to lead her along the boulevard. If her friend hadn't been there she didn't know if she would have been able to refuse Helen's invitation. The offer was obscenely tempting and dropped a smouldering coal of arousal in the pit of her stomach, and that irrefutable ache continued to plague her even when the sounds of Helen's climax were fading in the night's distance.

Nick appeared by her side and winked as though they shared a secret. He placed a muscular arm around Faith's shoulder and squeezed fraternally. Faith tried to pull away, and Claire yanked at her arm in an attempt to free her from his clutches, but Nick was strong and confident and seemed determined to remain at Faith's side. 'The silly bitch is overlooking the obvious, isn't she?' he laughed. 'You prefer a slice of pussy to a portion of cock, don't you?'

Faith frowned and didn't reply.

'How did my sister find such a charming suitor?' Claire murmured dryly.

Nick glanced in her direction. 'Shut it, fatty,' he snapped. 'I haven't bitten you yet, but if the night gets long and I get desperate enough I might risk the cholesterol.' Turning back to Faith, smiling with all his hatefully seductive charm, he said, 'How about I find you a tasty blonde? Something with legs up to her arse and a good set of jugs? Might that tempt you to feed?'

'I don't want…' Faith began, but she got no further for Nick released her from his embrace and rushed to the other side of the road. A slender blonde stood in a facing doorway, sheltering from the evening's mild breeze so she could light a *Gauloise*. Her sapphire-blue eyes looked briefly startled, then intrigued, when she saw him approach. 'Monsieur?' she whispered, as Nick loomed towards her. There was a hint of concern in her voice but it was clearly diluted by the attraction Nick inspired.

He boldly plucked the cigarette from the woman's lips and drew on its filtered tip. 'This is a very dangerous and dirty habit,' he said, speaking through plumes of smoke. 'Perhaps I could replace it with something equally dangerous but ultimately more satisfying.' Casually he flicked the cigarette aside and then waited until the blonde melted into his arms. They kissed with an animal need for each other and their bodies moulded together as though they'd been lifelong lovers.

Faith held her breath as she studied the pair. She could

122

understand why the blonde succumbed to Nick's charms so easily. He was devilishly handsome and blessed with the romantic allure she'd noticed in each of the coven's vampires. If she hadn't been trying to resist her own vile appetites, Faith felt sure she would have already given herself to Nick and enjoyed every sordid moment of his lascivious interest. Even thinking about it was enough to make her excitement swell and sharpen the edge of her hunger for blood. Unaware that she was doing it, she licked her lips as she watched Nick with the slender blonde.

He tore open the woman's coat and then rent her blouse. Her breasts were small and pretty, the nipples erect within the magenta rings of her areolae. The blonde gasped when he exposed her but she made no attempt to step away. With her chest bared she simply stared at Nick with an expression of fresh arousal and then pressed herself more eagerly into his embrace. He lifted her from the ground, easily managing her light weight, and manoeuvred one pert breast to his mouth. The blonde sighed when he took her nipple between his lips and her encouraging cries became more pronounced as he teased the hard bud of flesh between his teeth.

Seeming to savour the pleasure, Nick glanced towards Faith. 'How would you like to taste this one?' he teased, lifting his mouth from the soft breast. 'She's ripe for the plucking. We could take her together, if you want. But I'll let you have the first bite.'

Faith didn't want to listen, shocked by the images his casual words brought to mind. She could easily picture the three of them – she and Nick sandwiching his discovery – locked together in a sweaty, carnal embrace. It didn't tax her imagination to consider kissing the blonde, tasting her lips or possibly savouring further intimacies.

The prospects of caressing her bare flesh, touching a nipple or using her tongue against the woman's vagina, were all too easy to bring to mind. And even more exciting was the idea of drinking from her throat. Hesitantly she took a step towards him.

Claire pulled at her arm, gently trying to restrain her, but Faith knew she could easily escape her friend's hold. She took another step, thrilled by the thought of how she might be able to inveigle herself between the pair.

'She's game for it,' Nick encouraged, glancing dourly in Claire's direction. 'Or would you prefer me to find you something that's a little more on the chunky side?'

The insult against Faith's best friend was enough to break his spell. Blushing at the thoughts she had been considering, not wanting to dwell on the appealing atrocities she'd been contemplating, Faith turned away.

Claire tried to speak and Faith guessed she was only offering reassurance, but she was in no mood to listen. She hurried along *Boulevard de Clichy*, desperate to get to the *Cimetière de Montmartre* and begin her part of the ritual. It was only when she heard the clip of Claire's heels on the pavement and realised her friend was running to catch up with her, that she finally slowed down.

'You're doing well,' Claire said as she fell into step at Faith's side.

'It doesn't feel that way.'

'You're dealing,' Claire told her. 'No one could ask any more of you.'

Not wanting to dwell on whether she was resisting her urges or not, Faith tried to change the subject. She was about to ask Claire how long the ritual was likely to take but there was no opportunity for such a discreet question. Helen stepped between them and her presence meant they couldn't discuss the plans for Faith's salvation. Glancing

124

at the vampire, Faith saw a film of fresh blood glistening on her lips. The sight made her simultaneously ill and envious.

'You should have tried him,' Helen chuckled. 'He was surprisingly gifted.'

Faith knew, if she bothered to glance back down the road, she would see the fallen body of the vampire's most recent conquest lying forgotten on the street. But she'd seen enough drained victims since succumbing to Lilah's bite and she kept her head bowed as they hurried on towards the cemetery.

Untroubled by the lack of response, Helen glanced at Nick as he suckled against the blonde's throat. The couple's hips moved in a rhythmic union and they murmured with obvious passion. Faith followed the direction of Helen's gaze then quickly turned away before the sight could taunt her further. With obvious disdain Helen glared at the blonde and sniffed. 'Fucking slut.' Affecting an air of moral superiority, she linked her arm through Faith's. 'Where are we going?'

'Claire had an idea,' Faith began carefully.

'I'll bet it was lonely,' Helen quipped.

Claire rounded on her sister. 'At least there's more in my head than spent semen.'

Helen's eyes flashed crimson and she glared at Claire. 'What's the idea you had, fatty? Are you taking us to an all night patisserie?'

Claire tightened her hands into fists and Faith spoke quickly to try and diffuse the confrontation. 'She's trying to help me get the hang of this being-a-vampire thing,' she said defensively. 'She suggested I might feel more like feeding if I do something traditionally vampiric.'

'Such as?' Nick asked.

Faith hadn't seen him finish with his blonde or join them

as they walked from *Boulevard de Clichy* onto *Avenue Rachel*. 'Claire thought I might feel more like a vampire if I spent some time in a cemetery,' she said, struggling to remember their cover story, hoping it sounded convincing.

Nick and Helen exchanged a glance and Faith watched furtively, wondering if they knew of her real motives for suggesting such a location. Because Claire had told her so much about the ritual of the Bethesda Stone, and because the relevance of consecrated ground was still weighing heavily on her thoughts, Faith feared that one of them might make the tenuous connection.

'A cemetery is okay by me,' Helen said simply, touching Nick's arm. 'You made me in a cemetery.'

'I probably wasn't the first,' he grunted, then stopped her as she tried to catch him with a vicious claw. The pair briefly struggled, each fighting for dominance and control of the other. But as invariably happened between Nick and Helen, the pair soon forgot that they were supposed to be angry with each other and their aggression easily transformed into sexual passion. They joined their mouths, their hands exploring each other rather than trying to hurt, and they were soon involved in a furious clinch.

Faith followed Claire through the ornate gates to the *Cimetière de Montmartre* and, as she stepped into the tranquillity of the graveyard, she felt an unexpected confidence soothe her spirits. Her hunger remained, and she knew the temptation to feed would be just as irresistible if she dared to test it, but some intangible quality of the cemetery seemed to offer a promise that all would end well.

She walked peacefully alongside Claire, wading through an ankle-high mist that looked a little eerie, but somehow added to the graveyard's ambience. She already knew that the *Cimetière de Montmartre* was home to a wealth of celebrities, including Berlioz, Offenbach and Delibes, but she hadn't expected the tombstones to show such artistic individuality and flair. Looming out of the spectral white shadows were weeping widows, brooding angels and all manner of beautifully fashioned monoliths. But as macabre as the sights were, Faith was genuinely enjoying the moonlit stroll along a tree-lined avenue and no longer troubled that she could hear Nick and Helen pacing some way behind them.

'Is there a set time when we should do this?' she asked.

Claire checked her wristwatch and tapped the face with her index finger. 'Todd said you should be ready for midnight. That means we've got maybe twenty or thirty minutes.'

'And are there meant to be any preparations I should know about?'

Claire blushed and glanced back at Nick and Helen. Faith followed her gaze and saw Helen had her back pressed against one of the avenue's trees while Nick stood between her legs. A sea of white mist lapped around their ankles. It was impossible to tell if they were having sex or simply teasing one another in a form of malicious sport, and Faith was beyond caring which it might be.

'Todd said you should be naked,' Claire whispered.

Faith sniffed humourless laughter. 'He was joking, wasn't he?'

Studying the glimpses of leaf-littered paths that were visible through the mist, seeming suddenly uneasy with the concept of eye contact, Claire said, 'He sounded pretty sincere when he said it. He seemed convinced Hope would be stripping to perform her half of the ritual and he said it was vital you do the same.'

Faith quickly thought her way through her objections, then decided they were petty in the face of what she was trying to accomplish. So putting her reservations aside, unmindful of the cemetery's chill air, she plucked open the buttons of her waistcoat and exposed her breasts.

Claire gasped softly and Faith pretended not to hear the sound. She busied herself with the button on her leather mini-skirt and then unzipped it and allowed it to fall to the ground beneath the mist. Stepping out of her shoes, then shrugging the waistcoat from her shoulders, she stood before her friend with defiant pride.

'You look lovely,' Claire murmured, glancing hesitantly back towards the shadows where Nick and Helen writhed. 'But what are those two going to think when they see you naked? Aren't they likely to suspect something?'

'Undress,' Faith suggested. 'They'll be less likely to suspect a ritual if we're both naked. They might even think I've finally relented to my vampiric urges and that I'm trying to make or take you.'

After a moment's deliberation Claire began to peel the clothes from her body. Faith smiled at her friend's shy reluctance but her amusement soon evaporated when Claire revealed herself. Even though she had been touching and caressing her friend the previous evening, it still felt as though she'd been too long without properly seeing her naked. No longer restrained by the bondage, able to move freely and respond as she wanted, Claire looked breathtakingly beautiful in the moonlit gardens. The silver light played on the fullness of her figure, accentuating her breasts and highlighting her voluptuous curves, and Faith was stung by a need to have her.

Claire glanced hesitantly into her eyes and Faith could see her own lascivious desire was matched in her friend's. Her expression was conflicting: welcoming at first, then stern with denial. 'We shouldn't,' Claire warned her.

'No,' Faith agreed. She understood Claire's reasons for

saying the words and conceded that they were sage counsel. 'It would be wrong,' she admitted. 'But it might stop those two from guessing why we're here.'

She was ready to press her argument further in the hope that Claire might acquiesce, but no more words were necessary. Claire placed her naked body next to Faith's and they held each other as they quietly kissed. Claire's mouth was a smouldering haven, quickly exciting Faith as their tongues touched and intertwined. The pressure of her breasts was an infuriating torment and Faith marvelled that she had been able to resist the temptation of this pleasure for so long.

Then Claire moved her lips away and paused for breath.

'This could be my last night as a vampire.' Faith whispered, frowning solemnly.

'Don't let them hear you,' Claire shushed her, casting a nervous glance in the direction of Nick and Helen. 'Lilah's warned them to watch you, and while neither of them is particularly bright, they're both…'

Faith silenced her friend's reservations with another kiss. She didn't know which of them began to caress the other but it didn't take long before they were both stroking and touching. The chilly frisson of bare flesh beneath her fingertips was enough to heighten her desire, and after cupping the swell of both breasts and her hips, Faith encouraged her to lie down. She could see Claire was wanting to protest, and didn't know if her reservations came from modesty, a reluctance to dip beneath the white blanket of fog, or a general unease with the creepiness of being intimate in a graveyard. But it only took a little encouragement and she quietly relented.

The grass was wet, fine dewdrops from the mist caught in feather-light blades that caressed her thighs and ankles. Faith relished its chill and wondered if Claire felt the same thrill as the moisture enveloped her back and bare buttocks.

'Aren't we risking too much?' Claire asked quickly, but Faith placed a finger against her lips to silence her.

'We're not risking anything,' she whispered.

'Isn't there a danger this might prove too tempting for you?' Claire insisted. 'Your need to feed gets worse when you're…'

Her protests diminished as Faith pressed eager kisses to her shoulders and arms. Faith deliberately avoided her friend's throat and breasts, and for exactly the same reasons that Claire had been voicing her doubts. But as her mouth moved over her stomach, then slipped down to her mons, arousal made it easier to dismiss her fears. She savoured the sweet scent of Claire's musk and drank in the scent of her friend's growing need. Her hearing was attuned to every sound in the cemetery, from the rustle of indigenous rabbits scurrying through the undergrowth, to the faraway murmur of Nick and Helen as they bickered and fucked. Listening intently, Faith could only hear the urgent pulse of Claire's arousal. The muscles within her sex beat with a steady demand and Faith knew that, above all else, she had to sate that need.

Hungrily, she lowered her jaw to Claire's cleft. Claire stiffened and Faith sensed she was going to raise another argument as to why they shouldn't be doing this. But not allowing her the opportunity, acting quickly so that the moment couldn't be spoilt, she darted her tongue against the glistening pink pussy lips.

Claire sighed, the sob filled with obvious elation. Faith understood her friend's response because she could have happily moaned with the same degree of joy. The taste of Claire's sex was the divine pleasure Faith had expected and she stroked her tongue against the glistening lips for a second time. The labia were soft and sticky, moulding to the shape of her inquisitive probing as she gently lapped back and forth.

And all the time her heightened sensitivity made her aware of a thousand more elements of the moment. She could detect the acceleration of Claire's heartbeat, taste the subtle difference in flavour as her arousal intensified, and feel the blood pumping through her veins with renewed vigour.

Unaware she was doing it, Faith tested her teeth against the pulsing nub of Claire's clitoris. She had no intention of biting – not hard, anyway – but she savoured the sensation of the throbbing flesh resting between her canines.

Claire pulled away, covering an arm over her bared breasts and crossing her legs. Faith knew she could overpower her, push her to the ground and take what she wanted by force, but she didn't want to yield to that urge. Seeing the frustration and hurt in her friend's face was enough to make her feel shamed into an apology.

'Perhaps you were right,' she admitted. 'Perhaps we were pushing the temptation too far.'

'Maybe a little,' Claire agreed.

Faith laid by her side, not wanting to rekindle the intimacy but needing to feel the reassuring presence of Claire's nearness. 'Is there anything else I should know about tonight's plan?' she asked. 'Should I be in a specific location? Sitting in the lotus position, or doing anything in particular?'

'We're on hallowed ground,' Claire said, 'so that aspect is covered. 'And you're naked, like Todd said you should be.'

'Thanks for noticing.'

Claire grinned. 'But other than that I think your involvement in the ritual is pretty tertiary.'

'Ritual?' Helen repeated, looming through the mist from

nowhere.

Nick came rushing to her side, a black silhouette from the fog. 'What ritual?' he demanded. He glared from Claire to Faith, his brow furrowing with obvious anger. 'What ritual are you trying to perform?'

Faith saw Claire close her eyes and knew her friend was quietly cursing the lapse in concentration that had allowed her to be overheard. Unable to think of an excuse that might get her out of the situation, and steadfastly refusing to answer, she shook her head.

'Shit!' Helen cursed. 'I knew these bitches were plotting something.' She glared at Nick. 'Get them out of here. Get them out of here now.'

'What's wrong with here?' he demanded. 'It's only a graveyard.'

She rolled her eyes impatiently. 'It's hallowed ground, you arse. The whole cemetery is consecrated earth. If they're involved in some ritual she could be using that to her advantage.'

Nick reached out and grabbed Faith's wrist with one hand and Claire's with the other. 'Come on, ladies,' he said, 'I think it's way past the time we left here.'

Glancing at Claire's watch, Faith wanted to argue that he was wrong. The hands were edging closer to midnight and she didn't think it was time for her to leave at all. Unwilling to have the opportunity for salvation taken from her now, she tried to pull her arm from his grip but it was a futile struggle. If Hope's ritual didn't take effect within the next few minutes, Faith knew she would have to wait another twenty-four hours for a second opportunity, and she didn't think she would be able to resist further temptations for that long. Commonsense told her that if she could delay leaving the cemetery she might still be able to reap the benefit of Hope's ritual.

But as Nick dragged her down the tree-lined avenue towards the ornate gates, she didn't think there would be any way to delay leaving.

Hope

Act II, Scene III

'I haven't forgotten anything,' Lilah said sweetly. 'It seems more likely that I've just found what I was looking for.'

Hope glared at the vampire, horrified that the woman had caught her alone, trapped and naked. She tried to cover herself but Lilah was fast and Hope was no match for her supernatural speed. Before she could raise a hand Lilah rushed into the room, dropped her wooden box on Chalmers' desk, and was pressing her body close. The icy chill of the vampire's nearness filled Hope with conflicting rushes of dread and desire.

Smiling lewdly, Lilah placed her fingers around Hope's bared breast and squeezed. Her blood-red nails caused the pliant flesh to dimple and her smile grew tight as she made her grip more punishing.

Hope almost choked as she tried to splutter a refusal and she raised a hand to slap the fingers away. Lilah's challenging gaze made her think twice, but she still struggled to say something that would make the woman move her hand. It might have been easier to manage the words if her touch hadn't been so exquisite. The tip of Hope's breast was tenderly brushed, stroked by Lilah's cool palm, and shards of raw pleasure erupted from the nipple. Before she had properly accepted the danger she might be facing, Hope realised she was already close to succumbing to the vampire's every whim.

Lilah's lips parted to reveal her long, wicked teeth. They looked bloodstained in the office's dim light and Hope was disgusted to note that the observation didn't hamper her longing for the woman.

'Is this how you've been helping Toad?' Lilah asked, the scarlet glint in her eyes shining brightly, her laughter leaving nothing to the imagination. 'It's no wonder he said it would take a couple of days to sort out my late brother's affairs. He's obviously determined to get a lot of pleasure out of you before I cure him of his mortality.'

Blushing furiously, stung by the insinuation that she and Chalmers were involved in an intimate relationship, Hope finally found the strength to tear herself from Lilah's embrace. She stumbled back to the desk, trying to turn and conceal her body from the vampire's intrusive attention. It was automatic to try and fold an arm across her breasts but she hesitated, wary that the weight of her own hand might prove just as exciting as Lilah's touch had been. 'There's nothing between me and Mr Chalmers – nothing at all,' she snapped, trying to hide her confusion behind indignation.

Lilah chuckled. 'Not even a sheet?'

Hope glared at her. 'You shouldn't be in here,' she said, remembering something she'd seen in a film or a TV show. 'I thought vampires needed to be invited before they could enter a room. I didn't invite you in here, so you shouldn't be in this office.'

Lilah's derisive laughter rang from the walls. 'That particular rule only ever applied to Christopher Lee and Vincent Price.' Brushing her fingers against the back of Hope's arm, smiling as though she too savoured the pleasurable tickle, Lilah held Hope's gaze and added, 'Besides, even if that silly rule did apply, you look like a perfect invitation to me.'

Shivering, Hope tried to pull herself away from the woman's touch, but Lilah sidled closer. Stroking the back of her hand against Hope's cheek, sparking another elicit flutter of arousal, she lowered her tone to a confidential lilt. 'Have you and Toad been playing naughty games? Is that why you're naked.' Her gaze flitted to the flushed cheeks of Hope's bottom and she beamed with obvious approval. 'My word!' she exclaimed. 'He's been having some fun with you, hasn't he?'

Hope tried to turn away but Lilah was as adept at controlling subordinates as Todd had been. The vampire only had to place a hand on her arm and fix her with a warning look, and Hope knew she wasn't going to resist the woman any longer. Hating the embarrassment of her situation and despising the loathsome excitement that came with that response, she held herself motionless when the vampire's fingers touched the stripes on her rear. The lines of discomfort had been almost forgotten, their pain already fading to little more than a memory, yet it only took Lilah's gentlest caress to reawaken the fury of their agonising bite. Hope flinched from her touch.

'He can be a vicious bastard when he's got a cane in his hand,' Lilah observed. 'And he can be quite the little sadist when he sets his mind to the task.'

She spoke as though she had first hand knowledge of Chalmers' discipline, and Hope pondered on that idea for a moment before dismissing it as being too fanciful. Todd Chalmers was a powerful authoritarian, and Hope knew he was capable of administering punishment, but she couldn't imagine any situation where he would be able to dominate a vampire as wilful and single-minded as Lilah.

'Look how he's marked you up,' Lilah purred, the tip of her finger remaining in constant contact with Hope's bottom. She drew the nail slowly against the flesh,

136

inspiring a rush of tortured shivers to ripple through her buttocks. 'That must have really bitten hard.'

Hope had thought she was past suffering unwanted arousal this evening and believed her most recent orgasm might have fulfilled her body's traitorous appetites. Yet it seemed that her carnal responses were not so easily tamed. Shaking her head in silent refusal, she held her breath as Lilah smoothed her finger back and forth along one raised weal. With all the determination she could summon, Hope tried not to be swayed by the delicious torment.

Lilah winced sympathetically, teasing her hand over both buttocks before following the broken line down to the valley between them.

'No,' Hope whispered, but Lilah continued as if she hadn't spoken. Her ice-cold fingertips slipped down dangerously close to Hope's sex, brushing against the soft hairs there. Holding her breath, dreading the moment when the vampire's fingers would touch her labia, Hope fought against her desire to suffer more. Drawing on all her resources of willpower she dragged herself away and turned to glare at Lilah. The vampire frowned, as though she hadn't expected Hope to show such resistance.

'What do you want with me?' Hope demanded. She could hear breathlessness in her own voice and tried to tell herself it would sound as though she was containing her anger. 'Are you trying to get revenge on me because of what Faith did to your brother?' she asked, glaring defiantly at Lilah, praying the woman wouldn't notice how she'd been affected.

For an instant Lilah looked confused: then she brayed laughter, the mirth genuine, rich and hatefully condescending, and Hope understood that she had seriously misread the situation. 'Revenge?' Lilah roared happily. 'For that? You think I want revenge because your sister overthrew my brother?' She continued to laugh as Hope puzzled over the response. 'You haven't been following the plot, have you? Hasn't Toad told you what really happened? He helped me and my brother, so I'm sure he's aware of all the details.' Shaping the words deliberately Lilah held Hope's gaze as she explained. 'I trained your sister to kill my brother. I trained her, and Chalmers helped me every step of the way.'

Hope studied the vampire's face, sure she would be able to see some indication of the woman's lie, but in this instance it looked like she was telling the truth. Her doubts about Chalmers briefly resurfaced and she wondered if he was working to his own agenda, rather than for the benefit of her and her sister. Considering the little that she knew of him it was difficult to make an educated guess but she remembered Charity, saying that he lived by the motto: 'What's in it for me?'

Shaking her head, certain that Lilah would have her own motives for driving a wedge of distrust between her and Chalmers, Hope told herself she would think about the vampire's revelation at a more appropriate time. She knew that Lilah must have seen her doubts because the woman's voice became crueller.

'You ought to take time off from letting Toad spank you so he can fill you in on the full story. He was my brother's advisor for a good few years, and I guess he still would be if I hadn't taken control of the coven.' She winked as though sharing a confidence. 'Yet, for all the help he gave me, I have to take most of the credit. Chalmers simply got Faith to Rome so she was within my brother's reach. I was the one who trained your sister; I was the one who got her ready to face my brother. I was the one who made her rip the heart from his chest.'

Hope stared at Lilah, feeling ill and confused, but the vampire didn't seem to notice her distress. She nodded at the pulsing wooden box on Chalmers' desk. 'The cursed heart is in there, if you want to look.'

Hope's upper lip curled in disgust, but glaring at the pulsing box Lilah went on. 'The damned thing continues to beat, even though it's been out of his body for four days now.' With a shiver of distaste she added, 'Unless I take some decisive action I think it might carry on beating forever.'

Hope listened, not sure she understood what was being said and wishing she didn't have to hear any more. It seemed clear that Lilah was broaching the subject of a personal fear, but Hope couldn't understand how the knowledge might help her, or what it had to do with her plight. 'If you don't want revenge on me, then what do you want?' she asked.

Lilah's smile sparkled wickedly. 'I thought you'd never ask,' she breathed, and before Hope realised what was happening Lilah was kissing her enthusiastically. The vampire's chill lips grazed hers before a hungry tongue plundered her mouth. At first she was too stunned to move, then the pleasure was so great it was unthinkable to try and pull away. It wasn't just the meeting of mouths that fuelled her arousal – although that was painfully exciting – but Lilah had a way of ingratiating her body against Hope's and the contact sparked exquisite tremors. The leather of Lilah's waistcoat caressed Hope's bare breasts and fresh torrents of pleasure were wrung from her nipples, the friction intolerably enjoyable. One hand held her shoulder while the other slipped against the swell of her hip. Unable to resist, Hope pushed her tongue into the vampire's mouth as Lilah slipped her thigh between Hope's, pressing herself closer.

If her mouth hadn't been locked to the vampire's Hope knew she would have groaned as her pussy lips were teased by Lilah's thigh, and a rush of raw arousal made her want to melt in the woman's embrace. She was tingling with the need for satisfaction and knew it would only take the sacrifice of her surrender and her every need would be satisfied. The temptation bordered on being irresistible, but with an heroic effort she found the strength to pull away. She gasped with the exertion and regarded the vampire more warily. 'What do you want from me?' she asked. 'Why are you pursuing me like this?'

'Pursuing you?' Lilah laughed. 'What a wonderful way you have with words! It's so reminiscent of the eighteenth century.'

Hope glared at her, determined to have an answer. 'What do you want from me?'

Lilah regarded her with sudden solemnity. 'A gypsy has told me that you're a threat to my leadership of the coven,' she confided. 'I don't normally put a lot of trust in fortune-tellers but one of them recently told my brother his end was near, and she turned out to be right, so I figured it would be prudent to hedge my bets.' Shrugging apologetically she added, 'So because of the gypsy's warning, and for the sake of my position at the head of the coven, I'm going to have to take or make you.'

She said the words with such cool indifference that Hope had to struggle to remember they were discussing her life. Lilah was diabolically attractive and it would have been all too easy to be lulled by the mesmerising lilt of her voice as she casually discussed her plans for Hope's demise.

'But your death is scheduled for tomorrow night.' If Lilah's tone had been edged with any trace of regret before, it was now gone as she airily strove to change the subject. 'So there's no need to worry about your impending doom just yet.' She flexed a smile and Hope found the gesture absurdly reassuring. 'Toad has said I mustn't take you until tomorrow night,' Lilah continued, 'and while I know he's trying to usurp me with some treachery, I'm not going to risk the fate of my brother's fortune until I have a better understanding of the game he's playing.'

'Then, what is it you want?' Hope asked.

'Couldn't I just be teasing you for the pleasure of it?' Lilah suggested mischievously. 'If I make you into a vampire you might one day discover that there's a great deal of pleasure to be had from tormenting your victims, building their hopes and expectations, then dashing them when you've drained the last drop of blood from their throats.'

Hope shut that image from her mind, certain it would fill her with panic and terror. 'If you don't plan on killing me,' she began, faltering, 'if you don't plan on killing me tonight at least, why are you here? Why are you persecuting me like this?'

'You know why I'm here.' Lilah shook her head, seemingly puzzled by Hope's lack of understanding. 'I've told you what I want already,' she reminded her. 'I told you while we were in the bar downstairs. I told you when we were in the foyer of this damned casino: I want the Bethesda Stone.'

'You want…' She made herself pause, not knowing what she was about to say but sure it might be unwise. Alarm bells began to sound and she told herself not to speak until she had properly thought through the consequences. Whatever spell Lilah had worked on her was beginning to recede and Hope could see she was in danger of giving up her sister's last chance for salvation. She shook her head, partly to clear her thoughts and partly to show Lilah that they were no longer in agreement.

'The Bethesda Stone could save my sister,' she said

flatly, and as she spoke she deliberately kept her gaze from creeping down to the floor. She had already seen that the vampire was attentive and sharply attuned to every detail and Hope suspected, if she even glanced in the direction of her basque, Lilah might notice and discover the Bethesda Stone hidden in the garment's discreet hip pocket. 'You've hinted that I shouldn't trust Mr Chalmers, but he was right when he told me that much, wasn't he? The Bethesda Stone could save my sister.'

'There's a possibility it might help,' Lilah allowed, her eyes narrowing as she studied Hope.

'Then the answer would have to be no,' said the scrutinised girl, unnerved by the close attention but lifting her chin defiantly. 'Even if I did have the Bethesda Stone I wouldn't give it to you.'

Lilah considered her quietly; something about her composed expression making Hope think the woman was reading her thoughts. 'The Bethesda Stone is a wish stone,' the vampire said. 'The Bethesda Stone will grant your most heartfelt desire. If *you* use it – and only if you use it *soon* – the power of the stone will return your sister back to her mortal state.'

'I know that much,' Hope said. 'What's your point?'

'My point is simple enough for you to understand,' Lilah told her. 'The Bethesda Stone can grant your most heartfelt desire. But it's not going to.'

'Why not?'

'Because I want the stone to do something for me.'

Hope fought to remain unmoved by the vampire's threatening smile. It was still an effort not to glance down at the discarded basque and she struggled to continue with the conversation rather than give the vampire a clue to the stone's location. 'What do you need it for? What is there in this world that you could wish for that you can't simply take by force?'

'I have a need for a wish stone,' Lilah snapped, glancing beyond Hope's shoulder, glaring at the pulsing wooden box on Chalmers' desk. Then speaking quietly, as though talking to herself, she whispered, 'I'm not a great lover of unnecessary noise. The Bethesda Stone might be able to help me get a little of the peace and quiet I currently crave.'

Hope shook her head, uneasy with Lilah's obsession with the macabre wooden box and its grisly contents. 'Even if I had this stone I wouldn't give it to you,' she said, trying to end the subject before she could give herself away, throwing every effort into sounding convincing.

The vampire reacted with frightening speed. In one moment Hope was glaring at her with all the defiance she could manage, and in the next she was sprawled on her back across Chalmers' desk.

The wooden box was knocked to the floor, its lid remaining mercifully closed, but Hope could faintly hear its constant, lethargic pulse. Dismissing it she tried to think of how best to extricate herself from her position but it wasn't so easy to stay focused on that particular task. Her bare shoulders were buried on the leather-topped surface and Lilah towered between her spread legs. The vampire's icy hands traversed her body, stroking her arms, sides and hips as she slowly lowered her head. Hope's bare stomach was brushed by the feather-light whisper of the woman's raven fringe and, with growing unease, she realised where the kisses were headed. Panicked, she tried to sit up, but Lilah effortlessly pushed her back to the desk.

Because her stomach was twisting with arousal, Hope realised she wasn't putting too much effort into resisting. She steeled herself against the rush of excitement as Lilah's kisses neared her groin, and deliberately she tried not to shift as the teasing became unbearable.

'Stop acting as though you have a say in these things,' Lilah growled while pressing her lips against Hope's bare stomach. The tremor of each word echoed through Hope's flesh and she was crippled by the need to experience more. 'If you've something I want you'll damned well give it to me.'

Hope wasn't listening. The vampire's mouth had moved to her pubic triangle and she could feel the woman nuzzling her way through the neatly trimmed curls. The stimulation wasn't particularly strong – the caress of Lilah's fingers as they stroked her arms and sides was far more exciting – but the promise of what was going to come had Hope breathless with anticipation.

'It doesn't matter if we're talking about a mystical crystal,' Lilah went on, 'or if we're discussing your sweet, juicy cunt.'

The final word had a magical effect on Hope; as soon as Lilah said it she was focused on the sensations of that one small part of her body. And as though she had intuited as much, Lilah chose that moment to deliver her first kiss between Hope's thighs. Her tongue glided slowly upward, starting at the base of the labia and licking until she touched her clitoris. It was a languid caress, soft and enticing, and Hope wanted to scream in response. She considered putting a final effort into trying to pull away, sure that if she didn't break free now she never would, but it was impossible to make herself move. Lilah's tongue and lips were working divine magic between her legs and the thought of escaping was more of a sacrifice than she could contemplate. Knowing she was weak, and sure she should be putting up some resistance, Hope wallowed in bliss on the desk as the vampire continued to slide more gentle kisses against her pussy lips.

Lilah's mouth was wet as it rubbed against her sex, the tip of her tongue only slightly warmer than her ice-cool lips, and she used it to chase tiny circles against Hope's clitoris. Moving her face away, leaving her fringe to dance a tormenting tarantella against Hope's stomach, she said, 'You have to understand which one of us is in control here. You have to understand, if I say "give it to me", you're going to do as you're told.' She started to lower her face again and then paused with her mouth inches from Hope's sex. 'Do you understand?' she asked, glancing up, her scarlet gaze meeting Hope's silent plea.

Unable to voice a refusal, beyond caring what the consequences might be, Hope nodded acquiescence. 'I understand,' she whispered softly.

Lilah regarded her without attempting to disguise her hunger. She placed her mouth against Hope's sex for one last kiss, savouring the contact and teasing the clitoris with the tip of her tongue, and then she pulled away. Stealthily climbing up her body, making sure she made her presence known by rubbing herself against Hope's naked figure, she moved her mouth close to Hope's face.

The fragrance of sexual musk lingered on her lips and Hope squirmed with the delicious knowledge that she was inhaling her own scent on the woman's face. She considered tasting a kiss that was flavoured by her own pussy juice, and then resisted the urge, not sure Lilah would approve of such a bold demand. But she almost shook with relief when Lilah lowered her head and their mouths met. The flavours of sexual excitement coloured the vampire's kiss and Hope was transported into the throes of ecstasy. She rubbed her body hungrily against the woman's and relished every wicked moment. Her nipples were teased by the supple leather of Lilah's waistcoat;

her pussy lips were squashed as the vampire pressed a thigh between hers; but it was the taste of her own excitement on the woman's lips that made her pleasure complete.

Elated, she sighed, and Lilah lifted her face and smiled greedily down. 'You're too tempting to resist,' she purred, the sparkle in her eyes reflecting Hope's own hunger for more, and she understood perfectly when Lilah said, 'I don't care what promises I made to Toad. I'm going to have to take you tonight.'

Hope gasped sharply as the vampire's teeth pressed against her throat. She knew what to expect and she was willing to concede it was probably the one pleasure she needed to make her evening complete.

'The Toad has had you for long enough,' Lilah whispered. 'It's my turn to have you now, and this time nothing is going to stop me from enjoying you.'

As she started to bite a woman screamed, and caught between panic and pleasure, and yearning to experience Lilah's penetrating kiss, Hope couldn't decide if she might be listening to her own ecstatic cry.

Hope

Act II, Scene IV

'Toad!' Lilah cried. 'You bastard!'

Hope glanced up from her blissful reverie and saw that Chalmers had returned. She blinked to take in what was happening and was surprised to see he'd dropped a bulging hessian sack in one corner of the office along with a loosely packed sports bag. Those were only peripheral details, and they barely registered on her thoughts because of the confrontation happening immediately above her.

Chalmers wielded a large wooden crucifix and pressed it against Lilah's back. Wisps of pale grey smoke trailed up from between the vampire's shoulder blades as she thrashed in a frantic attempt to escape. The porcelain flesh on her back turned a painful red and then bubbled and blistered. Her venom and outrage were only matched by Chalmers' diligent efforts to keep her at arm's length.

'I'm disappointed in you, Lilah,' he grumbled. 'Don't you know how to keep to an arrangement?'

'Get that thing off me!' she roared, but prudently Chalmers kept the crucifix pressed hard against her and carefully manoeuvred so he was guiding her towards the door.

'We had a deal,' he said sourly. 'You were supposed to wait until tomorrow night and then I'd present this girl to you on a platter. Coming in here directly contravenes the verbal contract we agreed. I'm seriously disappointed.'

Lilah finally managed to squirm free and she stumbled

away from him. She snatched up her wooden box and glared at him with more outrage than Hope had ever seen. The vampire's hands were curled into claws and she looked ready to pounce in retaliation. 'You bastard!' she growled. 'You'll pay for that!'

'That wasn't quite the apology I thought I deserved.'

She tensed and prepared to launch herself at him, but Chalmers raised his crucifix as a warning. 'Go back to your coven,' he said firmly. 'We have an appointment for tomorrow night and I expect we'll sort out our differences then. Right now you're not welcome here and I want you gone.'

Lilah's features were twisted with impotent fury and it was with obvious reluctance that she took a step towards the door. Her eyes glowed with so much hatred Hope fancied she could see sparks spitting from them. 'The transfer of funds had better be complete by tomorrow night,' Lilah warned.

Chalmers studied her levelly. 'I'll be keeping to my side of the bargain,' he promised.

Lilah glared at him and Hope thought the woman would say more before leaving. She expected a final curse or a threat for retribution, but instead the vampire simply stormed from the office and disappeared into the corridor.

Chalmers turned to Hope, and after the shock of the fight and the vampire's expulsion she was left to feel embarrassed by her nudity and the compromising position in which she'd been found. Before she could try and cover herself, or explain what had happened, Chalmers was turning his back and locking the door. 'We might stand a better chance of saving your sister if you stopped trying to seduce Lilah each time you see her,' he admonished over his shoulder.

She stared at his back, incredulous that he could accuse

her of such an act. She didn't know if he had genuinely misinterpreted events or was trying to make light of what had happened, but his words still rankled. Before she had a chance to respond she saw he was struggling with the hessian sack and emptying its contents onto the centre of the office floor. With painstaking care, Chalmers poured out a flood of dark, wet earth, and it was so unexpected it quashed Hope's indignation and her curiosity took over. 'What the hell are you doing?' she asked.

He glanced at the wall clock behind his desk. 'Time's against us,' he grumbled. 'We have to act fast.'

'And acting fast involves pouring dirt on the floor?'

He paused with the half-full sack still in his hands and the remainder of its contents strewn in a large mound at his feet. The black clumps of soil looked unreal against the plush carpet and Hope wondered if Chalmers had finally snapped and gone insane.

'This is consecrated earth,' he explained. 'Don't ask me how I got it. Just don't be surprised if you think the flower beds around the *Basilique du Sacré-Coeur* look a little depleted tomorrow morning.'

Hope watched him pour the remainder of the soil onto the formerly immaculate floor and caught the sweet, woody scent of fresh earth. Granules of black dirt tumbled to the corners of the room and, as he shook the last of the contents free from the sack, she watched him accidentally grind a footprint into the rich pile.

'The ritual needs to be performed on hallowed ground,' she remembered. 'That's why you're dumping church soil on your office floor.'

He nodded and glanced again at the wall clock. 'The ritual needs to be performed on hallowed ground,' he confirmed. 'And it needs to be performed in the next five minutes.'

The urgency in his voice shook her from her reverie.

'Have you got the stone?' he asked.

She quickly retrieved it from the pocket of her discarded basque. Memories of how close she had come to parting with the stone made her blush. The embarrassment stung more painfully than the reality of her nakedness or the view she presented to Chalmers when she bent over. Reaching down for her basque meant turning her back on him, and bending over exposed the cheeks of her bottom and the split of her sex. If he'd been glancing at her, Hope knew he'd have an unhindered view of her sex lips, but that thought no longer filled her with the thrilling shame she had experienced before.

'It's here,' she told him, holding the stone up so he could see. 'Does that mean we're ready to begin?'

He used his hands to smooth a flat surface on the mound of soil, and then motioned for her to take her place while he went to the sports bag.

Gingerly, Hope knelt on the mound. She was beginning to feel ridiculous, ready to believe that the ritual and the vampires were nothing more than an elaborate charade to encourage her to undress at Chalmers' whims and submit to his perverted clan. But those worries were banished when she stepped onto the consecrated earth.

The cool wetness against her knees reminded her that she was naked, but it made her aware of much more than that. Although they were alone in the room, and she had watched Chalmers lock the door, she felt as though she'd suddenly become the centre of attention. The thought inspired a rush of delicious exhibitionism and she shivered with unexpected elation. The knowledge of her own daring – being naked and pliant and obeying Chalmers' strict instructions – made her tremble with unbidden excitement.

Lowering her gaze, not wanting him to see how she

was responding, she almost exclaimed in surprise when she noticed the Bethesda Stone glowed dully in her palm. A blood-red glimmer shone from within its depths and the light seemed to pulse in time with her heartbeat.

Hope couldn't understand why but the sight gave her a sudden rush of confidence. For the first time since Chalmers had told her about Faith's plight, Hope believed she had a genuine opportunity to make everything right. Suddenly eager to get the ritual underway, she glanced expectantly in Chalmers' direction.

After rummaging through the sports bag he had produced coloured candles and placed them on his desk and the office shelves. The pale flames warmed the room and added enough illumination so he could study the labels on a selection of miniature brown bottles that had been stuffed in his bag.

Ordinarily Hope knew she would have made a joke – asked if he was raiding the mini-bars, or speculated that they were going to play a drinking game – but she sensed this wasn't the time for levity. Since kneeling on the mound of cool earth her senses grew more alert and she felt as though a low-grade electrical charge was humming through her body. The idea of poking fun at the ritual had never been further from her mind. She waited patiently until he selected a couple of bottles from the cache and asked quietly what they were.

'Essential oils,' he said, sounding distracted. 'Clary sage and sandalwood. You need anointing before we can perform the ceremony.'

As he came closer Hope could smell the distinctive scents he mentioned. The clary sage was florid and invigorating while the sandalwood was more medicinal. 'I can smell almonds as well,' she said, sniffing critically.

'The carrier oil is almond-based,' he explained as he

stepped behind her.

She wanted to say more, suddenly uncomfortable with the idea of being anointed, but she realised her attempts at conversation were little more than delaying tactics and she knew there was no time for hesitation. Remaining motionless she braced herself for his touch and said nothing when he placed his hands on her shoulders.

His fingers fell smoothly against her back. The scented oils perfumed the air and coloured every breath. The blend of their aromas made her dizzy, and yet peculiarly more focused. She could feel the grain of his fingerprints rubbing coarsely over her bare flesh, the rough caress made smooth by the lubrication of the oils.

Chalmers' broad hands massaged in circles against the tops of her arms and then down to her sides. The touch was more intimate than she wanted but she knew better than to stop him. Once he had rubbed her buttocks, oiling the cheeks and stirring a low-level of arousal in the pit of her stomach, he climbed from the mound and returned to the sports bag.

If she had bothered to glance in his direction, Hope would have seen Chalmers pouring more oil into his palms, but she didn't need to look at him. She was already aware of what would happen next and it came as no surprise when he sat down in front of her and placed his hands against her breasts. She couldn't completely stifle her gasp but the sound wasn't enough to disperse the thickening atmosphere creeping between them. His palms were a broiling balm against her orbs and the heels of his thumbs were aggravating against her nipples. The tips of her breasts were annoyingly receptive and each caress fired her with a fresh rush of responses.

Initially she tried to fight the reaction, unwilling to have him excite her so easily, but lulled by the fragrances, the mood of the lighting, and the delicious friction of his massage, she eventually lost the will to resist.

He moved his hands from her breasts, stroking the lower curves of her ribcage, and leaving a sheen of scented oils glistening in their wake. Delving deeper, warming her waist with his febrile touch, his hands went to her hips while his thumbs pushed close to her sex. Frightened by the rush of guilty pleasure he inspired, she glanced doubtfully into his face.

Chalmers' features were a mask of deliberation as he worked the oil into her skin. His lips moved, and although she was only inches from his face she could hardly hear what he was saying. The little she could catch had a foreign twang to it that could have been Latin, or might simply have been one of the local Parisian dialects. Whatever he was saying – she assumed it was some chant pertinent to the spell – it was clearly taking up all his concentration as he carried on with the anointing. His hands smoothed over her thighs, sparking enough excitement to leave her dizzy.

Not wanting to appear too willing, but unable to resist the impulse of the urges he'd awoken, she eased her legs slightly apart for him. As he continued to rub the oil against her a soft smile broke Chalmers' lips. The tips of his fingers crept dangerously close to her sex and she held her breath as she waited for him to touch her there. It was an agonising moment where she was torn by the desire to suffer his touch and appalled that she could make herself so available for him. But she didn't want to do anything that might jeopardise the ritual they were performing, and she repeatedly told herself that was the only reason she wasn't moving away from him.

Chalmers opened his eyes and briefly appraised her naked body. 'You need to hold the stone in both hands,' he said, shaking his head and glancing at her lap. 'And always keep the larger half in your right hand.'

The bizarre instruction wrenched her from the warm mood he'd created, and puzzled, she watched him return to his sport bag and wipe his hands dry on a towel he kept within. She tried to tell herself that he was unaffected by the massage, and that was why he could still remain focused on the mechanics of the ceremony, but she could see the shape of his erection distorting the front of his trousers.

'Why do I need to keep the larger half in my right hand?' she asked. 'Is it important?'

He rolled his eyes and glanced at the wall clock as though the question was an annoying distraction. The hands were creeping inexorably closer to midnight. 'The Bethesda Stone is a wish stone,' he began with forced patience.

'I know that much,' Hope said testily.

'You are the conduit…'

'Yes.'

'…and used in connection with the correct ritual, the Bethesda Stone can grant the conduit's most heartfelt desire.'

Hope chewed her lower lip, wanting to tell him that she was already aware of her role as the conduit and the stone's ability. She had only wanted to know why she needed to keep the larger half in her right hand and it was a struggle not to tell him as much in her most contemptuous tone. She glared at him but he seemed determined to make his explanation as detailed as possible, even though midnight was getting dangerously close.

'As you've been told before,' he continued, 'the Bethesda Stone always demands a price, and as well as granting the conduit's most heartfelt desire, it also realises their darkest fear.'

This was a fact she hadn't heard before and she stared at him with sudden unease. After glancing at the dully glowing stone in her left hand, she quickly transferred it to her right. A prickle of disquiet scurried down her spine and the warmth of the room seemed to have suddenly vanished. 'The stone's going to make all my dreams come true?' she asked nervously. 'The good ones and the bad ones?'

'That's why you need to keep the larger half in your right hand,' he said solemnly. 'Mystics, palmists and fortunetellers are usually agreed that the right hand is associated with positive dreams, goals and aspirations. Whereas the left hand has more sinister connotations.'

Hope considered what Chalmers said, not doubting a word but wishing he had explained about the negative aspect of the Bethesda Stone earlier. She supposed he had said that the stone always demanded a price but she hadn't expected the price would be the realisation of her worst fear. Not sure what that might actually be, but knowing she would have to face that personal demon if she wanted to save her sister, she drew a deep breath and nodded agreement. 'All right,' she said. 'If that takes care of all the minor details, then let's get on with it.'

He glanced at the clock again, and even though the hands hovered over midnight he didn't seem in a particular rush to instigate proceedings. 'Are you sure you're ready?'

'I'm as ready as I'm going to be.'

'You understand your role in this?'

She nodded.

'You know that you're meant to hold the Bethesda Stone in both hands…'

'The larger half in my right hand,' she broke in impatiently.

'…and concentrate on your heart's desire.'

155

'I understand what I'm supposed to do,' she snapped anxiously, glancing at the clock too. 'Shouldn't we be getting on with it?'

He nodded and reached into the sports bag. Hope had thought she was prepared for the ritual, believed she was ready to do whatever was necessary to save her sister, but doubts and reservations came rushing back when she saw what he took from the bag.

'What on earth is that?' she demanded.

Chalmers glanced at the whip in his hand, seeming puzzled she could ask something so obvious. 'It's a knout,' he explained. 'It was a favourite amongst the Russian Czars and a forerunner of the notorious pelti, although the knout isn't quite as barbaric.'

Glancing at the wooden-handled whip, with its formidable lengths of bound leather and the trailing tip that dangled from its end, Hope thought it looked more barbaric than anything she had ever seen. She didn't know if he was correct in calling it a knout, and had no idea what a pelti might be, but she guessed this wasn't the time for such a gruesome history lesson. 'And what do you think you're going to do with your knout?' she asked.

He didn't lower his gaze from the challenge in her eyes. 'It's part of the ritual, Hope,' he said quietly. 'It's a *necessary* part of the ritual.'

Shivering at the thought of what she was doing, Hope nodded, and with an air of resignation she lowered herself back to the kneeling position. 'Go on, then,' she said. 'Like you said before: time's against us. We might as well start.'

He moved behind her and she heard him draw a reluctant breath. Stiffening her shoulders, preparing herself for the punishment, she wondered how badly the knout was going to hurt. It was small consolation to realise she would discover all too soon, and even less comforting to realise the muscles of her sex were already clenching in anticipation.

The relationship between his discipline and her growing arousal hadn't escaped Hope. She was loath to acknowledge that the punishment and her excitement went hand-in-hand, but she couldn't deny that a voice at the back of her mind was quietly encouraging him to hurry up and deliver the first blow. On a rational level she could have argued that she didn't want to be hurt. But she knew there was no honest way she could refute her eager need to feel the stinging bite of the whip.

The wall clock made an electronic beep to signal midnight.

In the silence that followed Hope thought it sounded like even the candles were holding their breath. She held herself motionless, still drinking the perfumes of clary sage and sandalwood, and waiting fretfully for the sting of the first blow.

The whistle of leather hissing through the air broke the silence. It struck loudly between her shoulder blades like the spit of fat from a griddle. Her nipples hardened and she felt her sex clench and grow more fluid. The excitement was as exhilarating as she had expected and she snatched a short, grateful breath. Not sure if she was trying to shun some part of the pain, or if it was an instinctive part of the ceremony, Hope closed her eyes. However, rather than swathing herself in the comforting blackness of any release, she found herself seeing vaguely familiar sights.

Surprised and unnerved she opened her eyes, just as Chalmers lashed the tip of the knout against one buttock. He scored a direct hit against the centre of the flesh and Hope thought the pain couldn't have been more severe if he'd spiked her with a steel barb. Her response was galling – she drew an excited breath and crushed her thighs together in an attempt to stave her growing arousal – and again it was instinctive to close her eyes.

As before, rather than allowing her the relief of darkness, she found herself seeing things that weren't in the room. The sights around her were vaguely familiar – she recognised the overpass of *Rue Caulaincourt*, and the ornate gates leading from *Cimetière de Montmartre* to *Avenue Rachel* – but she couldn't recall seeing them from such a frantic angle previously.

Chalmers sliced the tip of the knout against her side, and distantly Hope shrank from the pain. It was unnervingly close to her breast, and the whisper of the whip's descent stroked her with a chilly caress. But with her eyes closed she was away from Chalmers' office and only physically involved with the punishment. Mentally she was in the *Cimetière de Montmartre*.

The clarity of the image was marred by its lack of colour. Her view of events was almost monotone, except instead of seeing in only blacks and whites, the paler colours were all varying hues of red. If she had been given the time to think about it she would have said it was like viewing a black and white film through a blood-red filter.

But the distraction of Chalmers' knout striking her thigh was enough to stop her thoughts from making that connection. The flaming weal burnt brightly against her leg, making the muscle ache and secreting a liquid fire that burnt all the way to her pussy lips and beyond. She arched her back, keeping both hands tight on the stone and her eyes firmly closed. With an air of detachment she noted that her body was veering close to an orgasm, but the shrill rise of pleasure seemed of secondary importance compared with the events she was watching from behind her closed eyes.

A couple loomed into view and Hope recognised Nick and Helen from her encounter with them in the foyer. She caught a glimpse of Faith's friend, Claire, in the background, but she couldn't understand why she should be seeing those three when she was trying to concentrate on her sister.

Chalmers' mumbled chant rang briefly louder in her ears before he slashed the knout against her hip, the sting of the tip burning brightly within her flesh, but she wouldn't let herself be pulled away from the connection she felt she was making. The Bethesda Stone pulsed warm between her fingertips, its heat radiated slickly against her lap, and she was convinced that some greater power was on the verge of reversing Faith's plight.

It was the *Cimetière de Montmartre*, she was sure of that, and the gates loomed ever closer. Helen's mouth was a scream of constant curses and instructions and Hope tried to understand what she was saying. But in the stark illumination of crimson moonlight it was impossible to read her lips and Hope gave up rather than wasting valuable time. She could see that Nick was swearing and grunting, and although she didn't fully understand what she was seeing, Hope felt sure comprehension was close to hand.

Chalmers landed the knout against her back. It struck the flesh of her buttock and this time the shock was enough to push her body beyond the brink of a climax. She gritted her teeth and sighed with bitter frustration as the torrent of pain and pleasure intermingled in a furious roar.

Glancing up, seeing the overhead arch of the cemetery's gates, she realised she was on the brink of making a vital connection. She caught a fleeting glimpse of Nick's stern features, a passing glance of Helen's anger and a moment of Claire's dismay.

Chalmers landed the knout again. No longer able to see anything other than darkness, Hope opened her eyes. The vision had ceased abruptly and she was left alone with Chalmers, no longer able to see what was happening in the cemetery. Her body was still trembling from the throes of elation and after echoes of that delight were rekindled as Chalmers struck her twice more. She would have been happy to suffer further blows from the knout if she'd thought it might help, but Chalmers seemed to realise that the moment had passed them by and he angrily tossed the whip to the floor, the clatter of the wooden handle making Hope glance in his direction. His disappointment was as obvious as the bulge pushing at the front of his trousers.

'We'd better stop,' he growled, nodding at her lap while he lit a cigar. 'The stone's stopped glowing. And the clock says it's well past midnight. It looks like we either missed tonight's window of opportunity or something scuppered our plans.'

Hope grasped the stone more tightly, silently willing it to resume the connection she'd made. 'What are you saying?' she asked. The stinging in her buttocks, back and thighs was subsiding to a maddening ache and the tremors that had pulsed through her sex were becoming memories. 'What happens now? What are we meant to do?' She feared she already knew the answer to her own questions, but she wanted to hear Chalmers say the words.

He regarded her solemnly. 'It means we have to try again tomorrow night.' His frown was severe and she could see he was annoyed by the development. 'It means we have to try again tomorrow night with Lilah and her coven breathing down our necks.'

Hope glared at the cold black stone in her fist and remembered what Chalmers had said about its abilities as a wish stone. Miserably she realised it hadn't been able to grant her most heartfelt desire, but she had a sneaking suspicion that it had just realised her worst fear.

Interlude

Part Four

'Give that back,' Claire insisted. 'It's not yours and you have no right taking it off me. Give it back!'

Lilah kept her at arms length while she studied Claire's mobile phone. The coven's leader looked exquisite in her black silk gown. Like a snakeskin it clung to her athletic frame and the shimmering fabric moulded the shape of her slender arms and narrow waist. It was cut deep at the neckline to accentuate her cleavage, and split high up to the hip to reveal an enticing length of stockinged thigh. Her lips were puckered into a thoughtful kiss and her brow was twisted with concentration. 'I'd begun to think that Toad was awfully well informed about our movements,' she mused. 'I wondered if he had a crystal ball, or was maybe employing a psychic. Now I know different.'

Claire made another attempt to snatch the phone back but Lilah shoved her into the waiting grasp of Marcia and the mulatto. The two vampires easily restrained her, the mulatto teasing a hand against the shape of Claire's breast while Marcia extracted a long, lingering kiss and, when she finally moved away, her lips were rouged with excitement.

Studying the suite's mirror, cocking her head as though appraising an exhibit in a gallery, Faith made no attempt to intervene. None of the vampires were reflected, there wasn't even the ghost of her own image lurking behind the glass, and she was only able to see Claire struggling to escape an unseen adversary. Distracted, and looking for something in the mirror that remained annoyingly out of view, Faith didn't react to her best friend's obvious distress.

Lilah walked to the mini-bar and strummed her fingers on top of the wooden box she'd left there. She held Claire's mobile in her other hand and studied the keypad with an expression of rueful understanding. 'I was puzzled by the coincidence that Faith was on hallowed ground at the exact moment when the Bethesda Stone ritual needed her to be there,' she said slowly. 'But now I'm beginning to put the pieces together.' A smile crept slowly across her lips. 'You've been contacting Toad Chalmers, haven't you?' she said, using the phone's stubby aerial to point at Claire.

'Give that phone back,' Claire demanded, and glaring at Marcia and the mulatto she made a fresh attempt to pull free, but the vampires only laughed. The mulatto plucked open two buttons on Claire's blouse while Marcia stole a hand against her hip. Their caresses were a cruel tease with one of them unfastening her clothes while the other snatched punishing kisses against her lips, throat and shoulders. Their overlong canines had come into play and Claire gasped each time her flesh was caught with a vicious nip. The crucifix around her neck made the pair hesitate but it didn't properly ward away their interest.

Still in front of the mirror, Faith remained oblivious to Claire's struggles. She tilted her head slightly, narrowing her eyes and concentrating hard as she stared into the glass.

'You've been contacting Toad,' Lilah told Claire. The tone of her voice was balanced and it was impossible to tell if she was speaking with admiration or fury. 'You've been contacting Toad and you've been keeping him updated on what's happening with Faith.'

Glaring furiously, Claire remained silent. The mulatto released the final button on her blouse and the over-filled cups of Claire's bra were made visible to the room. Both breasts were round and full, and because of the kisses and touching the thrust of her nipples was visible through the lacy fabric. Marcia touched the right button of flesh while the mulatto pressed a teasing finger against the left. They both chuckled and Claire's cheeks flushed red with embarrassment. Clearly mortified she switched her angry gaze from one vampire to the other.

Lilah wasn't watching the torment. She stroked the lid of the wooden box and frowned thoughtfully. 'But why would you be doing that? What's in it for you?' She glanced in Faith's direction and asked Claire, 'Do you share the silly belief that the Bethesda Stone can help her? Is that what this is all about?'

'It's not a silly belief,' Claire snapped indignantly. 'The Bethesda Stone will cure Faith and then…' she stopped herself abruptly, and if Faith had turned at that moment she would have seen Claire's face cringing with self-recrimination.

Instead, Faith continued to tilt her head while she studied the mirror. She was desperately trying to catch a glimpse of her reflection. The image she had seen two nights earlier – a smoky haze that vaguely resembled her own form – had offered the promise of some chance for change. But that was two nights ago and since then she had almost succumbed to the unwholesome cravings of her vampiric appetite. Aware of her own limitations she knew she would be unable to resist much more temptation and she wanted to glimpse her hazy reflection in the hope that it would give her the encouragement to continue fighting those impulses.

'And then?' Lilah encouraged, mimicking Claire with a high-pitched whine. 'The Bethesda Stone will cure Faith, *and then*…?'

Claire shook her head. She was defiantly refusing to answer but it seemed clear that she had already said too much.

Lilah placed her hand over the wooden box and strummed her fingers quickly against its lid. The pulse inside throbbed lethargically almost as though it was answering. 'Toad wants Faith cured?' Lilah sounded as though she was talking to herself. 'But what possible use could he have for…?' her voice trailed off as understanding crept across her face. She took her hand from the wooden box and placed it over her mouth. 'My God! How could I have been so dumb? Why didn't I see it before? The answer's obvious, isn't it?'

Marcia and the mulatto exchanged a baffled glance. While the mulatto continued to caress Claire's left breast through the fabric of the bra, Marcia released the right and was teasing the rigid nipple between her finger and thumb. But sensing something important in their leader's exclamation, both vampires ceased their torment and turned expectantly to face Lilah.

'Why would Toad want to cure Faith? What possible use could he have for a virtuous little bitch who's already proven herself able to overthrow the strongest vampire?'

Claire glared at the coven's leader with bitter frustration.

Marcia shook her head, clearly not making the connection. 'What use would he have for her?'

The mulatto rolled her eyes.

'At tonight's meeting, Chalmers is supposed to hand me all titles to my late brother's estate.' Lilah made the explanation with a surprising amount of patience. Barely listening, Faith guessed the vampire was speaking more for Claire's benefit than Marcia's: taunting her with her newfound knowledge. 'As soon as Chalmers hands me the titles he will no longer have access to the coven's considerable wealth. And, because I no longer require his services, he'll be left penniless and without prospects.'

She paused. Her smiled glinted malevolently in the muted lights.

Claire's nose wrinkled with disgust.

'However,' Lilah went on. 'If Toad was able to cure Faith, and then have her kill me, he'd be able to keep all the money.'

'Doesn't Chalmers own this casino?' the mulatto broke in.

Lilah shook her head, clearly irritated by the distraction. 'The title deeds are in my brother's name. He'll be handing them over to me tonight.'

'What about her sister's rock band?' Marcia asked, nodding in Faith's direction. 'I thought Chalmers managed BloodLust?'

'Their management contract means they were signed to my late brother. As of tonight, they'll become my property.' Her smile flashed momentarily wicked as she considered the acquisition. 'Trust me,' she assured them, 'Chalmers has no assets. And he knows unless he puts me out of the picture, he'll be borrowing a pen and paper to write himself a "Homeless and Hungry" sign.'

Marcia blinked and regarded the coven's leader with obvious admiration. 'Is that really what he was planning?'

Lilah glanced at Claire's dour frown. 'I think that just about sums it up,' she gloated. 'Am I right?'

'What if that is what he's planning?' Claire demanded, her voice sharp with pent-up fury. 'It's not like you'll be able to stop him now.'

Lilah's smile blossomed into something cruel and obscenely sexual. 'You silly little bitch,' she snapped, shooting her glance in Faith's direction. 'All I have to do is get her to feed once. As soon as she's done that Chalmers' masterplan is screwed.'

'And you think you can manage that?' Claire sneered. She finally managed to tear herself away from Marcia and the mulatto and pushed her face defiantly closer to Lilah's. She seemed oblivious to her state of semi-undress and only determined to make her point. 'You haven't been able to get Faith to feed for the best part of a week. What makes you think you can manage it in the next four hours?'

Lilah glowered and raised a threatening hand, but rather than striking a blow across Claire's cheek she pointed at the mulatto. 'Take this bitch down to the *Notre Dame* crypt. I'll be along shortly.'

Claire struggled to resist being led out of the room but the vampires were determined to follow their leader's instruction. Her struggles were brief and futile and Lilah waved a sardonic farewell as she was dragged from the room. As soon as the three had left, the coven's leader retrieved her box from the top of the mini-bar and then stepped behind Faith. Amicably, Lilah placed an arm around her shoulder.

Faith turned to her slowly. 'What's your worst fear, Lilah?'

Smiling, Lilah shook her head. 'Let's not talk about my fears.' Her voice had slipped to a seductive whisper. 'Why don't we talk about what you want?'

Faith shrugged and allowed herself to be guided away from the mirror. Her reflection had remained frustratingly absent and she doubted she would ever see it again. Lilah took her to the couch and spread herself feline-like along its length, then rather than letting Faith have the chance

167

to join her, she indicated a place on the floor.

Obediently, Faith knelt where she'd been told. She realised she was being forced to assume a servile position, but that thought didn't inspire any notions of rebellion or dissent. Even when Lilah crooked her knee, allowing one leg to appear through the split in her skirt, Faith made no complaint about the obvious demands about to be made on her. She simply studied the coven's leader and waited to be told what to do next.

Lilah reached out and stroked a finger against her face. 'Are you hungry, Faith?' she whispered.

Seeing no benefit in lying, Faith nodded, the vampire's caress wickedly exciting against her cheek. It was natural to smile for her and with that expression Faith felt the familiar rise of her arousal. She struggled to quell the emotion, sure she should still be trying to resist her appetites, then decided there was no longer any point in fighting. Her reflection hadn't appeared in the mirror and that seemed to indicate that her chances of salvation were now gone. All she had left was her obedience to Lilah.

'You haven't fed since you joined the coven,' the vampire remarked.

'No.' Faith couldn't think of much else to say. 'No, I haven't.'

'You must be ravenous,' Lilah murmured, and languidly stroked her fingers through Faith's hair. She stopped when she reached the back of her neck and gently pulled her closer. Faith watched the vampire part her legs, allowing the split of her skirt to fall further open and reveal the tops of her stockings. With a casual flick of her wrist, Lilah pulled enough of the skirt aside to show that she wasn't wearing underwear. 'You must be ready to devour anything,' she sighed.

Her sex lips glistened slickly in the room's muted

lighting. The musk of arousal was only subtle but Faith found the sweet fragrance intoxicating. Unable to stop herself she drew a deep breath as she drank in the rich aroma. Lilah continued to guide Faith's face closer, making her unspoken instruction implicit.

Obligingly, Faith extended her tongue and lapped against the vampire's sex. The pussy lips were cool and soft. The frisson of the hesitant kiss was as electric as the caress of the stockings that rubbed against Faith's cheek. The sudden spark of excitement that flourished between them made both sit back, each regarding the other with sly, lurid respect.

Lilah released a throaty giggle. 'Gosh,' she whispered, 'you do that awfully well. Are those the same sort of kisses you give to that voluptuous girlfriend of yours?'

Faith broke the eye contact they shared, reluctant to answer the question. She didn't want to talk about her hunger and she most certainly didn't want to discuss the relationship she shared with Claire. Although she was content to be the vampire's slave Faith didn't want to unwittingly give Lilah any information that could be used against her or her friend. Defiantly, she remained silent.

Seeming untroubled by the rudeness, Lilah gently coaxed Faith's mouth back to her sex. The black bands of her stocking-tops pressed into the flesh of her thighs and the stark band contrasted sharply with her pallid, porcelain flesh. The flush of her excited labia was an inviting cerise that begged to be tasted.

Unable to resist, Faith thought the chore of licking a welcome respite from the prospect of questions and took to the task eagerly. She stroked her tongue against the velvet folds, savouring the forbidden flavour of the vampire's wetness. Trilling the tip of her tongue against Lilah's clitoris, relishing the responding throb as the bead of flesh squirmed beneath her attention, she worked her lips eagerly against the soft, moist entrance.

Lilah responded with a wistful moan. She held the wooden box against her chest and stroked the heel of her hand against its polished lid. In a breathless whisper she said, 'I'm sorry, we weren't talking about your special friend, were we?'

Faith lifted her mouth to reply, and the brief break in contact allowed her to savour the syrupy taste of the musk on her lips. 'No,' she said quietly, 'we weren't.'

Lilah smiled and guided Faith's face back between her smooth thighs. 'We were talking about your hunger, weren't we?' she purred. 'We were talking about the distressing fact that you haven't fed yet and you've been a vampire for almost a week.'

Faith was no longer sure what they had been talking about, but she could see she was being given a clear choice. Lilah wanted to either discuss Claire, or talk about Faith's inevitable first feed. Not wanting to betray her friend, sure there was only one way to avoid saying something she shouldn't, Faith mumbled, 'That's right, we were talking about the fact that I haven't fed yet.'

From the corner of her eye she saw the flash of Lilah's teeth as the vampire smiled again. Pushing her face closer to the woman's sex, burying her senses in the feel, flavour and fragrance of Lilah's pussy, Faith tried not to think that the vampire looked like she was on the brink of victory.

'Do you know what makes us vampires hungry?' Lilah asked.

Faith brushed the tip of her nose against the woman's clitoris, and the vampire shuddered and pressed one hand harder against the wooden box. She slipped the other behind Faith's neck, grabbing a fistful of hair and pulling tight. 'Do you know what makes us vampires hungry?'

she repeated.

Faith gasped with the sudden discomfort and realised she would have to answer. Making an effort to keep her voice stable she said, 'No, I don't suppose I do know.' Glancing up the contours of Lilah's supine body, she asked, 'What does make vampires hungry?'

Lilah guided Faith's face back to her sex before continuing. She waited until a tongue was lapping her before drawing a heavy breath for her reply. 'Not feeding is an obvious way,' she began. 'But did you know, sexual excitement makes the appetite worse? Seeing others feed always makes me hungry,' Lilah went on. Her tone faltered with arousal and she intermittently tightened her hold on Faith's hair. 'And if I feed from a Chinese person, you can guarantee that half-an-hour later I'm ready to feed from another. But there's one other thing that makes the craving unbearable in every vampire. Do you know what that is?'

Lilah moved her hand from the wooden box and caressed Faith's cheek. 'Would you like to me to whisper it to you?' she asked in a sultry tone, and Faith realised she had no chance to politely demur when the vampire's grip tightened at the back of her head. Lilah continued to smile with a pretence of affection and warmth as she dragged Faith away from her sex. 'Do you want to know?' Lilah purred, nibbling playfully at her earlobe, drawing her tongue against the microscopic hairs.

Shivering with a premonition of excitement Faith considered shaking her head, then realised there was no chance for such a movement. Lilah was maintaining a tight hold on the back of her head and she knew, if she managed to make the slightest movement, it would end the delicious kisses the woman was delivering to her ear.

'Do you want to know?' Lilah repeated. 'Do you want

to know what always guarantees an appetite in newly-made vampires?'

'Tell me.'

'Being drained.'

She locked her teeth against Faith's throat and bit hard. The hand that entwined in her hair gripped more tightly and Faith knew there was no chance to escape even if she had wanted.

'Being drained does it every time,' Lilah assured her, but Faith didn't hear. The pain was sudden and shocking and every bit as enthralling as she remembered from the night when Lilah first made her. The vampire's penetrating kiss was exciting and a more powerful union than any sex Faith had ever known or imagined. Intimacies with Claire might have inspired her passion, but the thrill of having Lilah drink from her neck went beyond the realm of that mortal pleasure. Faith arched her back and pressed her body eagerly against Lilah's lithe form. She relished the sensation of being drained and savoured the exquisite rush of having the blood sucked from her throat.

The usual symptoms of arousal – the tightening of her inner muscles, the stiffness around her nipples, and the delicious wetness that lubricated her sex – all seemed amplified and exaggerated. Instead of wallowing in the stimulation of her erogenous zones she could feel her entire body being overwhelmed by an encroaching orgasm.

'I've known many fledgling vampires who tried to resist their first feed,' Lilah gasped. She moved her lips from Faith's throat to speak and spent droplets of blood spilled from her mouth. Her tone was low and husky and it occurred to Faith that, for the first time this evening, she was hearing genuine arousal in the vampire's voice. 'Neophytes often try to suppress their hunger. They can sometimes battle the desires of their sexual appetites, but once they've been drained, almost to the point of death, it's only a matter of time before the new instinct takes over.' Without another word Lilah pressed her mouth back over the wound in Faith's throat.

Faith understood what had been said – and understood all the implications about what would now happen – but those matters were of peripheral importance. As Lilah continued to grace her with her kiss, greedily sucking the lifeblood from her body, Faith could only revel in the glorious joy of climax. She was aware of briefly losing consciousness and could never decide if that lapse came from too much pleasure or too little blood. But when she came back to herself, her face was pressed between Lilah's thighs. The woman's sex gaped enticingly, and although she felt weak and hungry, the urge to devour the vampire had never been stronger. She nuzzled the dewy lips, slipping her tongue against their succulence, before plundering the sweetly scented wetness within.

Lilah groaned and made a feeble attempt to pull away but it was a half-hearted effort. Faith guessed the vampire's resistance was little more than a token gesture and felt sure the woman would stay beneath her tongue until she was satisfied. Confident in her understanding of the situation, Faith teased the pulsing clitoris for an instant before nibbling lightly on the bead of flesh.

Lilah's groan grew louder. Faith glanced up from between her legs, smiling when she saw the consternation on the vampire's face. Lilah still held her damnable wooden box and had it clutched against her chest with one arm. Her other arm flailed helplessly and Faith couldn't work out if the vampire was trying to caress her, push her away, beat the side of the couch, or simply rake her nails against the furniture's plush fittings. Seeing the elated confusion in Lilah's eyes she guessed the vampire couldn't properly work out which choice she wanted to make either.

'Your friend is very lucky to have you,' Lilah growled.

Faith tried to bury herself in the chore of licking Lilah's sex, commonsense telling her that thinking about Claire at this time was a bad idea, but once her friend's image was in her mind she was unable to shake it away. It was all too easy to picture herself doing this for Claire, and then doing a lot more for her. The hunger within her stomach – inextricably linked with her voracious sexual appetite – made her eager for Claire and eager to feed.

'Just think how much fun you and she could have if you made her,' Lilah mused.

Faith frowned with the effort of trying not to think about that possibility. But the idea was infuriatingly tempting. She knew she had suggested something similar to Claire and remembered that her friend had refused, but Faith couldn't recall the reason why. Racking her brains to recall Claire's protestation against being made, Faith could only think that her friend might need a little more persuasion.

Lapping more greedily, trying to lose herself in the task of pleasuring Lilah rather than consider what she could do with Claire, Faith sucked and nibbled until the vampire screamed. She continued through the throes of Lilah's orgasm, relishing the leakage of arousal that daubed her cheeks and nose and chin. Even when it was clear that the coven's leader was spent, and that her appetite was fully sated, Faith continued to work her mouth against the woman's sex.

Lilah forced herself to sit upright and pulled Faith's face from between her legs. 'Are you ready to feed, Faith?' Lilah gasped through the final shivers of her orgasm. 'Are you ready to feed on that succulent, pious friend of yours?'

Faith didn't have to consider her answer. There was no

longer anything to consider. 'Yes,' she whispered. She used the back of her hand to wipe Lilah's musk from her mouth and realised she would make the same gesture after she'd fed from Claire's throat. The prospect made her inner muscles clench with fresh fury and another tingling rush of joy coursed its way through her body. The idea of denying her appetite was no longer an option; she was hungry, excited and more than ready to feed. 'Yes,' she confirmed. 'Take me to her.'

Hope

Act III, Scene I

The casino was busy enough to keep her distracted from thoughts of the impending ordeal. Enthusiastic players pushed at her table, and because she was caught up in the immediacy of their demands there wasn't the time for Hope to think about vampires, wish-stones or her sister's plight. She didn't want to dwell on what might come this evening and knew, if she did give herself time to brood, panic would triumph over her sense of duty.

'*A rien ne va plus,*' she called, enjoying the moment's reprieve from work as she set the ball spinning within the wheel. 'No more bets.'

Avril stepped to her side with a flourish of uncharacteristic ebullience. Normally, during the busier evenings, the serious-faced croupier would rush through her work without taking the time to smile or share a friendly comment. But this evening she seemed to have been affected by a miraculous transformation. She grinned incessantly, flirted playfully with the more forward customers, and the throaty sound of her laughter regularly chimed across the casino floor. 'It will be a profitable night for Monsieur Chalmers, no?' she offered.

'It's going to be a busy one,' Hope agreed. She kept her voice dutifully low, knowing the customers were concentrating on the roulette ball as it span around the wheel. 'Not that the extra workload seems to be troubling you,' she said with meaning.

Avril smiled shyly, her lashes fluttering as she lowered her gaze. 'You have seen the change that has come over me?'

'It would be hard to miss,' Hope grinned. 'What happened? Have you discovered drugs? Found Jesus? Got a pay rise? Or is there a new man in your life?'

Avril's cheeks flashed briefly rouge as she nodded.

Hope wanted to ask her about the love interest – who he was, where they met, and a hundred and one other details – but the roulette wheel chose that moment to clatter into its final few turns. Avril stepped from her side and began to clear chips from the table while Hope called the winning number to a mixture of elation and disappointment from the players. The casino was busy enough to absorb them for five minutes before they had another chance to speak, but Hope pounced on the opportunity. The past two days had been a disheartening blend of bad news and sexual passion and it was good to be involving herself in the minutiae of gossip and everyday life.

'So, who is he?' Hope asked. 'How long have you known him? What's he like? And when do I get to meet him?'

Grinning excitedly, Avril said, 'He is a very exciting man. Surprisingly exciting for an Englishman.'

'He's English?'

'Yes. I did not know him before last night but he has made on me a very big impression. I think you might also know him. He mentioned your name last night while we were…' she hesitated for a moment, looking as though she was searching for the correct English phrase, and eventually she completed the sentence by saying, '…while we were getting to know each other.'

A snake of unease shifted its coils inside Hope's stomach. 'Who is he?' she asked warily. 'What's his name?'

Avril seemed oblivious to Hope's concern. She continued to smile blithely and nodded towards the slowing roulette wheel. 'The table,' she murmured, preparing to return to her duties. 'The ball has—'

Hope grabbed the croupier's wrist. 'Who is he, Avril?' she insisted. 'What's his name?'

A flash of concern twisted Avril's pretty features, and then disappeared. She glanced behind Hope and her smile flourished again. 'There is no need for me to tell you about him,' she said cheerfully. 'He's here now and can tell you all about himself.'

Hope followed the croupier's gaze and her gravest fears were confirmed.

Nick strode confidently into the casino with Helen hanging from his arm. He waved in the direction of the roulette table and Hope didn't know if the gesture was meant for her benefit or as a greeting intended for Avril.

Turning her back on the vampire, ignoring the slowing roulette wheel, Hope glared at Avril and shook her head. 'He's a very dangerous man,' she whispered urgently. 'You shouldn't have anything to do with him. He's not a healthy person to be around.'

Surprising her, Avril laughed. 'He warned me about your games. He said you had previously frightened a girl away from him by pretending he was a vampire.' She brushed the hair away from her neck to reveal a fresh bruise that had been hidden by the tresses. Within its purple depths Hope could see two puncture wounds from Nick's bite, and the worries she'd been trying to forget came rushing back with sickening force. 'As you can see,' Avril said, wincing softly as she caressed the damaged flesh, 'his story inspired us to play a fun game. Did I not say that he is surprisingly exciting for an Englishman?'

'I'm deadly serious,' Hope told her, layering her voice

with insistence. 'Nick really is a vampire and his interest in you is nothing more than a device to get to me.'

Avril grimaced and Hope realised she was squeezing too hard on the croupier's wrist. She snatched her hand away, apologising and still trying to get her message across, but the demands of the roulette table had become more pressing. The losers sensed the absence of concentration at the wheel and dispersed themselves amongst the blackjack tables and the slots. The few customers who had won made belligerent grumblings about the amounts they were due to collect.

'Pay the winners then close the table,' Hope told Avril, and the croupier stared at her as if she'd been slapped.

'Close the table?' she echoed. 'I think Monsieur Chalmers would not approve.'

Hope pressed her lips to Avril's ear. 'Pay the winners. Close the table. Then get as far from here as possible.' She nodded in Nick's direction. 'Your new boyfriend is a *very* dangerous man.'

She didn't get the chance to register the uncertainty on Avril's features, or work out if her instructions would be heeded, for Nick settled himself on one of the stools near the wheel, Helen took the seat next to his, and they both smiled expectantly. Hope waited for the last of the winners to be paid before finding the courage to face him, ignoring Helen, knowing it was Nick she would have to deal with on this occasion. 'What do you want?' she asked.

Nick held a chip between his finger and thumb and tried to spin it against the baize. Intent on the chore, sticking his tongue out of the corner of his mouth while he concentrated, he said, 'Your presence is required on the *Île de le Cité*.'

'I've got plans to go there later.'

Nick made a second attempt to spin the chip. It fell

over as soon as he let go and he grumbled. 'Lilah has asked me to escort you to the *Île de le Cité*,' he said, without looking up. 'She wants me to take you there now.'

'Todd Chalmers is taking me there later.' Hope spoke with quiet authority. 'I'll be going as soon as I've finished my shift.'

'Chalmers is already…' Helen began, but Nick silenced her with a sideways glance. He shrugged for Hope's benefit, finally sent the chip spinning, and smiled easily.

'All right,' he said, 'I can see I'm not going to win this argument. I'll catch up with you later. I might even follow you down when you finally decide to go.'

His indifference was unsettling and Hope wondered if she had misjudged the threat the vampire represented. 'Aren't you going to try to force me?' she asked uneasily.

'I doubt it would do much good.' He fixed her with an expression that bordered on innocence. 'Besides, if you have no plans to accompany me just yet I can spend a little time with my new girlfriend.' He glanced in Avril's direction and his razor-sharp smile glinted wickedly beneath the casino chandeliers. 'She's quite a tasty little piece,' he said, licking his lips.

Helen giggled, and Hope glared at Nick but he ignored her disapproval.

'Avril enjoyed our little role-playing game last night,' he boasted. 'Did she mention what we did? She was the helpless victim and I was the naughty vampire. I think we might play that game again tonight. But this time I'm going to make it a little more convincing. I might make her a little more helpless. I might play my part with a little more naughtiness.'

Hope knew she couldn't leave Avril to suffer the fate Nick had planned. 'Wait here,' she snapped, despising the way he could manipulate her – despising the way everyone seemed able to manipulate her these days. Flouncing away from the table, heading towards the staff cloakroom, she called back over her shoulder, 'I'll fetch my coat.'

He stepped beside her, matching her brisk pace across the casino floor and maintaining an air of jaunty good humour. 'You don't need to grab your coat,' he said cheerfully. 'I could happily kill a couple of hours with Avril until you're ready. I could take her out for a bite, or we could just find a quiet corner of the bar and share a drink.'

They left the floor and pushed through the doorway that led to the staff locker room. Hope was reaching for her coat when he spoke, the words making her bristle with fury and she rounded on him with a warning finger. 'You'll leave Avril alone,' she growled. 'You'll leave Avril alone or I'll—'

He was fast. She had been pointing the finger between his eyes, making the gesture as ferocious as she could, but Nick was less than intimidated and had supernatural speed on his side. He snatched hold of her wrist, tugged to unsettle her balance and pulled her into a loose embrace. The scent of his cologne disguised the fragrance of something dark and animal and Hope couldn't decide if she was inhaling the manly odour of his sweat or the coppery flavour of a recent feed, but the distinction seemed immaterial as she gazed into his crimson eyes and was warmed by the flicker of desire that lurked there.

She didn't want to be held by the loathsome vampire, she only wanted to keep him away from Avril, but his lustful interest made her yearn for something else and she was disgusted with herself when she realised what that was. Inside the basque her nipples began to ache as they strained against the cumbersome fabric, and deep within her sex the tingling of arousal began.

Nick raised an eyebrow and she wondered if, on some intuitive level, he had become aware of the quickening pulse between her legs. Not daring to lower her gaze, fearful of the consequences if she showed she was intimidated or excited, Hope met the challenge of his mesmerising stare.

'You're quite the bossy little thing, aren't you?' he teased. 'Are you always this demanding, or am I just lucky enough to be getting special treatment from you?'

She forced herself not to be lulled by the musical chant of his voice. 'Whatever relationship Avril thinks she has with you, I want you to end it. I want you to end it *now*.'

He leant closer. His teeth were viciously sharp and his lips looked so ruddy they were almost effeminate. Yet Hope was desperate to experience his kiss. The possibility of feeling his lips against her skin was invigorating and the prospect of having his teeth pinch her flesh was enough to make her tremble. She tried not to let those thoughts sway her judgement but the desire was a difficult force to fight.

'Avril and I were going to play some very exciting games this evening,' Nick confided. 'What can you offer to make up for what I'll be missing?'

Hope missed the intonation in his voice and struggled to think how she could bargain with him. Arousal and frustration were clouding her thoughts but the chance of securing Avril's safety remained at the forefront of her mind. 'I'll go with you to the *Île de le Cité*,' she offered. 'I'll go with you now, like you asked.'

Nick shook his head and lowered his mouth, his lips dangerously close to her face. 'You were already going to go there,' he reminded her. His gaze briefly dropped and she saw he was appraising the swell of her breasts.

Still held in his embrace it was impossible to see if the shape of her nipples could be discerned but she felt sure he had to have noticed something to make his smile inch wider. 'If you want me to pass up my fun with Avril, you'll have to give me something better than that.'

This time she didn't miss the intimation. As she had often thought before, there was always a price to be paid, and this time she could see Nick was determined to extract the highest rate possible. She swallowed before speaking, aware that they were alone, in the discretion of the locker room. A CCTV camera lurked in one corner but Hope recalled that Jean Duval had told her the locker room was never monitored. Steeling herself before speaking, aware of the sacrifice she intended making, she whispered, 'What do you want from me?'

The arm around her waist tightened fractionally and Nick pulled her closer. The swell of his concealed erection pressed against her thigh as he deliberated his response. 'I wouldn't want to take you,' he mumbled, licking his lips as though tasting the idea. 'Lilah would be furious if I denied her that pleasure. And I wouldn't want to make you. That would complicate our situation far too much.' Smiling playfully, he disclosed, 'I think I just want to play with you for a little while.'

Hope moaned. She hadn't wanted to make the sound but it was torn from her as his mouth moved closer. The promise of his kiss and the constant caress of his hands were an unbearable combination. He had shifted position and the swell of his erection nestled over the crotch of her basque. The pressure against her sex inflamed her, filling her with a furious, insatiable need. Rocking her hips gently she revelled in the friction of his arousal rubbing against her.

'I guess that might satisfy me.' Nick made the

183

concession as though bestowing upon her a great favour. 'But you'd better be good,' he quickly warned.

She shivered when his hand brushed between her thighs, not knowing if he was popping the fasteners of the basque or releasing his own straining length, and it was only afterwards that she realised he was deftly doing both. An icy finger brushed the gusset of her panties, and her excitement grew when he pulled the underwear aside and his chilled hardness pressed against her pussy lips.

'You'd better be damned good,' he growled, pushing forward.

She held her breath, bracing herself for the brutal penetration, certain that this pleasure was going to be despicably marvellous. Unable to bare the teasing, anxious to have him satisfy the animal need he'd awoken, Hope pushed onto him as he stabbed with his hips and his frigid length impaled her. Nick sounded gruffly content and pleased with himself; Hope didn't know if she gave a moan of protest or a sigh of contentment.

He eased his pelvis back, drawing his erection from within her and leaving her pussy achingly empty. She tried to reach for him, intending to urge him back inside so she could writhe against his thickness, but he slapped her hand away. His casual gesture left her in no doubt who was in control and she almost submitted to his dominance. It was only with an effort of concentration that she was able to grab hold of his jacket's lapel and shake until she had his attention.

'You are going to leave Avril alone, aren't you?' she pressed, thrusting a hand between their bodies, not pushing him away but preventing him from fully entering her again. 'I have your word on that, don't I?'

A flicker of impatience creased his brow. 'You have my word,' he grumbled, and from behind her Hope heard the derisive sound of a woman's laughter.

Shocked, she twisted to see who was watching them, the tip of Nick's erection remaining wedged just inside her sex and its cold, lethargic pulse beating dully through her pussy. The stiffness of her nipples was a perpetual agony of bliss and every nerve-end screamed for the pleasure to continue. But she ignored all those responses when she saw Helen leering over her shoulder.

'Nick's good at making promises when he's in that position,' Helen confided, and Hope's stomach muscles clenched with shame. It was galling to know their intimacy was being watched but it was even more sickening to realise that she could continue without caring. Nick's erection was between her legs, he seemed capable of satisfying the need that simmered inside her, and nothing mattered more than sating that appetite. Even when Helen reached for the neckline of her basque, stroking seductive fingertips against the swell of her cleavage, Hope made no complaint.

Nick placed a hand on her jaw and turned her face so she was forced to look at him. Gently nudging his cock forward, pushing slightly deeper, he said, 'You can consider my relationship with Avril ended.'

Sighing with relief, Hope moved her hand and allowed him to sink deeper. The vicious chill of his erection and the caress of Helen's hand were proving to be an intoxicating blend. She could have given herself over to the thrill of a climax in that moment but Nick seemed to think she wanted more from him. 'I'll get Helen to break the bad news,' he said loftily. 'That way you and I can get out of here as soon as you've squeezed the last drop of come from my balls.'

Hope glared at him, despising his coarseness but still wanting him to continue. She nodded grudging consent to his suggestion, willing to accept any solution that kept Avril from his clutches. As he ploughed slowly in and out of her she closed her eyes and heard him whisper something unintelligible to Helen. The words were indecipherable and Hope only understood they were an instruction when the female vampire drew her hand away and walked idly out of the locker room.

'Does that satisfy you?' Nick asked.

Rather than voicing her reply, Hope grabbed his hip and pulled him deeper. Her sex was full to bursting and the prospect of an orgasm had never seemed closer. His mouth fell over hers and she was treated to the invasion of his tongue. Giving herself over to the thrill of the moment, no longer caring about the impropriety of letting him have her, she clenched her inner muscles in an attempt to wring more pleasure for herself. He gasped, grinned, and then readjusted his hold on her back.

Hope wrapped a leg around his side and felt a surge of different sensations flood her pussy. She almost lost balance, was briefly grateful for his intimidating strength as he continued to support them both, and then he was taking her with increased ferocity.

His shaft pushed furiously in and out, battering the lips of her sex and exciting a wet, liquid squelch. Their embrace grew tighter, his grunts of excitement became more obscene, and she groaned as the climax crept inexorably nearer.

'What a delightful little ride you are,' he growled.

Nearing the precipice of her orgasm, Hope said nothing as she waited for the pleasure to cleanse her thoughts of guilt and shame. Unconsciously she threw her head back, exposing her throat for him and leaving herself open and vulnerable. Attuned to every nuance within her body she could feel the pulse at her throat beating hard. It briefly crossed her mind that the sight might prove too much of a temptation for Nick's macabre appetite, but that didn't stop her from flaunting herself as she surfed the burgeoning waves of pleasure.

'You bitch!' he exploded, pushing himself deeper. She had felt full while he was riding her, but as he nestled deeper for the final thrust she was sure her sex had taken more than it could accommodate. His ejaculation was a douche of scalding wetness that pushed her beyond the limits of her own endurance. She rocked her pelvis, rubbing her clitoris deliberately along his shaft, and was rewarded with her own glorious climax.

The release was physically satisfying and spiritually draining. The orgasm she had craved convulsed its way through her body leaving her weak, sated and filled with self-disgust.

Nick pulled his cock from her sex and his grin curled like a sneer. 'Lilah is going to be so pleased with me,' he chuckled.

Hope regarded him warily and waited for him to elaborate.

'Your sister was feared because of her virtue,' Nick explained. 'The entire coven – even Lilah's brother, the dark one – they were all scared of Faith because she was so good and chaste and pure.' His noisome chuckle deepened as he fixed her with his disapproving expression. 'I guess virtue and purity aren't something we need worry about with you.'

As she quickly straightened her panties and refastened the poppers on her basque, Hope couldn't bring herself to look at him.

Nick held his spent length in one hand and looked ready to push it back inside his trousers. He appraised her with a lewd smile and asked, 'Do you want to play some more before we leave?'

Horrified by what she had just done, and appalled that she had found enjoyment in the act, Hope shook her head. The suggestion was grossly tempting and she didn't doubt Nick would make any intimacy intensely pleasurable, but she couldn't bring herself to submit to him again. 'Let's just go to the *Île de le Cité*,' she said.

He shrugged good-naturedly, straightened his clothes, and then extended an arm to escort her out of the casino. Ignoring the gallant gesture, Hope snatched her coat then stormed out through the foyer towards the main door. When she glanced back, to catch a brief glimpse of the casino floor, she was struck by the idea that she might never see the inside of the building ever again. The thought saddened her and exacerbated her worries, but she knew it wouldn't make her change her mind about what needed to be done. Hesitating, searching for any reason to delay the moment of leaving the casino, she paused and said stiffly, 'Someone should inform Chalmers that you've taken me early for tonight's gathering.'

'There's no need for that,' Nick scoffed. 'Chalmers will already be there.'

She studied him guardedly, convinced he was telling the truth and wondering why the revelation inspired fresh doubts about Chalmers and the trust she had invested in him. She supposed it was the idea of him being comfortably alone in the presence of the vampires, and the knowledge that he was afforded some degree of immunity from the coven's appetites. But she also wondered why he had lied to her. Their plans had involved travelling down to the crypt together, and discovering he was already there made it easy for her to imagine he was setting her up as a sacrifice for Lilah. She tried to stop herself from harbouring such worries, knowing they would wear at her courage for the night, but it was a difficult battle to fight. Trying to put her fears behind her, she took a final glance around the foyer and asked, 'Where's Helen? I thought she'd be coming with us?'

'Helen's doing what you wanted her to do,' Nick said gruffly. 'She's putting an end to my relationship with Avril.' He had the good grace to blush after glancing in the direction of one corner.

Hope followed the line of his gaze and was horrified to see Helen and Avril in a passionate embrace. She immediately remembered the redhead who'd been with Nick and Helen and realised Avril was in a potentially lethal situation. She started towards the pair but Nick placed a hand on her arm and his grip was firm enough to stop her from intervening. 'There isn't time for you to stop her,' he stated.

Hope tried to shake his hand away but he was clearly practiced in the art of restraining young women. Seeming to know she had an audience and basking in the attention, Helen pressed her teeth against the croupier's bared shoulder. She flickered her gaze in Hope's direction, and when they made eye-contact Hope realised the vampire was mocking her before biting.

Hope closed her eyes and shivered. She could see her sacrifice had been for nothing, and although Nick had managed to satiate the need that had smouldered within her, the transaction of sex for a favour hadn't saved Avril from the vampires. Maybe worse, there was also the risk that she might have jeopardised Todd Chalmers' carefully laid plans. Disgust and self-loathing enveloped her like a cloak.

Nick placed his arm around her shoulders and patted her reassuringly. 'Don't go worrying about your friend,' he said kindly. 'Helen will take real good care of her.'

Hope wasn't listening. She was sure that Avril's bleak fate was an indication of what she could look forward to this evening and felt certain she was doing nothing more than giving herself to vampires. Trying not to let herself be pulled down by that thought, convinced there was still a chance to save her sister, she realised the night's success all depended on the integrity of Todd Chalmers.

It was the first comforting thought she'd had since seeing Nick because, deep in her heart, she felt sure Chalmers wouldn't disappoint her or her sister. Wanting to believe that, she silently repeated the words as Nick escorted her from the casino. *'Chalmers wont let me down… Chalmers won't sell me out to Lilah… Chalmers won't let me down…'*

Hope

Act III, Scene II

'Get on your knees, bitch,' Chalmers roared. 'Get on your knees and pay proper homage to Lilah.'

Hope stared at him with the same stunned dismay she would have shown if he'd slapped her face. Nick had brought her to the crypt on the *Île de le Cité*, beneath *Notre Dame*; Marcia had torn the coat from her body as soon as she entered the underground lair; the two subordinate vampires had gleefully stripped away Hope's basque and underwear; and now she found herself naked and sprawled at the feet of the coven's leader.

Chalmers pointed at Hope as he bawled his instruction, his voice echoing from the hidden walls, but it was Lilah who held Hope's attention. The vampire looked both feminine and imposing – dangerous and desirable – even though she still held the cumbersome wooden box under one arm. Her features were an inscrutable mask except for her eyes, which sparkled with an emotion Hope didn't want to understand.

Slowly a smile crept across the vampire's lips. Hope wanted to look away but there was something hypnotic about the way the woman held her gaze. She didn't know if it was the eerily exciting charm of her body – Lilah's muscular physique was shown to perfection by her black satin gown – or something about the sultry air of sex appeal that exuded from her like a perfume. Whatever reason, she was caught in the snare of the woman's seductive powers and didn't doubt she would submit to Lilah's every whim if ordered to. The thought left her twisting between feelings of apprehension and anticipation.

'Get on your knees and pay homage to Lilah,' Chalmers growled.

Hope fixed her glare on him, unsure if this was part of his charade or if he was serious in his instruction. Knowing there was no excuse for defying him – knowing she had to do whatever he said regardless of whether he was helping her or preparing her as a human sacrifice – Hope pulled herself to her knees and glowered at Lilah.

The stench of must and decay lingered within the crypt's dank air. The soil beneath her knees was as clammy as a sweaty hand. The flickering sconces on the wall made the shadows shift as though a hundred more vampires lurked impatiently in the corners. Yet Hope noticed none of these distractions as she stared reverentially up at Lilah.

'What do you expect me to do with her, Toad?' the vampire asked coolly.

Chalmers' grin slipped a notch. 'I'm keeping my half of the bargain here, Lilah,' he said stiffly. 'And now you're holding all the cards.' Pointing at one of the shadowy doorways that led further underground he said, 'In that crypt you've got the mulatto checking the transfer of accounts was conducted correctly.' Shifting his hand to the right, pointing to a second doorway, he said, 'Faith and her chubby friend are ensconced in there. And, in here,' his accusatory finger dropped in Hope's direction, 'you've got the other virtuous sister you wanted.'

Nick laughed derisively when Chalmers described her as virtuous and Hope glared at him.

'I wanted the Bethesda Stone as well,' Lilah said. She kept the wooden box clutched under her arm as she extended a hand. 'I'll take that now, please.'

Chalmers' air of confidence faltered a little more and Hope watched him cast a sly glance at his wristwatch. She guessed the time was around the eleven o'clock mark, and figured he wanted to refrain from bringing out the wish-stone until it was closer to midnight and the spell could take effect, but she couldn't imagine how he would delay a creature as single-minded as Lilah.

'I'll see you get the stone in plenty of time.' Chalmers' easy tone should have been a balm to the vampire's obvious ire, but Lilah remained with her hand outstretched as though she was waiting for him to pull the stone from his pocket and give it to her. 'Before you take control of all that's rightfully yours,' he continued, 'don't you want to amuse yourself a little with your latest acquisition?' He used his open palm to gesture in Hope's direction and the vampire finally deigned to glance at her.

With a twist of unease, Hope suddenly fretted that Lilah knew of Chalmers' plans. There was something about the way she held herself, something more than simple confidence or arrogance, that made her look like she was only acting the role of an unsuspecting hostess. Watching the sly glances she cast in his direction, noticing the knowing exchanges between the leader and her subordinates, Hope grew more convinced that Lilah was merely pretending to go along with Chalmers' plan.

'Amuse myself with her?' Lilah asked innocently. 'And how do you propose I do that? I've already fed twice this evening.'

Chalmers disappeared to the corner of the room and returned holding a cane. Offering it to Lilah as though presenting her with a holy artefact, he said, 'I believe you enjoyed disciplining Hope's sister before you left Rome. Why don't you see if you get the same pleasure from striping this one as well?'

193

Hope switched her gaze to him, incredulous at the suggestion. Watching Lilah, Chalmers didn't notice Hope's shock.

'You're good, Toad,' Lilah purred, stroking the length of cane before plucking it from his hands. 'You're very good.' There was genuine approval in the vampire's voice as she stepped from his side and started to circle Hope.

A blade of arousal twisted inside Hope's stomach as she struggled not to show her nervousness. She knew her body should have been acclimatised to the sensations of being naked and vulnerable – it had happened so often over the last couple of nights she should have considered the condition passé – but still she squirmed with embarrassment and yearned to be somewhere else.

Lilah paced around her, slicing the cane haphazardly through the air as she familiarised herself with its weight. 'Is this what you've been preparing her for?' the vampire asked. 'Have you been training her so she'll take a proper session of discipline?'

Chalmers shrugged. 'Tonight marks the end of the coven's requirements for my services,' he responded. 'I thought you might appreciate this gift in the spirit of a farewell gesture.'

'Shouldn't it be the other way around?' Lilah asked, turning on him with an inquisitorial stare. She was standing behind Hope and the cane scratched like a skeleton's finger against her buttocks. Hope stopped herself from shivering and listened for Chalmers' reply.

'Since the coven no longer has any requirement for your services, shouldn't we be giving you a present?' Lilah asked. 'Golden handshakes and farewell carriage-clocks: isn't that the way these things are normally done?'

Chalmers' politic laugh echoed from the walls. 'You're letting me leave with my life,' he explained diplomatically.

'I think that's a greater severance gift than any other aide has ever received from a coven.'

Lilah fixed him with a puzzled frown. 'We're letting you leave with your life?' she asked doubtfully. 'When did I agree to that?'

The three vampires enjoyed a cocktail-party chuckle, and while Chalmers joined their merriment Hope could see the amusement didn't reach as far as his eyes.

Dismissing the distraction, stepping into Hope's line of vision, Lilah glowered down and pointed at her with the cane. 'Do you want me to strike you with this?' she asked sternly. 'Would you like that? Would you get pleasure from it?'

Hope stared past the vampire and saw Chalmers was fixing her with a silent plea. She could see the response he expected and knew, now they were this close to actualising his plans, there was no other option. Suppressing the refusal that wanted to spill from her lips, wilfully not thinking about what she was agreeing to, Hope held Lilah's gaze. 'I'd like that very much,' she said.

Lilah stepped past her and Hope watched Chalmers close his eyes with relief. The vampire disappeared again and for an instant she was sure a vicious blow would sting her buttocks. Bracing herself, holding her muscles as taut as steel, Hope listened to the dull pounding of blood through her temples. Instead of the hurt she expected, she was surprised to feel Lilah's cool hand smoothing against her bottom. The caress was hateful and more punishing than any blow from the cane might have been. The vampire stroked the rounded cheek of one buttock and her fingertips brushed near the moist crease of Hope's sex. Drawing her hand away, too quickly putting an end to the unwanted stimulation, Lilah lightly patted Hope's bare behind.

'Are you going to be a good girl and endure everything I want of you?' Lilah asked.

Hope gritted her teeth, wishing she didn't have to reply but knowing some response was needed. Chalmers glared at her, his impatience looking set to boil over into anger, but he wasn't the focus of her attention. 'I'm here for your pleasure, mistress Lilah,' she said, concentrating only on the sound of Lilah's voice, knowing she had to defer to the vampire.

The first blow came without warning. Hope didn't hear the cane shriek through the air or even catch the grunt of effort as Lilah hurled the weapon down. The first thing she noticed was the howling stripe of pain that blazed across her backside. A line of fire nestled deep within her cheeks, its smouldering edges seeping warmth to the tops of her thighs then ebbing on to her sex.

'I did this for your sister.' Lilah gasped the words as she sliced another blow against Hope's bottom. 'I'm going to enjoy doing it for you,' she grunted, striking again. 'And I might even do it for your other sister, Charity.'

Unable to think of a response, not trusting herself to open her mouth for fear she would scream for the torment to end, Hope said nothing. The cane wasn't as vicious as the knout had been but she thought it came a close second. Lilah administered each shot as if she was threshing a harvest and Hope tried to accept the punishment with the little dignity she could muster.

Nick stood before her, his lascivious grin reminding her of the depths she had already sunk to this evening. Marcia was by his side, holding him in an intimate embrace with one hand behind his back while the other rubbed the front of his trousers. The blonde had one leg wrapped around his hip and she rocked her pelvis urgently against him. Her lower lip was thrust out in a sultry pout.

Behind the couple Chalmers repeatedly glanced at his wristwatch. Hope tried to get his attention, hoping he would see that she needed this torment to end and trying to believe that he might have some way of intervening, but in her heart she knew he would be unable to help. As that depressing thought filled her with futility, Lilah striped another cutting blow against her rear. This one bit more viciously than its predecessors, scorching the sensitive flesh at the tops of her legs. Hope cringed from the anguish, and then surrendered to the aftermath of warming arousal the pain generated. She arched her back as waves of delight spread through her body and then mumbled a guttural thank you to the cruel vampire.

'You've trained her remarkably well,' Lilah told Chalmers.

Standing in shadows, Chalmers sounded more relaxed than Hope expected. 'What sort of going away present would she be if I hadn't trained her well?' he said.

'Can she take more than just a cane?'

Hope fixed him with a warning expression, but Chalmers didn't bother to glance in her direction. 'What would you like her to take?' he asked, smiling easily for Lilah, with all the oily charm that could make him so despicable. 'I've got a paddle, there might be a slipper in my bag, I may even have something quite special and rare.'

Hope's eyes widened and she had to stop herself from screaming a refusal as he hinted about the last item. Subconsciously she shook her head.

'You've certainly come prepared,' Lilah observed. Her peculiar tone puzzled Hope, and while she thought the vampire might simply be deliberating her choice, she was struck again by the idea that Lilah knew what Chalmers was planning. She didn't know where the notion came from, or why it was so compelling, but she felt certain the coven's leader was wise to Todd's delaying tactics.

'Which do you want to use on her?' Chalmers asked.

'Which do you think will excite her the most?' Lilah returned.

'Is that what you want to do? You want to excite her?'

'Naturally. If I'm going to feed from the little bitch I want to taste the adrenaline and the endorphins.' Seeming to come to a quick decision, she tossed the cane to him and snapped her fingers. 'Give me the paddle,' she commanded. 'Let's see if that can get her good and wet before I drain her throat.'

With her hearing attuned to every nuance in the room, able to detect the whisper-soft rustle of satin gliding over the sheer denier of silk stockings, Hope listened as the vampire lowered herself to her knees. Without needing to look back she knew Lilah was squatting beside her exposed rear. The idea was simultaneously exciting and frightening, and Hope held herself rigid for fear of suffering the vampire's touch. When an icy finger brushed one punished cheek, the cruel caress rekindling the torment of one particularly punishing stripe, it took every effort of willpower for Hope to contain her cry. Her heartbeat hammered at an accelerated pace and she could taste the bilious flavour of excitement at the back of her throat.

'That is…' Lilah had dropped her tone to a husky drawl, '…that is, if she isn't already good and wet.'

Hope knew what was coming yet still it seemed her body was unprepared for the vampire's assault. The chilly finger slipped to her sex and an icy tip brushed the centre of her heat. Her pubic curls were teased aside as Lilah stroked the dewiness of her labia. A shiver of raw pleasure bristled through her pussy. The vampire's cold touch was a lit taper to her growing desire and, Hope thought, it would only take a little more stimulation before she was revelling in the throes of an orgasm. Softly, she sighed.

'Are you wet?' Lilah enquired, and as she spoke she slid her finger between Hope's pussy lips.

Hope tried not to be won over by the unwanted intrusion but her body's responses were treacherous. The inner muscles of her sex convulsed elatedly, and when Lilah slipped her finger deeper Hope groaned with the glory of impending release. The vampire chuckled and placed a second finger alongside her first.

Hope opened her eyes wide with surprise. She noted Nick's lurid grin, Marcia's condescending leer, and Chalmers' frown of concern. But she remained unmoved by everything except the euphoria being wrought inside her sex. Lilah rubbed her fingers back and forth, eliciting a wet squelch that was both embarrassing and stimulating. A third finger joined the first two and Hope's tight inner muscles were stretched wider. Her pussy lips were pressed aside as Lilah eased her wrist back and forth and coaxed fresh shards of pleasure from Hope's sex. She continued until the nearness of an orgasm was so close Hope could almost savour its electric flavour.

'I think we can get her a little wetter,' Lilah decided, snatching her hand away.

In any other circumstance Hope would have screamed in protest and demanded that the vampire finish what she had begun, but prudence told her this was neither the time nor the place for such a show of petulance. So accepting her frustration without complaint, keeping her curses to herself as she watched the vampire go to Chalmers, she tried to remember that she wasn't there for her own pleasure.

She was there to save her sister.

'Have you got that stone ready for me yet?' Lilah asked Chalmers, and he handed her a paddle.

Hope stared at the implement, her horror returning as she regarded its studded leather faces. She knew the knout was unbearable, and had already decided the cane was nearly more than she could be bear, but the paddle looked just as gruelling as either of those vicious torments.

'I'll see you get the stone in plenty of time,' Chalmers assured her. 'For now, like I said before, you should enjoy yourself with this latest acquisition.'

Even though she believed his ruse would ultimately benefit Faith, Hope couldn't stop glaring at him as he invited the vampire to inflict more punishment upon her. She watched Lilah take the paddle, saw her take a step away, and then pause as though a thought had just occurred to her.

'How long do you think this virtuous girl can delay me?' Lilah asked innocently.

Hope wondered if Chalmers would now see that the vampire was aware of his plans. She tried to read his face, searching for some glint in his expression that showed he understood that Lilah wasn't fooled by his charade, and that she was only playing along. 'How long?' Lilah repeated.

'Hope's here for as long as you want her,' Chalmers said evenly. 'But I wouldn't have said she was delaying you.'

Pursing her lips, clearly keeping her own thoughts to herself, the vampire took the paddle and walked out of Hope's line of vision.

Having already suffered the woman's chastisement once, Hope half-expected her to begin the punishment with another hatefully exciting caress. She was trying to think of a way to make herself immune to the arousal, steeling herself against the potential thrill that would come when Lilah's freezing fingers stroked her buttocks. Yet instead of playfully teasing her, the vampire simply slapped the paddle against her backside.

It didn't land with the same invasive bite of the cane, but Hope thought it was more insidious because of that. The flat slap of discomfort slowly evaporated to a redness and warmth and each subsequent blow only exacerbated that friction. She clenched her teeth, trying not to be won over by the growing tug of arousal, but she knew she was fighting a losing battle.

The leather hurt more fiercely than the slap of an open palm. The rounded surface of the studs added a vicious pinch that made her want to weep with unsatisfied frustration. Rather than elegantly slicing air, the paddle only landed. But each blow fell with a resounding crack that shook through Hope's frame. Growing attuned to the vampire's rhythm, she started to brace herself in preparation, but still the slaps managed to catch her unawares. She quietly cursed the discipline and struggled not to glance back over her shoulder and glower at her tormentor.

Lilah paused from the paddling, appearing in front of Hope with a glistening smile on her lips. She squatted on her haunches, allowing the split in her skirt to fall open and giving Hope full view of the unclothed secrets hidden within her gown. Shadows lingered at the tops of her thighs but Hope could see enough of the vampire to notice that she wasn't wearing panties. A sheen of wetness glistened on her flushed pink pussy lips and Hope realised the lustre of arousal had come from Lilah's enjoyment of her predicament.

'Are you enjoying this, Hope?'

Not trusting herself to speak, not sure if she would beg the vampire to stop, or demand that she satisfy the urge she'd awoken, Hope fought to meet Lilah's gaze and nodded.

'You're not thanking me any more,' Lilah complained. 'I expect you to thank me after each blow, if you want me to punish you properly.'

Hope nodded again and drew a deep breath as she struggled to find the words. The warmth across her rear was unbearable and the arousal that pulsed inside her vagina inspired a demand that had to be satisfied. She held the vampire's gaze, not caring if her expression gave away the inner turmoil of her excitement, and whispered, 'Thank you, Mistress Lilah. Thank you for paddling me.'

Rather than moving with her usual swiftness, the vampire stood slowly in front of her. The split of the gown remained open, continuing to reveal the delicious glimpse of her sex, and Hope was enchanted by the scent of musk that exuded from the wet lips. She didn't want to acknowledge the vampire's arousal, or compare it to her own swelling need, but she believed that she and Lilah were attuned on some level, even if it was only through their mutual excitement.

When the vampire stepped away Hope almost sobbed with frustration. However, there was little time to bemoan her predicament. Lilah started to sweep the paddle down again and Hope was treated to the punishing sting of the studs as they bit into her cheeks.

'Thank you, Mistress Lilah,' she mumbled, hating her own servility and meaning every word of gratitude. 'Thank you.' She caught herself praying for the punishment to end, or at least for it to become so severe that it pushed her beyond the brink of an orgasm, but neither of those scenarios seemed likely. Lilah continued to slam down the studded leather until Hope was wriggling impatiently beneath each blow.

'Thank me again,' Lilah said, appearing in front of her.

Hope's gaze flitted briefly over the vampire's confident smile, and then fell between her legs. The vision of the vampire's sex was painfully exciting and she couldn't seem to get enough of the torrid sight. Swathed in shadows, and clearly beyond her reach, secretly glimpsing Lilah's sex made her arousal burn more brightly than ever.

'Thank me again,' the vampire repeated. 'And if you make it convincing enough I might just give you the special reward you so obviously want.'

Hope regarded her curiously, certain the vampire was referring to something depraved and satisfying. She wanted to ask what Lilah might be implying and would have voiced the question, if Chalmers hadn't intervened.

He stepped to Lilah's side, making her the offer of a length of leather. Hope tried not to show her fears when she recognised the familiar knotted ends of the knout. 'Why don't you try using this on her?' he suggested.

Lilah turned on him scornfully, pushed the paddle against his chest and walked away.

Chalmers fell to his knees and pressed his mouth close to Hope's ear. 'You're doing well,' he whispered. 'Lilah's distracted, her mind's away from the stone – and the time – and there's every chance we could get out of this with Faith returned to normal and our heartbeats still working. I might even get to keep the dark one's funds in my own name. That would be a bonus, wouldn't it?'

She glanced at him, amazed that he could think about money when their lives were in jeopardy, and surprised that his words really did give her a promise of hope. The pain and humiliation were easy to forget as she realised she was on the verge of achieving her sister's salvation. She was about to thank him, and let him know that she now understood what they were working towards, when a figure loomed out from one of the crypt's shadowy doorways.

Holding a burning torch in one hand, the flickering flames casting sombre shadows across her dark features, the mulatto entered the room and coughed to gain Lilah's attention.

'What is it?' the coven leader demanded.

'There's an error in the accounts,' the mulatto replied.

Marcia gasped, Nick mumbled 'shit', and the silence in the crypt was deafening as four pairs of crimson eyes turned to glare at Chalmers.

'An error in the accounts?' Lilah repeated.

The mulatto nodded. 'I think Chalmers has been trying to deceive you,' she said, speaking boldly, using her flaming torch to point at him.

Interlude

Part Five

Faith inhaled deeply and caught the mingled scents of fear and excitement. Light in this annex of the crypt was poor, even with a flame burning lethargically from one sconce, but if nothing else her time as a vampire had taught her to see quite effectively in the dark. It was a powerful ability, surprisingly useful, and this time it helped her pick out the shape of Claire, chained in an unlit corner. Some of the clothes had been torn from her body – she looked pitiful, ravaged, alone and defenceless – but rather than evoking sympathy, the sight only made Faith lick her lips.

Claire glanced up from a sullen reverie and Faith was gratified to see terror widen her eyes. If not for the ropes at her wrists and ankles she knew Claire would have been backing fearfully into the corner. Even with those restraints she still made a plucky attempt to sink deeper into the shadows as she shook her head in refusal. 'It can't be far from midnight,' Claire hissed. 'You've resisted the temptation this long, Faith. Don't give in now. Don't let that bitch Lilah win. Hold out for a little while longer.'

Faith stepped quickly to Claire's side. She traced her fingers against one exposed arm, savouring the sensation of blood pulsing beneath the flesh, and the heightened perfume of Claire's disquiet. It was gratifying to caress her helpless friend, stroking the shape of one rounded breast and then teasing her leg between Claire's spread thighs. The effects of power and control were potent aphrodisiacs and almost as formidable as her ravenous hunger. 'Do you *want* me to hold out a little longer?' she asked sweetly, relishing the moment, chasing her fingertips up to the ropes that bound Claire's wrists.

Claire bit back a sob, the sound so resigned to suffering it made Faith's pussy tingle. 'Wait until after midnight,' Claire moaned softly. 'At least leave it until then.'

Faith brushed the hair away from Claire's shoulder and was faced by the sight of the silver crucifix. She didn't want to look at the hateful jewellery, unable to say why it upset her but knowing it made her feel ill, yet she knew she would have to do more than just look. Gingerly she pushed her finger against the small cross and guided it to the other side of Claire's neck. It was an exercise in personal torment; the cross scalded her skin and produced a trickle of acrid white smoke that reeked of burning flesh. But Faith wouldn't let herself be deterred. Blinking back tears that were caused by the pain, she slipped the jewellery out of sight.

'Please, wait until after midnight,' Claire begged.

Faith didn't respond, and as soon as the crucifix had been moved aside, she placed her lips over Claire's throat. The pulse of the jugular vein pounded against her lips, the tempo growing faster as she licked the taut flesh. The temptation to bite was painfully strong and she didn't know if she resisted because of Claire's plea, or because hesitation gave her the opportunity to prolong the torment. 'You're asking an awful lot of me,' she whispered, and Claire's pitiful moan made Faith squirm with fresh hunger. 'How can you stand here, looking like such a temptress, and ask me to wait until after midnight? Don't you think I've shown more than my fair share of restraint?'

'Please,' Claire begged. 'You can see I've got no option

about standing here.'

Her voice had taken on the strident whine of the truly terrified and Faith found the tone intoxicating. She brushed her fingers over the thrust of Claire's nipple and wasn't surprised to find the bead of flesh standing hard and temptingly erect.

'I'm tied to the walls,' Claire protested. 'All I'm able to do is stand here and beg.'

'And you're doing it so well,' Faith said, stealing another kiss from her friend's neck. Through the pulse of her jugular the echo of Claire's heartbeat trembled against Faith's lips. The temptation to feed had been unbearably strong before but it was never this irresistible. She pressed her canines against the alabaster skin of Claire's throat and seriously contemplated biting.

'Please,' Claire sobbed.

Faith's fingertips finally reached the rope around her wrist. The flesh was beautifully smooth and made her ache to satisfy her immediate desires. But Faith forced herself to hesitate. Releasing the knot, allowing Claire's arm to fall free from the binding, she pushed her body against her friend's and held her in a loose embrace.

Claire regarded her doubtfully. 'Are you saving me?'

Faith's wicked chuckle sounded like an imitation of Lilah's diabolical mirth. It rang from the crypt's walls with the macabre ferocity of a death knell. It was a mocking laugh that suggested Claire was foolish for even thinking she had a chance of salvation. Faith writhed against her, savouring the sensation of the helpless body as it jostled her own, and was rewarded by the increased scents of Claire's terror and arousal. 'Do you want to be saved?' she asked, trying to disguise her wicked glee, enjoying her friend's confusion.

'You know I do. I want us both to be saved.'

Faith released the rope from Claire's other wrist. Freeing both arms, allowing her friend partial freedom, she cajoled herself more intimately against Claire's weary body. Stroking her hands over both buttocks, pushing her leg more forcefully between Claire's parted thighs, she resisted the urge to kiss her throat again. 'Why don't you beg me not to take you?' she asked in a placatory tone.

Claire glared at her, but Faith was no longer stung by the animosity.

'Why don't you get down on your knees and beg me not to take you?' Faith suggested. 'I think that would be a damned fine place to start.'

'Is that really what you want me to do?'

'Unless you'd rather I just fed from you.' She stole a finger against Claire's throat, shivering as the frisson of electricity excited them both. 'If you'd rather I just fed from you, then I'll happily do that.'

Claire dropped to her knees, and Faith could imagine her own scarlet smile glistening in the torchlight as her friend's head bobbed close to her sex. Caught up in the moment, revelling in the thrill of control, she caught a fistful of Claire's hair and guided her mouth towards her pussy.

Before rushing from the casino, and only to give her some degree of modesty as they hurried through the city's streets, Lilah had draped a coat over Faith's shoulders. Now it was simply a matter of unfastening the cinched belt at her waist, allowing the garment to fall open, and Claire's face would be a mere breath away from her sex. The power of being in control made her feel strong and alive and her excitement burnt brightly.

'You shouldn't be making me do this,' Claire said softly.

Faith pulled hard on her hair. 'That doesn't sound like begging.'

'But—'

Faith yanked until she heard her friend squeal. A small part of her felt guilty for inflicting pain on Claire but it was easy to ignore that tug of conscience. Her senses were attuned to every subtle change within the crypt and she felt sure she knew the real needs Claire was trying to conceal. Admittedly her friend was frightened and clearly worried about the repercussions of their actions, but the scent of her fear was a pale backwash beneath a dark musk of excitement. Drinking deep breaths of the air, revelling in the fragrance, Faith knew Claire was looking forward to the submission as much as she was personally enjoying the control. 'You've never complained about doing this before,' she said. 'You're only complaining now because you think there's a danger that I'll get excited and feed from you.'

Claire started to speak again but Faith shook her by the hair until she fell silent. 'I've got you down on your knees so you can do one of two things,' Faith said firmly. 'Begging is one of your options. I don't think I need tell you the other.'

Claire glared up at her. 'This isn't you, Faith.'

Faith pulled harder and forced Claire's mouth against her sex. 'Are you sure it's not me?' she sneered. 'Why don't you have a proper taste before you make such a bold statement? I can't have changed that much since the last time you tasted my cunt.'

The tickle of Claire's fringe brushed her inner thighs, and the warm tip of her nose buried into Faith's pubic mound. The caress of her nervous breath was shockingly exciting and Faith eased her legs further apart as she prepared for the rush of euphoria. Claire's hands went to her hips, and Faith was briefly troubled by the idea that her friend might use her hold to try and exert some sort of advantage, but after a few moments she realised her doubt was misplaced. Claire only held lightly, and then just so she could more ably lick, kiss and nuzzle. Her lips fell gently onto the tops of Faith's legs, and occasionally she lapped her tongue against the glistening wetness of her labia.

Faith ground her teeth together, relishing the rush of delicious pleasures. Her sex lips were already wet but Claire's tongue added heat and lubrication. She licked the sensitive flesh and skilfully teased the folds apart before dancing the tip of her tongue against Faith's clitoris.

It was the subtlest of dark kisses, a connection that was almost accidental, but enough to push Faith to the verge of a climax. She continued to hold Claire's head in position, using her other hand to massage the back of her own neck while her body was buffeted by waves of growing delight. The nearness of an orgasm only began to recede when Claire snatched her head away and pulled her hair from Faith's grip. Faith glared down at her, annoyed that the mood had been broken.

'You don't want me to do this,' Claire gasped.

'I bloody do,' Faith growled indignantly. 'And despite your pious protests I think you want it too.' Outraged that Claire could pretend to be against what they were doing, Faith dropped to the floor and pushed her back. The ropes that still bound Claire's ankles kept her legs spread and Faith had no difficulty stealing a hand beneath the hem of her skirt. She saw the resentful glare being shot in her direction but that didn't stop her from guiding her fingers to the gusset of Claire's panties and easing the fabric aside.

Claire made a muted shriek of protest and tried to stop her, but Faith swatted her hands aside. Not allowing her conscience to interfere she pushed her hand forward and found the haven of warm wetness that nestled between Claire's legs. The pussy lips were slick with heat, and with the panties pushed aside the scent of her arousal had never been stronger.

'Are you sure we shouldn't be doing this?' she asked, snatching her wet fingers from under the skirt and thrusting them beneath Claire's nose. The viscous smear glistened like liquid gold in the glow of the torchlight. 'Are you sure this isn't what you want?'

Claire's gasp was an inarticulate sob. Wiping her fingers on her friend's face, leaving the sticky residue like a battle scar on her cheek, she lowered her hand back to the heat of Claire's sex. Her vampiric smile grew more menacing. She teased the inner labia apart and rested the weight of two fingers over Claire's entrance, then not hurrying, relishing the sultry friction, she began to slide them inside.

Claire shook her head and mumbled something too soft to be heard properly. It could have been a protest, but sounded more like encouragement to Faith, and she pushed deeper. With her fingers inside Claire's tight confines she could once again feel the tantalising pulse of her lover. The temptation to feed welled within her as did the greedy need to share Claire's pleasure. Rubbing gently back and forth, enjoying the reluctant sighs she was inspiring, Faith brushed the pad of her thumb over Claire's clitoris. The tiny ball of flesh throbbed and it only took the lightest touch to reduce her to a quivering mass of ecstasy.

'Are you really trying to tell me you don't want this?' Faith enquired sweetly, but held in the throes of bittersweet pleasure Claire said nothing. She slapped her palms impotently against the crypt's soil floor and moaned with bliss-fuelled fury. The flaming sconce offered little illumination and Claire was only a silhouette in the darkness. But that didn't stop Faith from catching the scent of her excitement, or noticing the gratified shivers that coursed through her body. 'Are you really trying to tell me that this is something you don't want?'

Claire groaned and finally found the breath to reply. 'Of course I want this,' she sighed impatiently. 'I still find you irresistible, even when you're being an evil bitch. But I want something more.' Grabbing hold of Faith's wrist, making another attempt to push her hand away, she said, 'I want something wholesome.'

Faith rubbed her clitoris again, squashing the bead of flesh between her thumb and Claire's pubic mound. She didn't care if she was causing pleasure or pain but she wasn't disappointed to hear her friend sigh with excitement. The inner muscles around her fingers convulsed with elation and the wetness became warmer and more copious. Claire's husky breaths dropped to a rasp of raw arousal.

'Wholesome?' Faith repeated. 'What could be more wholesome than this? We're just two friends enjoying a little innocent pleasure, aren't we? Isn't that wholesome?'

'We're in a crypt,' Claire pointed out, her voice strident with emotion, and Faith could hear the nearness of frustrated tears underscoring each word. 'We're in a dank, smelly crypt, and rather than treating me like a lover you're taking me as though I was a victim. There's nothing wholesome about this.'

Unable to think of a response to justify her actions, and stung by the accusation that she was ignoring her friend's needs, Faith said nothing. Their difference of opinion threatened to sour her mood and she struggled to be more like Lilah and less bothered by Claire's opinion. It would have been easier to ignore her friend if Claire hadn't continued talking and Faith wondered if she should simply give in to the demands of her dark appetite and drink from her throat.

'I thought we were going to be an item,' Claire complained. 'I thought you and I had a future together.'

Faith worked her fingers back and forth, pleased that her efforts were rewarded by Claire's augmented shivers. She could sense the swelling climax between her friend's legs and knew it would only take a little more teasing before she wrung the orgasm from her.

'We can still be an item if I make you,' Faith argued. 'And it would be a much better future than we'd ever planned. We'd be immortal and have a longer future together – longer than either of us ever imagined. And more satisfying.' Struggling to understand her own argument, and trying hard to win her friend over, she spoke quickly to prevent being interrupted. 'There are a lot of drawbacks to being a vampire; I won't pretend there aren't. But the benefits are unbelievable. You can *feel* more when you're a vampire. You can enjoy more. It turns sex into an experience that's nothing like any mortal has ever experienced.'

'Are you saying that vampire sex is better than what you and I experienced together in Rome?'

Faith opened her mouth to answer, and then closed it quickly. She didn't want to be involved in this argument, and wasn't willing to discuss the difference between physical satisfaction and spiritual fulfilment. 'I just said it's like no mortal has ever experienced,' she growled. Working her fingers faster, lowering her voice so Claire had to strain to hear, she said, 'I'm just suggesting that you should try it for me. I'm just saying it would be a way for us to be together for always.'

Claire shook her head and tried to squirm away. It was clear that she was basking in the same furious pleasure that Faith was enjoying but she was struggling to resist. 'That was never what we wanted and it's still not what I want,' she said, panting breathlessly, forcing each word with gargantuan effort. 'Are you suggesting we could become a vampire couple, like my pathetic sister, Helen? And that bastard boyfriend of hers, Nick?' No longer disguising her contempt she spat with disgust onto the crypt's floor. 'Those two feel nothing for one another. They spend half their time bickering, and when they're not rutting like dogs together they're casually fucking potential victims.'

Faith considered this, but she was unable to discount the option as easily as Claire. She didn't particularly care for Nick and Helen, and knew the couple's existence was built on the pain and suffering of others, but she felt defensive and couldn't bring herself to condemn the lifestyle so readily. She supposed a part of the attraction came from her personal knowledge of being a vampire and her understanding of the fundamental powers of passion and satisfaction. Admittedly it wasn't wholesome, but she wondered if that was a small price to pay in exchange for the tremendous benefits of immortality and unimagined joy. 'It doesn't sound like they have such a bad life,' she said quietly.

Claire shook her head. 'That was never what I wanted for you and I. And I don't really think it's what you want, is it?'

Silent for a moment, Faith couldn't think how to respond. She knew what Claire was saying, remembered the simple and undemanding fulfilment life had given her before she suffered Lilah's bite, and realised Claire's question wasn't one she wanted to answer. 'What do you think we want?' she asked, trying to avoid the issue, truculently lowering her voice.

'Just a normal relationship,' Claire said. 'Just you and me sharing long nights together and spending days in the sunlight. Just you and me holding hands, getting tans and then examining each other's white bits. Maybe doing something that can be a little kinky now and again. Maybe occasionally doing something that can be a little daring. But not doing something that always has to be dark, twisted and sadistic.'

Faith didn't want to hear any more. The memories that Claire's words evoked hurt worse than when she'd been touching the crucifix. Shaking her head, pulling herself away from the floor, she grabbed a fistful of Claire's hair and forced her face back to her sex. Reasoning that the chore would briefly silence her, or at least make it more difficult for her to continue her side of the painful argument, she pulled on the tresses and encouraged Claire to lap her pussy. 'I'm tired of listening to you now,' she complained. 'Carry on doing what you were doing before.'

Obediently Claire began to lick, and this time Faith tried to lose herself in the pleasure but it refused to come. Before she had been able to dance on the precipice of an orgasm as soon as her friend's tongue touched her, but now that joy remained hatefully out of reach. Claire's obvious reluctance to join the coven, her insistence that the life of the vampires was wrong and immoral, preyed viciously on Faith's thoughts. Her sex was being expertly teased, Claire trilled her tongue against her clitoris and repeatedly plundered Faith's moist depths, but she still found herself unable to respond with her former abandon. The thrill of being in control was meaningless in the face of Claire's resigned obedience and the pleasure was tainted by the knowledge that as a vampire she would never be able to experience anything more satisfying.

As though sensing the shift in her mood, Claire sat back

for a moment and glanced up from the floor. 'We could make it good between us again,' she promised. 'It's not too late. There's still a chance.'

Faith considered the words, trying not to be drawn by the temptation they offered. She considered demanding that Claire return to licking her, but it was impossible to find the strength to give that command. 'Would it be good?' she asked softly. 'Would it be as good as you're suggesting?'

'It would be better than good,' Claire assured her, and as though trying to prove her point, as though eager to show how wonderful their future could be, she grabbed Faith's hips and buried her face back against her sex.

With the promise of a fulfilling future lying ahead of them, Faith found she could give herself to the pleasure this time. She didn't bother to resume her hold on Claire's hair, gripping her own scalp as the waves of pleasure flowed through her sex. The joy returned more powerfully than before and she realised that, rather than dominantly demanding something from her friend, they were once again sharing an experience.

The first orgasm struck like a body blow of pleasure, surprising her with the brutal onslaught of pure delight. She stifled a shriek, not wanting to draw attention from the coven in the neighbouring annex of the crypt, then crested on a second wave of bliss. Explosions of euphoria echoed through her sex and she was torn between wanting Claire to continue and needing to make her stop so she could briefly recuperate.

It wasn't the beautiful experience she had always associated with Claire, but it was close and reminded her of exactly what she was missing. Shaking as the eddies of her climax faded, Faith could only see that the pleasure had one drawback. She almost sobbed when she realised she had been overlooking something so obvious. But rather than giving in to such a weakness, she simply reached down and stroked her friend's cheek affectionately.

Claire continued to lick and kiss between her legs, wreaking divine bliss through Faith's sex.

'Claire?' Faith sighed, touching her cheek again.

Claire glanced up from the floor, her mouth coated with a residue of wetness that glistened like bronze in the light of the flame. The excitement that lurked beneath her smile vanished when she saw the intent on Faith's face, her arousal instantaneously replaced with pure panic. 'You were going to wait until after midnight,' Claire reminded her. 'You were going to wait.'

'Did I say I would?'

'We had an agreement,' Claire wailed, her protests growing louder as Faith dragged her from the floor. 'You know we had an agreement,' she insisted. 'You promised.'

Faith gently brushed the hair from Claire's shoulder before placing her lips against the pulsing vein. Easily controlling her friend's struggles, effortlessly holding her in position as she prepared to bite, she lightly nuzzled Claire's ear and whispered, 'I don't remember promising. And I don't think I can hold out any longer. If midnight doesn't happen soon, I think my instincts are going to take over and I'm going to have to take you.'

Hope

Act III, Scene III

The stunned silence was thick enough to slice with a meat cleaver. The mulatto held her torch, using it to accuse Chalmers while all the other vampires turned to glare at him. Hope could sense the revelation caused an upset to his plans, but she couldn't think of a way to deflate the situation. Nick had pushed Marcia away from his embrace, no longer interested in the passion of her kisses. His frown was sullen and foreboding. Lilah flexed her long fingers and her manicured talons looked ready to spill blood. The sneer on her lips made her vicious smile appear all the more lethal.

Yet surprisingly Chalmers held the floor as though he was still in control of the situation. He studied his accuser doubtfully, gracing her with a playful smile. 'Are you sure there's been an oversight in the accounts?' he asked. 'Are you absolutely sure?'

The mulatto sneered. 'Yes, I'm positive. And it's more than a mere oversight. It's an error that leaves you in control of eighty-five percent of the coven's assets. I'd call that a damned sight more than an oversight. I'd call that...'

Not letting her finish, Chalmers shook his head and started to walk away. For an instant Hope thought he was making an escape, and she could see the others shared her low expectations of his intentions. Marcia took a step closer to the door and Nick stiffened, ready to hurl himself in Chalmers' direction should the need arise. But Chalmers walked to the corner of the crypt and snatched the cane from the floor.

Hope briefly wondered if he was going to try and fight his way out of the room; and was wholly stunned by the way he finally reacted. He stepped swiftly back to the centre of the crypt and sliced the cane down hard across her bare cheeks. 'You silly little bitch!' he roared, his face a mask of thunderous outrage. 'You stupid little cow!'

The pain was exquisite. While Lilah had been disciplining her, Hope experienced a rush of excitement with each stroke of the cane, and every punishing blow of the paddle had borne a tang of sultry pleasure, but this was nothing like those teasing slaps. This was gratuitous suffering without any of the benefits. A flare of anguish burst across both cheeks and she found herself infuriatingly close to sobbing.

'You were supposed to help me get the accounts ready for Lilah,' Chalmers declared, slicing another blow against her backside. 'I had you review the books to eliminate the risk of this sort of embarrassment, and this is how you repay me!'

Hope was half-prepared for the stinging shot this time but it still didn't get her any closer to dealing with the pain that seared her buttocks. She fixed him with a desperate plea for leniency, willing to do anything that would make him stop using the cane, but Chalmers seemed determined that his act should look convincing.

'How do you expect these vampires to deal fairly with us if you won't deal fairly with them?'

Hope didn't hear the question. Chalmers had scored another furious blow across her poor rear and the pounding of blood drowned every other sound out as it soared through her temples. Her bottom was ablaze with punished flesh, but the heat inspired a sensation she knew would soon spark fresh arousal.

'Are you saying the girl is responsible?' the mulatto asked.

Chalmers fixed her with a scornful expression. 'You don't really think I'd try and cheat the coven, do you?' His injured tone was so plausible that Hope briefly found herself believing him. She fixed him with a startled glance and was rewarded by another fierce stripe from the cane. This one stung hard enough to bring tears to her eyes. He was raising his arm again and Hope could see this shot would be just as punishing, when Lilah appeared at his side and grabbed his wrist.

'Why would the girl try and cheat the coven?' the vampire demanded. 'It doesn't make sense. What advantage would that give her?'

He glared at her with gruff impatience and tried to wrestle his hand free, but even though she was still holding her wooden box Lilah easily won the brief battle and eventually he stopped struggling. 'She's not trying to cheat the coven,' he growled. 'She's simply trying to make things awkward for me.' He fixed Hope with a look of bitter fury and went on. 'I don't think she's ever been comfortable with the prospect of being the night's sacrificial offering. I think she's been plotting mischief so that she's not the only one who suffers here this evening.'

Hope watched Lilah consider this and could see the vampire was giving him the benefit of the doubt. 'Go on, then,' she said, releasing her hold on Chalmers' wrist, stepping back and allowing him to continue. 'If she's been up to mischief then she certainly deserves some sort of reprimand. Get on with it, Toad.'

Hope glanced fearfully at her tormentors, scared that

this had been Chalmers' plan all along. She suddenly felt foolish for having believed in him, and wondered if she had been wrong to entrust her fate into his unscrupulous hands. Her worst fear – the prospect of being trapped by the vampires – had now been realised, and she could see she was no closer to executing Faith's salvation. The possibility that Chalmers had orchestrated the whole situation made Hope weak with despair.

'Go and check the accounts again,' Chalmers demanded. Hope glanced up at him and saw he was pointing at the mulatto. The dark-skinned vampire turned to Lilah for confirmation of the order, but Chalmers now seemed to be holding a position of authority on the floor. 'Get me an exact breakdown of where Hope has made errors so I can rectify matters to Lilah's satisfaction.'

Hesitant, and only after receiving Lilah's nod of assent, the mulatto took her flaming torch and returned to her private crypt.

'Why don't you two make yourselves useful?' Chalmers said, turning on Marcia and Nick. 'Hold this one in position for me. The undisciplined bitch is starting to squirm each time I stripe her.'

Hope glared at him, but Chalmers wasn't looking and she guessed he was deliberately refusing to meet her gaze. Movement in front of her made her realise that the pair of vampires were eager to become involved and they rushed to do as Chalmers had demanded. Nick grabbed Hope's left hand and easily pulled her from the floor. Marcia took hold of her right and placed a gentle kiss against her wrist.

'Hello again,' Nick whispered, his scarlet gaze shining with bright glee. 'I didn't think we'd get the chance to become reacquainted so soon.'

Dismayed by this turn of events, Hope shivered. Marcia's full lips were moist and gentle, subtly exciting

221

her and adding an unwanted frisson to the moment. Nick, more direct than his female counterpart, placed a hand over Hope's breast and squeezed. The tips of his fingers found her nipple and he casually teased until the button of flesh stood hard.

The combination of embarrassment, arousal and dread made Hope dizzy. She was briefly thankful that the two vampires were holding her because she knew her knees were on the verge of buckling. Miserably she glared at Chalmers, but he still didn't deign to look in her direction.

'Drape her over the sarcophagus,' he instructed, using his cane to point. 'It's time she was taught a proper lesson.'

Inelegantly, Hope was dragged to the stone box in the centre of the crypt. Her buttocks were pushed against its chilly surface and she was laid back as the vampires towered over her. Concerns of the cold weren't an issue – the frigid marble was a positive balm against her burning cheeks – and she was more troubled by the malevolent intent she could see in Nick and Marcia's smiles. Despite the pain that Chalmers had managed to inflict, and regardless of the discomfort of being laid naked over the chilly sarcophagus, she remained poignantly aware that the vampires still presented the greatest threat. She didn't believe either Nick or Marcia would feed from her without Lilah's permission, but she didn't think the coven's leader would refuse the request if made.

Marcia's subtle kisses moved from Hope's wrist to the inside of her elbow. Her gentleness was surprising and infuriating and, if she had been concentrating on the sensation more, Hope would have struggled to wrench her arm free. But once she was stretched across the sarcophagus Nick took his hand away from her breast and placed his mouth there. The hateful pleasure he inspired made Hope anxious to escape and she cursed him with a string of bitter expletives. Unmindful, he danced the tip of his tongue against her and coaxed the nipple to full erection, and as soon as it stood hard inside his mouth he rested the punishing pressure of his canines against its firmness.

Hope groaned and made another attempt to pull away. Both vampires were making their caresses more intimate. A hand stole against her right knee, stroking upwards and aiming for her sex. The fingertips brushed her inner thigh and continued travelling purposefully higher. Another hand rubbed against the curve of her left hip, gliding down in an urgent exploration. It was all too easy to imagine both sets of fingers meeting against her pussy lips and plundering the moist haven of her sex. When the first of the fingertips touched, sliding against her slippery flesh, she groaned with bitter frustration. The second set brushed through her pubic curls making directly for the centre of her wetness. Hope bit back another cry.

'I want to cane her backside,' Chalmers growled impatiently. 'Stop fondling the little bitch like that and turn her around.'

There was a moment's hesitation, and if Hope had bothered to open her eyes she guessed she would have seen the pair looking to Lilah for confirmation of Chalmers' instruction. But lost in the illicit pleasure the vampires evoked she didn't bother looking. She knew the teasing fingers shouldn't have been touching her, and she knew it was wrong to succumb to the joys they inspired, but that didn't make it any easier to resist. And there was no need for her to see what was happening, because with their unnatural speed the vampires turned her so her breasts were squashed against the cold stone and her bottom was thrust in the air. She was shocked by the sudden change in position, despising the fact that they all seemed able to excite her and then leave her frustrated and unfulfilled.

Her legs were coaxed further apart, Nick casually manhandling her thighs while Marcia continued to kiss her wrist and draw her teeth against her pulse. She took some consolation from the fact that Nick was no longer able to tease her nipples, but it was the only advantage that came from the change in position.

'Get her arse higher,' Chalmers directed. 'And get her legs a little further apart. I want to do this properly.'

Hope's shame wasn't as severe as her excitement, but it came a close second. She couldn't imagine a more humiliating position and wondered how it was possible for her body to continue functioning without simply closing down from the trauma of mortification. She tried to wrestle away from the vampires, but their superior strength left her in no doubt that she would be under their control until they deigned to let her go. And when Marcia tapped lightly against her inner thighs, Hope grudgingly spread her legs further apart.

She didn't want to assume the position – after the past couple of nights she was all too used to bending over so her bottom could be chastised – but she couldn't decide if she was loath to suffer the pain or the pleasure. Both were such diabolical torments she didn't know which she dreaded the most.

'Would you care to do the honours, Lilah?' Chalmers asked.

Hope glanced back over her shoulder, disgusted to see he was trying to present the coven leader with the cane. She shivered from the thought of being handed so casually from one tormentor to another, and tried not to let the idea inflame her excitement. It was easy to remember that in this same crypt she had accused Chalmers of plotting to hand her over to his vampire girlfriend, and she began to fret that the accusation had been more truthful than he let her believe.

'She's very well presented,' he encouraged, stroking Hope's buttocks. 'And I know you've been aching to have a proper go at her since you arrived here in Paris.'

Hope forced herself to remain rigid, not wanting to be won over by the maddening friction of his casual caress. Her rear remained a furnace of raw heat and she was discovering that made her exceptionally sensitive. The scrape of Chalmers' palm was almost enough to have her wallowing in a glut of dark passion. Fresh beads of sweat erupted on her brow and the flesh between her legs turned into a liquid mass.

'And,' he continued in the tone of a confidante, 'you deserve to punish her as much as I do. Since it was your money she messed with, perhaps you deserve to punish her more.'

On a level beneath her arousal, Hope could sense that he wanted Lilah to take control of the cane. She didn't know if he was genuinely trying to win over the coven leader, or if he had other plans to take care of while Lilah was distracted. Because Chalmers hadn't bothered to explain his intentions Hope could only pray they were still working toward the same goal, and that it wasn't too late to manage Faith's salvation.

'Why don't you take the cane and see how she responds?' he coaxed. 'You can see she's more than ready.'

Hope held her breath and listened expectantly.

'No, I'll let you begin,' Lilah said coolly.

Hope tried glancing back, wondering if she might see disappointment on his face, but Chalmers acted before she could properly turn. He drove the cane hard against her bottom, grunting with the effort. She didn't cry out –

she expected he would inflict more punishment if she made any noise – but it was a struggle to keep her protests contained. The whole evening was developing in a way she hadn't anticipated and the thought that Chalmers had deceived her was constantly at the forefront of her mind.

'You should be apologising,' he snapped, slashing another blow across her buttocks, but she bit her tongue, shaking her head from side to side in silent refusal. 'You should be begging me for forgiveness.' Hope contained the squeal that rose at the back of her throat. 'And you should be making us believe that you're truly sorry.'

Hope didn't know what to say, and wasn't sure she would have the breath even if she could think of the right words.

Nick no longer had access to her breasts but he was following Marcia's lead and exciting the flesh of Hope's wrists. His kisses weren't as subtle, he seemed unable to touch the sensitive skin without using his teeth to inflict playful nips, but that didn't make the pleasure any less powerful. Marcia continued to use her tongue against Hope's arm, murmuring meaningless platitudes about the sweetness of her flavour, but the vampires were only a minor consideration as she continued to suffer Chalmers' punishment.

He slashed the cane repeatedly, shocking her with the force of each blow and fuelling a deep-seated desire between her legs. The discomfort from the cane was infuriating but the arousal it inspired was worse. She arched her back, trying vainly to pull her arms away from the vampires and wishing she could simply give in to the thrill of release. Her body ached for a climax and she yearned for an opportunity to let the orgasm course through her, but she sensed that Chalmers would be disappointed if she gave herself over to the pleasure so quickly. She also thought he would make the punishment more severe if he thought she was enjoying the discipline.

'You've taught her to relish that,' Lilah observed.

Hope cringed from the vampire's voice. She feared the power of Lilah, and despised her for what she had done to her sister.

But most of all, she hated the way Chalmers was so eager to pause from the gruelling chastisement so he could reply to the coven's leader. Her blazing rear remained poised in the air, the desperate need within her sex continued to pulse unsated, and it was all she could do to listen to their conversation and wait impatiently for the torment to resume.

'I trained her for this moment,' Chalmers explained. 'If you want to try it yourself you're more than welcome.'

There was another pause, agonisingly long, as Lilah deliberated her response. Hope wanted to scream that she didn't care which of them finished striping her backside, as long as one of them hurried up and did it, but she remained dutifully silent. It was a struggle to contain her reaction, and when she heard Lilah take the cane from Chalmers' hands she began to wonder why she still craved for the chastisement to be concluded.

'Were you trying to cause upset here this evening?' Lilah asked.

Hope said nothing, expecting to feel a line of pain slash across her buttocks, but rather than delivering a blow Lilah drew the tip of the cane against one vicious weal. It was little more than a light caress and Hope knew she wouldn't have felt it on any other part of her body, but because the vampire was exciting the hurt of injured flesh, Hope almost screamed.

'Toad's been doing important work for me,' Lilah continued. She pressed the cane hard against the centre of one buttock, and Hope guessed she was resting the tip over the cross of two or more stripes, because the blazing anguish seared in all directions.

'He's been doing vital work for me, yet you think you can usurp his endeavours just because you don't like the way he disciplines you. Was that why you messed things up for him?'

Hope shook her head and tried to say it hadn't been like that, but the words refused to come. The cane was snatched away from her buttocks and the threat of another blow made her hold her breath in anticipation. But the agony never came.

She glanced back over her shoulder and saw Lilah was alternating her glare between Nick and Marcia. 'Turn her over,' she snapped. 'Chalmers might like to stripe bare backsides, but I can have much more fun on a face to face encounter.'

Hope's eyes widened in horror as Nick and Marcia obeyed Lilah's instructions. As before, there was no delay and before she realised it was happening she was laid with her back against the sarcophagus. She could see what was coming, and knew the cane would be slashed across the swell of her breasts, the idea so terrible it left her trembling.

She cast a quick glance in Chalmers' direction, wondering if there was a chance he might intervene and help her. But his smile of cruel approval told her that she was wasting her time even thinking he might come to her rescue.

Nick raised a hand, and Hope briefly thought she had found salvation from the most unlikely source. But when he lowered his mouth to the tip of her right nipple, then began to suckle gently, she realised he was only exacerbating the torment.

228

Marcia followed his lead, raised a hand to stop Lilah from hurling the cane down, and then placed her lips over Hope's left breast. Both vampires had chilly tongues and cool mouths, yet they inspired a heat that made Hope hurt with fresh excitement. The pair seemed to prefer her in this position because, once again, they took advantage of the opportunity to caress her hips and thighs. Their fingertips made a circuitous journey towards her sex before briefly meeting over the humid crease of her pussy lips.

'Get out of the way,' Lilah growled. 'It's my turn to punish her.'

'Two more minutes,' Nick said, shaping the words around Hope's nipple, and she almost climaxed as his lips buffeted fresh pleasure through the tip of her breast. She heard Marcia giggle but the sound came from a distance as the pleasure of an orgasm threatened to engulf her body.

But the torrid joy was snatched from her as quickly as it started when Lilah said again, 'Get out of the way.' The stern timbre of her voice was sufficient to make Nick and Marcia hesitate, but neither of them stopped. Their hands continued to explore her body and Hope feared they would carry on indefinitely. Glaring defiantly up at the vampire, she drew a deep breath.

Chalmers stepped to Lilah's side and placed a hand on her shoulder. The vampire fixed him with a venomous expression but he seemed undeterred. 'Rather than using the cane, and so you can properly punish this little bitch, why don't you try this?' he suggested.

Hope glanced up and her stomach folded with apprehension. The idea that he might still prove to be her ally was swiftly banished and she realised she'd been wrong to trust him. It was clear that the only reason he had brought her to the crypt was as a gift for the coven's leader and she wondered how she could have been so foolish. As she had feared would happen, she saw that Chalmers was presenting Lilah with a special weapon of torment. Even though the light in the coven was dim, and she could make out little more than shapes and shadows, she knew exactly what this was without needing to see it properly.

'A strap?' Lilah frowned, shrugging Chalmers' hand away. 'What makes you think I'd enjoy using a strap on her?'

Chalmers shook his head. 'It's not a strap.' The smile in his voice was despicably evil. 'It's not a strap at all. This is a ceremonial knout.'

Hope

Act III, Scene IV

Hope had always known there would be a price to be paid, and she had always feared it would be high. But she had never expected it would be this high.

'Just let me watch her come again,' Nick pleaded.

He spoke with Hope's nipple pressed between his canines. The piercing pain was almost enough to have her screaming in a meld of agony and ecstasy but she resisted the urge. Her hands were clutched into fists, the fingernails burying into the soft flesh of her palms. Sweat sheathed her body and she trembled through extremes of undiluted elation. Her heartbeat raced with a mixture of adrenaline and arousal.

'Just give me two minutes,' Nick insisted. 'I only want to watch her come.'

Marcia continued to suck on Hope's left breast, exciting undiscovered bliss with every movement, but it was Nick who seemed devoted to the task. Unlike Marcia he was devouring her, licking and sucking the nipple and making her wriggle with impatient arousal. Marcia continued to use the tips of her fingers, exploring Hope's hips, thighs and the secrets of her sex, yet Hope was barely aware of the female vampire's involvement. It was Nick's attention to her pleasure that was so hatefully satisfying and she knew, if Lilah did concede to let him use her for another two minutes, he would force her to climax from the simple act of foreplay.

'Go on,' Marcia urged, her voice possessing the plaintive whine of a spoilt child. As she spoke her fingers continued to stroke the smooth flesh of Hope's sex, brushing the lips apart, sliding against the clitoris and perpetually threatening to penetrate.

Hope felt dizzy with the effort of resisting her climax, but she knew that wasn't a battle she would be able to continue much longer. Her nerves were fraught with arousal and she suspected it wouldn't take much more stimulation before she was basking in the bliss of satisfaction.

'Just two minutes,' Marcia begged. 'Then we'll let you have her.'

Lilah snapped the knout against the crypt's low ceiling. The echo bounced crisply from the walls and a flurry of dirt fell to the floor. 'You'll let me have her now,' she growled softly. 'Get out of the way. It's my turn to punish her.'

Churlishly, Nick and Marcia eased themselves aside. They each remained on the floor and held Hope's wrists so she couldn't try to escape or protect herself, but it was obvious they were giving the leader clear access.

Lilah stood over her, eyes sparkling with appreciation. She viewed Hope's bare body while the knout trembled in her hand. Her entire frame shivered as though powered by an electric charge. As always she held the ever-present wooden box beneath one arm, but she seemed so used to its awkward presence that it no longer looked like a cumbersome accessory. Smiling cruelly, her scarlet gaze never leaving the swell of Hope's breasts, she drew the knout back and prepared to deliver the first blow.

Hope cast a fearful glance in Chalmers' direction, but he wasn't looking at her. Rather than concentrating on her, Lilah, or the other vampires, he seemed more preoccupied with surreptitiously retrieving something from the sports bag he'd dropped in the corner of the room. Wary that he might be doing something for Faith's benefit, and not sure why she was still trying to deceive herself that her sister's salvation could remain a part of his agenda, Hope snatched her gaze away from him and turned to glance back at Lilah.

She was in time to see the knout descend and watch its vicious tips land hard against her breasts. The anguish was stunning. Every other pain had been a forerunner to this indignity. Spikes of pure agony were torn through her sensitive flesh and she pulled from side to side in a futile attempt to escape the punishment.

Nick grinned with approval.

Marcia drew her tongue hungrily over her lips.

Lilah raised the knout and threw it down for a second time.

The lengths of leather whistled through the air and bit like bee stings. There was no sense in trying to back away from the punishment – the sarcophagus beneath her was stone and unrelenting – and Hope remained rigid as the knotted tips struck her breasts for a second time.

'Yes,' Nick drooled, a note of triumph in his voice, distantly puzzling Hope when she heard it. Understanding only came as she realised he had wanted to watch her achieve another climax and the punishment had finally driven her to the brink of an orgasm and beyond. The difference between pleasure and pain was indistinguishable and her relief came as the knout spat repeatedly against her breasts. She could feel the knotted tips snatching at her nipples, knew her body would never receive discipline to such an extreme ever again, and wallowed in the divine bliss of Lilah's punishment.

Marcia chuckled and dared to plant a kiss against Hope's

throat. The pressure of the vampire's lips added a delicious dimension to her throes of pleasure. Unable to contain the impulses any longer, and not bothering to resist the needs of her body, Hope moaned and allowed the climax free rein. Her eyelids fluttered as she crested on the verge of consciousness and it was only when she was stung by another blow from the knout that she deigned to glance at Lilah.

The vampire was smiling happily as she struck. The wicked tips of the knout bit sharply against Hope's breasts and her crimson smile grew broader.

'You do know,' Chalmers began tentatively, 'she doesn't need to be held in place.'

Hope had almost forgotten he was still with them and she glared at him for his interference. She didn't mind Nick and Marcia's presence; with their casual caresses and whispered words of approval the pair were adding untold pleasures to her satisfaction. Rather than trying to distract Lilah, Hope thought Chalmers should scurry back to a corner of the room and let the vampire continue using the knout.

'She doesn't need to be held in place at all.'

Lilah graced him with an expression of obvious doubt. 'You've trained her that well, have you?' she scoffed. 'Is that what you'd have me believe?'

Chalmers snapped his fingers for Nick and Marcia's attention. 'Let go of her,' he instructed. 'Go and join your bookkeeping friend,' he suggested, nodding towards the annex where the mulatto had disappeared. 'Maybe take her back to the casino so I can get the transfer of accounts sorted as soon as we've finished here.'

They both glanced at Lilah, who nodded grudging consent. 'If he says you're not needed, then perhaps it's best if you leave. Find out where Helen is,' she added, as the pair disappeared through the doorway. 'She's been away from the coven for too long.'

Hope studied Chalmers uneasily, still not sure she could trust him but now harbouring fresh doubts. She didn't know if he had dismissed the vampires so it was now only Lilah against the two of them, or if a part of his plan was to ingratiate himself into the affections of the coven leader. Admittedly, Faith and Claire remained through the doorway of the other annex, and Hope couldn't bring herself to imagine what might be happening there, but she thought it looked as though Chalmers was genuinely trying to make things right for her and her sister. She regarded him with renewed respect, inwardly chastising herself for having suspected his motives.

'Get on your knees and turn your back to Lilah,' Chalmers barked. He snatched the knout from the vampire's hand and hurled a sharp blow against her side. 'Show her that you can take a proper discipline,' he snarled. 'Don't make me tell you twice.'

She cursed herself for almost believing that he might be on her side. The depths of her own gullibility had sunk to a new level and she vowed that she would never again allow herself to be taken in by the duplicitous bastard. Biting back a sharp retort, convinced it would do no good to insult him, she started to do as he commanded.

'Get on your knees, and stay on your knees,' he shouted, stepping to her side as she did as she was told.

Then lowering his voice, bending down so he could thrust something into her hand, Chalmers hissed, 'Remember what I told you about this.' She glanced down and realised he was discreetly passing her the Bethesda Stone. 'Keep the larger half in your right hand,' he whispered. 'And concentrate on your most heartfelt desire.' She studied him, amazed that she was trusting him again and wondering if this time her faith might be justified. 'It's vital that you keep the larger half in your right hand,' he hissed. 'Don't forget that.'

Hope risked a hesitant glance over her shoulder, scared that Lilah might overhear, but it seemed clear that the vampire was preoccupied with the craftsmanship of the knout. She held it in one hand, smiling fondly as she examined the strips of knotted leather. 'I can't take much more of her punishment,' she whispered to him.

He glanced at his wristwatch and shook his head. 'You won't have to take much more. It's almost midnight.'

She switched her gaze from the wish-stone, then back to Chalmers, and decided she'd been wrong to doubt him. His methods might have been suspect, and she still thought he was trying to cheat the coven of their money, but he wasn't the out-and-out rogue she had believed. 'You really want us to try and save Faith, don't you?'

'It's good of you to notice,' he snarled sarcastically. 'I'm glad you didn't leave it much later before you realised what we're doing.'

There was no chance for Hope to reply because Lilah chose that moment to use the knout again. The lash of knotted leather screamed through the air then cracked against her buttocks. She gaped in surprise, shocked that the pain could be so vivid.

Jagged waves of pleasure scratched through her backside and she gripped the stone tightly as she tried not to be dragged down by the rush of another climax. Her breathing had deepened to a guttural moan, her heartbeat was pounding hard and she knew the onset of another orgasm could come with the next lash.

'You're right,' Lilah cried gleefully. 'She really can take the discipline, can't she?'

Hope listened for Chalmers to reply, but he didn't. She

dared to glance over her shoulder, in time to watch the knout descending yet again, and saw he was standing in the furthest shadows of the crypt. He was almost hidden from view, but she could see enough of him to notice he was sprinkling something on the floor, and she thought she could see his lips moving. The scent of mystical fragrances – subtle, but strong enough for her to notice – wafted from his corner of the crypt. It was almost impossible to be sure, Lilah was now using the knout with hateful ferocity, but Hope thought Chalmers' lips were shaping Latin words.

'Go on,' Lilah barked, the enthusiasm in her tone telling Hope that the vampire was thoroughly revelling in her position of control, 'start thanking me for doing this. And make it bloody convincing.'

Hope shook her head, not sure if she would be able to do as the vampire asked. She was wary that she might jeopardise the magic of the Bethesda Stone by obeying such a command, and although it meant defying the vampire's direct instruction, she kept her mouth firmly closed. She was wilfully trying to concentrate on her most heartfelt desire – the wish that Faith might be changed back from being a vampire – and she didn't want to spoil those thoughts by responding to Lilah's facile demands.

'Thank me,' Lilah insisted, hurling the knout down harder, and blisters of pure anguish sparkled against Hope's buttocks, making her cringe and shriek. Above that sound she could just hear Chalmers' Latin, and when she glanced down at the stone in her hand she realised the spell was beginning to work.

'I'll hear you thank me if I have to do this all night,' Lilah warned.

Hope grimaced as another blow struck between her shoulder blades. She'd thought Chalmers could be punishing whilst wielding the knout, but he was nothing like the sadistic taskmaster that Lilah had become. The vampire struck blow after blow, reddening her poor bottom and scourging the tops of her legs. Her skill with the knout was a remarkable ability that Hope hadn't anticipated.

'Thank me, you little bitch. Thank me!'

Hope glanced down at the stone in her hands and clutched it tighter. She could feel a growing heat building in her hands, and the Latin chant was now being shouted. Hope wondered why Lilah's suspicions hadn't been raised by his sudden lapse into an archaic language, but she seemed oblivious. It was only when she dared risk another glance, studying Lilah as curiously as the circumstances would allow, that she realised the vampire was completely absorbed in delivering the punishment. Thankful that things finally seemed to be going right she closed her eyes, tried to ignore the pain and sexual excitement, and concentrated on the stone in her hands.

'What the hell is that?' Lilah demanded, and Hope glanced up from her thoughts to find the vampire towering over her. The light coming from the stone had become so strong it was impossible to hide, and with growing horror Hope saw that Lilah had noticed its pulsing glow. It wasn't surprising; the light shone so brightly it was like an illuminated glove around her fist. With her eyes flaring furiously Lilah threw the knout to the floor and dropped to her knees by Hope's side. 'It's the fucking stone, isn't it?'

Unable to think of a convincing lie, and sure that nothing she could say would conceal the truth, Hope didn't reply.

'Give that to me,' Lilah growled, but defiantly Hope shook her head. She could feel the magic of the stone coursing through her, and although she didn't believe it was imbuing her with any special powers, she felt strong enough to refuse the vampire.

'Give it to me,' Lilah insisted. She reached out and snatched one half of the stone from Hope's fingers.

'No,' Hope cried, keeping hold with her right hand. She tried to slap the vampire aside but Lilah was only holding the stone with one hand and blocked the blow before it could land. Hope was ready for a greater struggle and resigned to losing in the face of Lilah's formidable strength, but that didn't happen.

Chalmers' chant became louder, rising to a thunderous crescendo before he clapped his hands.

Unable to tear her gaze from the stone, Hope saw the terrible illumination now throbbed between her and Lilah. The misty glove of light covered both their hands and grew brighter with each passing second. A charge of pure energy tingled through the tips of her fingers, and for the first time since she'd heard mention of the stone she was fixed with the absolute certainty that it was going to work.

A crackle spat from her fingertips, sharp enough to make her release her hold, but her brief worry that Lilah now had control of the stone was relieved when she saw the vampire had dropped her half at the same moment. Hope wanted to retrieve the stone from the floor, sure she must need to do something else before the ritual could be fulfilled, but she saw it had already crumbled into a pile of loose and worthless ashes.

'What the...?' Lilah began, but a cry from the annexed crypt silenced her and Hope felt her heart swell with elation. She recognised her sister's jubilant shriek, and although she would never be able to explain the subtle difference in tone, she knew it was free from all vampiric influence.

She glanced nervously at Lilah, expecting the vampire

239

to react to the cry, but Lilah's attention was focused uneasily on the wooden box she'd been holding. Hope watched in awe as the miniature treasure chest trembled in the vampire's hands and then turned quickly away when it shattered like a bomb.

She shielded her eyes from the risk of flying debris and it was only when she heard a gasp of surprise that she dared to peer back and see what happened. Where the box had been resting, tucked under Lilah's arm, there now stood a tall, formidable stranger. His brooding countenance and menacing smile made it obvious that he was a vampire, and although Hope didn't consider herself an expert, she thought it was clear he was a powerful vampire.

'The dark one,' Chalmers gasped.

'My brother,' Lilah whispered meekly.

Chalmers grabbed Hope from the floor and pulled her to her feet. Echoes of pleasure continued to make her dizzy but she was fast regaining her focus and realised they had to make their escape as quickly as possible. 'What's happening?' she squealed. 'What's going on?'

He shook his head and encouraged her towards the crypt's second annex. 'I think these two have a little catching up to do,' he explained carefully. 'Let's find Faith and her friend and get out of here while we have the chance.'

'Did it work?' Hope asked. 'Did the stone do what it was meant to?'

He regarded her solemnly, casting his glance back in the direction of Lilah and the dark one before replying. 'I think it did that, and some more besides.'

Epilogue

Hope Harker knew there was always a price to be paid but she now saw it was a lesson that Chalmers was only just beginning to learn.

'Is this some sort of penance?' he demanded.

Sunlight streamed through the glass windows of Orly airport, bathing them all in a brilliant yellow glow. Hope glared at him with hands on her hips and defiance in her eyes. Behind her Faith and Claire held hands, uninvolved in the conversation and constantly exchanging sultry glances with one another.

'Are you giving me this errand because you want to pay back some of the punishment I made you suffer?' Chalmers asked. 'Is that what this is all about?'

'Faith needs to recuperate from her ordeal,' Hope said flatly.

'And Hope is the only one I'd trust to help me look after her,' Claire broke in.

Faith squeezed Claire's hand and the pair exchanged a lingering kiss. Hope was trying to discreetly not notice them but she kept catching glimpses of their reflections in the polarised glass of the windows. For some reason she couldn't explain, Faith's reflection seemed to shine with its own inner light.

Chalmers ignored Faith and Claire, settling his dour frown on Hope. 'I should be looking after my interest in the casino.'

'Avril and Duval can manage that for you,' Hope

returned. 'They managed to fight off Helen. I'm sure they can run the place while you take a week off to do something this worthwhile.'

He shook his head and glared at her. 'You're making me pay, aren't you? This is nothing more than vindictive revenge on your part.'

'The gypsy's curse said that the vampires would be defeated by a virtuous girl.' Hope tried not to sound weary as she spoke but it was difficult to conceal the emotion. Along with Faith and Claire, she and Chalmers had pooled their collective knowledge on the motives and plans of the vampires. Over a breakfast of croissants, orange juice and strong black coffee, they worked out that the Bethesda Stone had granted Hope's greatest wish and realised Lilah's darkest fear. They also rationalised that, while Faith had been saved, a danger to the three sisters still remained. Claire had pointed out that the vampires would no longer see Faith as a threat, because she had been tainted by her involvement with the coven. And she then went on to tactfully suggest that Hope's submission to Nick might invalidate her claims to retaining any virtue.

Which only left one sister who the coven might consider a threat.

'Charity's at risk if one of us doesn't go and warn her,' Hope told Chalmers. 'And you're the only one who can give her that warning and maybe protect her.'

'I had enough difficulty convincing you,' he grumbled. 'And you always struck me as being gullible.' He shook his head despondently and continued to scowl. Hope could see, from the way he glared at the *Non Fumeur* sign that he badly wanted a cigar, and she almost felt sorry for him.

Almost.

'I still think you're making me pay,' he complained.

'And I think you're demanding a bloody high price.'

Hope said nothing and waited for him to pick up his luggage and head towards the departure gate. The electronic sign above the entrance said the flight was leaving for Heathrow and she knew that would take him back to Charity and hopefully an end to her family's threat from the vampires. A tight smile thinned her lips as she watched him disappear through the gate.

She knew there was always a price to be paid, and she also knew the price would always be higher than expected. But with her bottom still aching from the torment of the previous evening, she now realised that sometimes the high price was worth paying.

The story concludes in:
The BloodLust Chronicles – Charity

More exciting titles available from Chimera

1-901388-09-3*	Net Asset	*Pope*
1-901388-18-2*	Hall of Infamy	*Virosa*
1-901388-21-2*	Dr Casswell's Student	*Fisher*
1-901388-28-X*	Assignment for Alison	*Pope*
1-901388-39-5*	Susie Learns the Hard Way	*Quine*
1-901388-42-5*	Sophie & the Circle of Slavery	*Culber*
1-901388-41-7*	Bride of the Revolution	*Amber*
1-901388-44-1*	Vesta – Painworld	*Pope*
1-901388-45-X*	The Slaves of New York	*Hughes*
1-901388-46-8*	Rough Justice	*Hastings*
1-901388-47-6*	Perfect Slave Abroad	*Bell*
1-901388-48-4*	Whip Hands	*Hazel*
1-901388-50-6*	Slave of Darkness	*Lewis*
1-901388-51-4*	Savage Bonds	*Beaufort*
1-901388-52-2*	Darkest Fantasies	*Raines*
1-901388-53-0*	Wages of Sin	*Benedict*
1-901388-55-7*	Slave to Cabal	*McLachlan*
1-901388-56-5*	Susie Follows Orders	*Quine*
1-901388-57-3*	Forbidden Fantasies	*Gerrard*
1-901388-58-1*	Chain Reaction	*Pope*
1-901388-61-1*	Moonspawn	*McLachlan*
1-901388-59-X*	The Bridle Path	*Eden*
1-901388-65-4*	The Collector	*Steel*
1-901388-66-2*	Prisoners of Passion	*Dere*
1-901388-67-0*	Sweet Submission	*Anderssen*
1-901388-69-7*	Rachael's Training	*Ward*
1-901388-71-9*	Learning to Crawl	*Argus*
1-901388-36-0*	Out of Her Depth	*Challis*
1-901388-68-9*	Moonslave	*McLachlan*
1-901388-72-7*	Nordic Bound	*Morgan*
1-901388-80-8*	Cauldron of Fear	*Pope*
1-901388-73-5*	Managing Mrs Burton	*Aspen*
1-901388-77-8*	The Piano Teacher	*Elliot*
1-901388-25-5*	Afghan Bound	*Morgan*

1-901388-76-X*	Sinful Seduction	*Benedict*
1-901388-70-0*	Babala's Correction	*Amber*
1-901388-06-9*	Schooling Sylvia	*Beaufort*
1-901388-78-6*	Thorns	*Scott*
1-901388-79-4*	Indecent Intent	*Amber*
1-903931-00-2*	Thorsday Night	*Pita*
1-903931-01-0*	Teena Thyme	*Pope*
1-903931-02-9*	Servants of the Cane	*Ashton*
1-903931-03-7*	Forever Chained	*Beaufort*
1-903931-04-5*	Captured by Charybdis	*McLachlan*
1-903931-05-3*	In Service	*Challis*
1-903931-06-1*	Bridled Lust	*Pope*
1-903931-07-X*	Stolen Servant	*Grayson*
1-903931-08-8*	Dr Casswell's Plaything	*Fisher*
1-903931-09-6*	The Carrot and the Stick	*Vanner*
1-903931-10-X*	Westbury	*Rawlings*
1-903931-11-8*	The Devil's Surrogate	*Pope*
1-903931-12-6*	School for Nurses	*Ellis*
1-903931-13-4*	A Desirable Property	*Dere*
1-903931-14-2*	The Nightclub	*Morley*
1-903931-15-0*	Thyme II Thyme	*Pope*
1-903931-16-9*	Miami Bound	*Morgan*
1-903931-17-7*	The Confessional	*Darke*
1-903931-18-5*	Arena of Shame	*Benedict*
1-903931-19-3*	Eternal Bondage	*Pita*
1-903931-20-7*	Enslaved by Charybdis	*McLachlan*
1-903931-21-5*	Ruth Restrained	*Antarakis*
1-903931-22-3*	Bound Over	*Shannon*
1-903931-23-1*	The Games Master	*Ashton*
1-903931-24-X	The Martinet	*Valentine*
1-903931-25-8	The Innocent	*Argus*
1-903931-26-6	Memoirs of a Courtesan	*Beaufort*
1-903931-27-4	Alice – Promise of Heaven. Promise of Hell	*Surreal*
1-903931-28-2	Beyond Charybdis	*McLachlan*
1-903931-29-0	To Her Master Born	*Pita*
1-903931-30-4	The Diaries of Syra Bond	*Bond*
1-903931-31-2	Back in Service	*Challis*

1-903931-32-0	Teena – A House of Ill Repute	*Pope*
1-903931-33-9	Bouquet of Bamboo	*Steel*
1-903931-34-7	Susie Goes to the Devil	*Quine*
1-903931-35-5	The Greek Virgin	*Darke*
1-903931-36-3	Carnival of Dreams	*Scott*
1-903931-37-1	Elizabeth's Education	*Carpenter*
1-903931-38-X	Punishment for Poppy	*Ortiz*
1-903931-39-8	Kissing Velvet	*Cage*
1-903931-40-1	Submission Therapy	*Cundell*
1-903931-41-1	Caralissa's Conquest	*Gabriel*
1-903931-42-8	Journey into Slavery	*Neville*
1-903931-43-6	Oubliette	*McLachlan*
1-903931-44-3	School Reunion	*Aspen*
1-903931-45-2	Owned and Owner	*Jacob*
1-903931-46-0	Under a Stern Reign	*Wilde*
1-901388-15-8	Captivation	*Fisher*
1-903931-47-9	Alice – Shadows of Perdition	*Surreal*
1-903931-50-9	Obliged to Bend	*Bradbury*
1-903931-48-7**	Fantasies of a Young Submissive	*Young*
1-903931-51-7	Ruby and the Beast	*Ashton*
1-903931-52-5	Maggie and the Master	*Fisher*
1-903931-53-3	Strictly Discipline	*Beaufort*
1-903931-54-1	Puritan Passions	*Benedict*
1-903931-55-X	Susan Submits	*Heath*
1-903931-49-5	Damsels in Distress	*Virosa*
1-903931-56-8	Slaves of Elysium	*Antony*
1-903931-57-6	To Disappear	*Rostova*
1-903931-58-4	BloodLust Chronicles – Faith	*Ashton*
1-901388-31-X	A Kept Woman	*Grayson*
1-903931-59-2	Flail of the Pharaoh	*Challis*
1-903931-63-0	Instilling Obedience	*Gordon*
1-901388-23-9	Latin Submission	*Barton*
1-901388-22-0	Annabelle	*Aire*

***

The full range of our wonderfully erotic titles are now available as downloadable e-books at our website

www.chimerabooks.co.uk

We now also offer hundreds of the best and most innovative adult products from around the world, all intended to help you enjoy your sexuality.

Are you shopping for sexy lingerie, sex toys, lotions and potions, fun and games or bondage play? Whatever your desire, you'll find it in the **Chimera Emporium** at **www.chimerabooks.co.uk**. Or write to our Readers' Services for a copy of our **Emporium Catalogue**.

We know you'll enjoy our selection, which includes all your favourites and many new items – all products to set your pulses racing!

***

Chimera Publishing Ltd

22b Picton House
Hussar Court
Waterlooville
Hants
PO7 7SQ

www.chimerabooks.co.uk

chimera@chimerabooks.co.uk

***

Sales and Distribution in the USA and Canada

Client Distribution Services, Inc
193 Edwards Drive
Jackson
TN 38301
USA

***

Sales and Distribution in Australia

Dennis Jones & Associates Pty Ltd
19a Michellan Ct
Bayswater
Victoria
Australia 3153

Don't miss the first in this superb series...

BloodLust Chronicles – Faith

by

Lisette Ashton

The dark one is the cruellest of all vampires: renowned for his evil deeds and notorious for his depraved appetites. When a gypsy foretells his demise at the hands of the virtuous Faith, he plots to avoid the fate by robbing the girl of her virtue.

The beautiful and austere Ms Moon is on a mission to train Faith for her forthcoming battle with evil. Employing a regime of the most punishing discipline, she exhibits a depravity that almost matches the dark one's perverse tastes.

And the innocent and naïve faith – scared, alone and vulnerable in a foreign city – knows she has to endure Ms Moon's twisted tuition in order to meet the challenge of slaying the dark one.

1-903931-58-4 ● £6.99

Or the breathtaking climax to the trilogy...

BloodLust Chronicles – Charity
by
Lisette Ashton

The dark one, cruellest and most sexually depraved of all vampires, has been brought back from the grave. Lilah, his beautiful yet warped and sadistic sister, once again reigns by his side, and together they vow to exact revenge on those who dared to challenge them.

Youngest and most innocent of three virtuous sisters, Charity learns that she will be called on to fulfil an ancient prophecy. She is told there will be pain; she is warned there will be humiliation; and she is prepared to suffer a regime of cruel, degrading discipline.

But nothing has prepared her for the fact that she might – just might – relish these torments...

"And now abideth faith, hope, charity, these three; but the greatest of these is charity." I Corinthians: 13:13

1-903931-61-4 • £6.99

Two more great titles coming in April 2004...

Angel Faces – Demon Minds
by
Jessica Rael

In the desert, no one gives a damn if you scream...

The Cruza: A ruthless, all female crime syndicate that has been building its power base over generations. More secretive than the CIA, more deadly than the Mafia, its main interest: *White Slavery*.

Miss Rebecca, *The Inquisitor*, head of the powerful San Diego division, oversees a lucrative operation, feeding the insatiable perverted appetites of the Cruza's wealthy lesbian clients by preying on the millions of vulnerable illegal immigrants that flood over the Mexican border each year. So successfully, that even the notorious Russian Mafia is knocking on her door, looking for a partner in their own sex slave operations.

In contrast to Rebecca's own icily cruel but sophisticated style, her young protégé, Amber, was forged in the burning hatred of white-trash America. But now the girl's sadistic talent for inflicting sexual torment upon the Cruza's collection of slave girls may be crucial as Rebecca attempts to hunt down a renegade assassin and her twisted creation, *The Dolls' House*, before the woman's growing insanity leads the FBI straight to the Cruza's door.

1-903931-62-2 ● £6.99

Ruled by the Rod
by
Sara Rawlings

The three nubile daughters of a Victorian vicarage are subjected by their guardians to strict discipline by cane and restraints.

Never free of stripes, they must relieve the men of that turgidity that female proximity induces.

In the course of their education they see much of the justice system; stocks, whipping post, ducking stool, and the harsh life of a women's prison...

1-901388-62-X ● £6.99